SHADOW STATE

Also By Andy McNab

Nick Stone Series

Remote Control
Crisis Four
Firewall
Last Light
Liberation Day
Dark Winter
Deep Black
Aggressor
Recoil
Crossfire
Brute Force
Exit Wound
Zero Hour
Dead Centre
Silencer
For Valour
Detonator
Cold Blood
Line of Fire

Street Soldier Series

Street Soldier
Silent Weapon

Boy Soldier Series

Traitor
Payback
Avenger
Meltdown

DropZone Series

DropZone
Terminal Velocity

War Torn Series

War Torn
Battle Lines

Liam Scott Series

The New Recruit
New Patrol
The New Enemy

Tom Buckingham Books

Red Notice
Fortress
State of Emergency

Non-Fiction standalones

Bravo Two Zero
Immediate Action
Seven Troop
Spoken From The Front
Today Everything Changes
The Good Psychopath's Guide to Success
Sorted! How to get what you want out of life
The Hunt

Fiction standalone

Whatever It Takes

ANDY McNAB

SHADOW STATE

WELBECK

First published in 2023 by Welbeck Fiction Limited,
an imprint of Welbeck Publishing Group
Offices in: London – 20 Mortimer Street, London W1T 3JW &
Sydney – 205 Commonwealth Street, Surry Hills 2010
www.welbeckpublishing.com

A CIP catalogue record for this book is available from the British Library

Hardback ISBN: 978-1-80279-480-9
Trade paperback ISBN: 978-1-80279-482-3
Ebook ISBN: 978-1-80279-481-6

Printed and bound by CPI Group (UK) Ltd., Croydon, CR0 4YY

FSC
www.fsc.org
MIX
Paper | Supporting
responsible forestry
FSC® C171272

10 9 8 7 6 5 4 3 2 1

CHAPTER 1

The fourth punch didn't draw blood. But the fifth one did.

Nathan Pike tasted the warm tang of iron in his mouth and pressed his tongue up against teeth that felt loose but, if he was lucky, a few more hits away from freeing themselves from the fleshy prison of his gums.

He staggered backwards and smacked into thick metal bars, dislodging flakes of faded blue paint and hoping the impact made a loud enough noise to draw some attention. He waited a couple of half-seconds before he spat out a gob of red liquid. The pause was for dramatic effect, and to buy himself some time.

The guards had been overly vigilant ever since Pike had been hauled into the police station shortly before one a.m. three nights ago. Since then, he'd slept, eaten, drunk and relieved himself under the constant watchful eyes of various members of the Sihanoukville police force. But now that something worthy of their interest was actually happening they were conspicuously absent. He'd wondered if the old security camera half-bolted and half-taped to the ceiling outside his cell worked. Now he was sure it did, and that his beating was being viewed by an audience who were enjoying him finally getting what was coming to him.

Pike spat again – a weak spray of blood and grey phlegm this time – and shook his head slightly from side to side, seeing just how much the room in front of him would keep spinning and how long it would take for it all to slow down and stop in place.

His cellmate, who Pike guessed had been waiting to see if he'd slump down the thick bars and crumple over onto the cell floor in a heap, pulled his right arm back and struck again, a powerful hook sending fist into face and bone into metal.

Pike was taller than the other man. Literally head and shoulders above him. But his short assailant looked stronger – the skin across his muscles tight from exercise or labour rather than the dehydration caused by spending a week propping up beach bars and not drinking enough of the right kind of fluids. His compact, lean frame made Pike's six feet look lanky, gangly in comparison. He was also faster. He landed another punch before Pike had a chance to block the quick left jab.

Once again, pain shot through Pike's head and bounced around his skull. This time his legs did almost buckle and give way under him, but he managed to stumble diagonally onto the thin shelf of his bunk and another brief respite.

The raised concrete oblong was hot and slick – not from his body heat, sweat, or blood, but because the cell he was interred in was on the southern coast of Cambodia and didn't have air conditioning. Everything in it was warm, and damp.

'Any time now would be good,' he called out as he wiped a bubble of blood from the corner of his mouth, in case the invisible guards were listening for a desperate plea for help.

Pike reminded himself that he couldn't be too angry at what the other man was doing. After all, pretty much ever since he'd appeared on the bunk opposite him twenty-four hours ago, dragged in shoeless, beltless and vestless by two silent, hard-faced uniforms, Pike had been goading him to attack.

For the first day of his incarceration, Pike had been alone. In the cell at least. There had always been at least one pair of eyes on him from beyond the bars. He'd periodically tried to engage the guards in conversation, offering up a joke when they brought him a plate of rice, or asking for a phone call, or when they were planning on charging him with something and he sensed them stifling yawns caused by their own inaction. But they either didn't speak English or enjoyed the fear they thought their silence and blank looks provoked in Pike – the slow-burn impotence of being locked up far away from home with no way of knowing when or if he might be released.

He'd slept for a few hours on his first night, and more on his second – no matter how disastrous or uncertain a situation Pike ever found himself in, he could always sleep – and, after a couple of cheery good mornings to the day shift, he'd settled into a few hours of solitary confinement. Yes, the temperature in his cell rapidly climbed back over thirty degrees celsius, the humidity was close to one hundred per cent, and the lack of airflow did nothing to stop the short-drop toilet set in the

3

floor by the wall between the two shelf-like bunks from occasionally stinking like someone had shoved several dead bodies down it a few weeks ago. But Pike had stayed in worse places in his time and, more importantly, he'd always been able to get on with just his own company.

It was a trait that had seen him described as a quiet soul when he was young, then odd, weird, and a loner as he got older. He wasn't cripplingly introverted, or a sociopath who was incapable of normal social behaviour. He liked being around people, if he liked the people. But if he didn't, he was content to be by himself.

He'd whiled away his second morning, keeping his senses light and letting the ceiling and walls drift in and out of focus, the sounds of the police station wash over him and the fetid stench of the toilet go mostly unnoticed, until his lunch arrived and, with it, the man who was currently beating the crap out of him.

Pike hadn't been able to tell if the Cambodian had been coming up or down when he'd been dropped on the bunk opposite his, but it became very obvious very quickly that he wasn't happy that his chemical rollercoaster had carried him into a police station holding cell in the middle of the day, and especially one that also contained a foreigner. Pike would have been more than happy to let him ride out the high or low he seemed to be in the middle of alone, but it was clear from the guards' lack of reaction to the other man's angry protests that they didn't seem similarly inclined. So, Pike had decided to force the issue.

He'd started slowly, a few hours after he'd handed his empty plate through the bars and the other man had finally stopped shouting and curled up on his bunk facing the wall, pretending that Pike wasn't there, or he wasn't, or both.

He tapped incessant, off-beat rhythms against the wall, pausing for a few moments when the body across from him shifted before starting up again. Then, as the afternoon ticked on and the air in the cell reached its hottest and the man had to stretch out on his back to spread out his body heat, Pike started murmuring through unmoving lips, his nonsense whispers just loud enough to be heard but not consciously registered.

A couple of well-timed screams in the middle of the night pushed the man nearer the edge, half an hour of counted press-ups, star jumps and sit-ups shortly after dawn took him right up to it, and Pike's loud, open-mouthed chewing of his breakfast plate of rice finally sent him over it.

The man threw his own battered dull metal dish at Pike, followed by his first punch and a long list of what Pike guessed were expletives.

He'd been bounced around the cell, and now he was back where he'd begun, only face down on his bunk with his plate on the floor a foot away from him surrounded by rice grains.

Pike had originally calculated the other man would get no more than five strikes in before the guards arrived and intervened. He was rapidly approaching ten, and Pike wasn't sure how many more he could take. He also suddenly started to worry he'd made a serious and possibly fatal mistake with his timing.

Neither of them had been given a spoon or a fork to eat their breakfast with but it occurred to Pike that, with enough force, the plate itself could do a lot of damage. He had a vision of the Cambodian pressing it into his throat, crushing his windpipe and cutting into his skin. This idea apparently occurred to the other man at the same moment because he reached down, picked up the plate, and brought it over his head ready to slam it down on Pike's neck.

Finally, the guards decided to call time on their entertainment. The cell door was thrown open and voices erupted, barking orders. The plate was grabbed, and more hands pinned the man's arms to his side.

Pike looked up at his cellmate as he stopped resisting being restrained. He offered him the slightest, faintest curl of a smile that was meant to communicate something along the lines of, 'Thank-you, now we can both get a bit of peace and quiet alone.'

Unfortunately the Cambodian misinterpreted the sentiment and clearly thought Pike was trying to goad him one last time. So, instead of acknowledging the cleverness of Pike's plan with a grin or subtle nod that broke his mask of suddenly constrained rage, he lashed out a leg, landing a heel-kick square in Pike's face and knocking him unconscious.

CHAPTER 2

Pike woke up in another cell. It wasn't all that different to the last one. The same concrete floor and walls, the same bars across one of its sides, the same sweltering heat. The only differences were that his cellmate was absent, and there were no bunks facing each other but a plinth – you couldn't call it a bed – in the middle of the room, which he was lying on.

There might have been a short drop somewhere, but for the moment his body was more interested in staying still than propping itself up and twisting around to check, and his nostrils weren't currently working at peak efficiency. He could live with that particular little mystery a little longer.

He doubted the police station had a dedicated infirmary. If it did, it would probably have some equipment in it, and maybe even a doctor or a nurse. More likely he was in the morgue, lying where who knew how many other travellers who had been too naive about the dangers of straying far from home or too trusting of the exotic substances they'd imbibed and ingested had lain before him.

He glanced up at the ceiling through the bars. There was no decrepit security camera tenuously gripping at the ceiling for its life. No one to watch over the dead, or the beaten-up. He was alone.

If anyone had asked, Pike would have said it had been his desire for solitude that had led to him ending up in a beach town on the thin strip of coast Cambodia had managed to keep from its neighbours on the Gulf of Thailand in the middle of the wet season. He'd wanted to get away. Off the grid. Off the beaten track.

However, it had turned out that this particular track had recently become surprisingly well-worn. Because Sihanoukville was actually two places.

One was a sleepy, post-hippy idyll of salt- and sun-bleached bungalows and bar shacks populated by a slow rotation of backpackers who had either realised their money went much further in Cambodia than Thailand or Vietnam or were drawn to the apparently excellent scuba diving off the nearby islands of Koh Rong and Koh Rong Sanloem.

The other was a vast construction site of towering, half-finished glass and steel carcasses racing up into the sky.

Labourers toiled and sweated through the day to build the casinos, hotels and shopping malls that were going to persuade Chinese tourists to stay in Cambodia a little longer and part with a little more of their money after they'd marched around Angkor Wat in their selfie-stick-wielding battalions.

Flickering rainbow-coloured strips, oversized signs and enormous adverts in hanzi were already being bolted to the sides of towers that hadn't topped out or had all their sides.

In the day it looked like a not-quite-right Florida. At night it transformed into *Blade Runner* on Sea.

Pike had spent a week with the backpackers, lounging on the beach, drinking two-for-one cocktails with generously irregular shots of alcohol in them, thinking about turning the cooling dips in the sea into a few hundred metres of exercise but never actually bothering, fending off offers of pedicures and accepting ones for massages, and working his way through the seemingly endless supply of roadside cafes that competed to serve the lowest price pad thais on the wobbliest tables.

Then, three nights ago, he'd ventured into the other Sihanoukville.

Had his curiosity got the better of him, or was he looking for trouble? A little from column A, a little from column B.

As the sun started to dip, he finished his fourth potent mojito and, instead of finding something to eat or heading back to his bungalow, he walked north along Ochheuteal Beach and past the island ferry terminal to the part of town where every next hotel was five storeys taller than the one before and all charged at least ten times what his did for a bed for the night.

After another beach, Sokha, which was littered with people swirling straws through the last inches of their sundowners and ended abruptly with an inlet that might have been created by the tide or a river – the water was still and Pike was not an expert on erosion direction patterns – he cut inland, through the manicured grounds of one of the open casinos to a succession of narrow streets.

The Khmer Rouge had robbed Cambodia of a generation of people and progress over the course of its brief, bloody rule during the 1970s. For four years, the regime isolated the nation from the rest of the world, abolished its currency, closed its schools and hospitals, emptied out its cities, and killed almost a quarter of the population.

The brightest, most educated minds, the political classes, and anyone who displayed any signs of belonging to a religion or a foreign ethnicity were murdered by the Santebal, the Khmer Rouge's secret police. And millions more perished as a result of the regime's aims to turn Cambodia into a society of uneducated and poorly trained peasant farmers.

The country was trying its best to make up for its stalled development now. Between every bar and cafe in old Sihanoukville was a stall that would download the latest movies onto your phone or tablet for a couple of dollars in a couple of seconds. But its digital infrastructure was built on incomplete physical and social ones.

Outside Phnom Penh, the capital, and Siem Reap, the gateway to the Angkor temple complexes, there were few public services, and those that did exist weren't well maintained or integrated. Rubbish collection was sporadic. Recycling was done out of personal economic necessity rather than fashionable sustainability guilt.

Main roads were tarmacked, minor ones might be. Both would be potholed, and neither would have many street lamps. This wasn't a problem where the buildings were low and the starlight and moonlight were plentiful, or where pavements were bathed in perpetual neon glow from several storeys above. But, where unfinished cathedrals of capitalism faced each other, the streets at their bases were turned into pitch-black gullies that threatened anything but a good time and the chance to win, lose or spend a life's savings.

Pike passed three of these chasms, only glancing into their gloom to check for vehicles that might have forgotten to turn on their headlights and might somehow speed at him without making a sound.

Then, as he was halfway across the fourth something caught his attention. He didn't know if it was a movement or a sound that pricked the edges of his senses but was too quiet to fully register, but he stilled himself in the middle of the road, turned and focused on the darkness, waiting for his eyes and ears to find what had caused his heartbeat to jump a couple of bpms.

It took a few seconds, but then the scene half-resolved.

Pike could see three men standing in a semi-circle next to a wall about twenty metres from him. And, at their feet, another figure, prone on the ground, face down. Pike's pulse quickened again. He instinctively took two steps forward towards the group, letting the darkness envelop him before any of the people he was watching had a chance to realise they'd acquired an audience.

Now he could make out more details. The man lying on the ground was Cambodian. He was wearing a vest and shorts and he was breathing and moving, both sluggishly, as he turned onto his side. The three standing over him were better dressed and better fed. Shirts stretched over their larger, flabbier frames. A lighter setting fire to the end of a cigarette in one of their mouths briefly illuminated their faces – they were also locals, and they looked like they were enjoying themselves.

Pike had no idea what had occurred to result in the three men standing over the other one. They could be local drug dealers, teaching a lesson to a desperate customer who had run out of funds to pay for their latest hit. Or they could be tourists, down from Phnom Penh for a few days of rest and relaxation, exacting a bit of quick street justice against someone who had tried to relieve them of their wallets or phones.

Whatever it was, it was none of Pike's business. And yet, as soon as one of the standing men's legs pulled back and his foot swung into the stomach of the body beneath him, he found himself striding towards the group, his steps muffled by three voices laughing and one groaning.

Closer, he could pick out a few more specifics of the men. The one on the ground's skin was sunken and sallow, his eyes bulging. The smoker had a wispy goatee, and a scar that ran from the tip of his temple all the way down one side of his face to his jaw and neck. The remaining two were the largest of the bunch, and they seemed like twins or clones of each other – the same height, the same slicked-back hair, the same distended paunch, the same oddly high-pitched chuckle directed at their victim.

'Three against one doesn't seem very fair,' Pike said, announcing his presence once he was only a couple of metres away.

He couldn't tell if any of the trio understood what he'd said. But that wasn't the point. The point was to confuse them all so they were off balance when Pike sprang forward, hurling himself at the man closest to him in a move that looked like the kind of rugby tackle someone would attempt if they'd never played the game.

Pike barely missed headbutting the man's belly. Instead, one shoulder smacked into him and, a second later, the other slammed into the ground, along with the rest of both their bodies. Again, and by fluke more than skill, Pike managed to avoid his face making contact with a pavement slab. And his plan to surprise had worked – his victim hadn't had enough time to register what was going on and protect his own head before the back of it bounced loudly off a slab.

With one of the three now out of action for at least a minute or two, the numbers were even. At least they would've been if the man who had been taking the beating hadn't used the distraction of Pike's sudden arrival to spring up and start sprinting away into the night.

Pike was outnumbered once more, and the chances of another good Samaritan appearing out of nowhere to come to his aid were slim.

The two Cambodians squared up to him with confident, arrogant sneers across their faces – like whatever was going to happen next they knew they'd come out of it a lot better than Pike, even though their friend was now lying at their feet, possibly concussed but certainly in a fair amount of pain.

The fight was over quickly.

Pike dodged a punch from one of them, but that just moved him to within reach of the other, who grabbed at his t-shirt then shoved him over their friend, sending Pike tilting backwards onto the pavement again. He landed on his backside. This time, the shots of rum in his system didn't do anything to dull the shock of impact and a jarring spasm shot up his spine. Then his arms were grabbed and forced behind his back and he was twisted over onto his front, taking almost the identical place of the stranger he'd saved and who apparently had no intention of returning the favour.

He felt the weight of one of the larger men on him, knees pressing into his lower back and arms holding his hands across each other near his shoulder blades. And he watched as goatee leaned over, opened a small, leather card holder and slid it next to his face. Then he flicked his lighter so that Pike could see what was inside.

It was a police ID card.

And that was how Pike had ended up in a holding cell with no passport, no way to contact anyone in the outside world, and not enough money to bribe his way out. It was also why his guards had no interest in making his stay with them a particularly pleasant or short one.

He could tell from the light, the heat and the humidity that it was still daytime, but not how long he'd been out for. He imagined he hadn't been out for over eighteen hours – more likely just two or three.

Pike ran his tongue along his teeth again. They were all still there. Then he reached a hand – unshackled he was pleased to discover – up to his face.

He felt small shards of pain under his fingertips but couldn't detect any oversized swelling or bruising. Flakes of dried blood caught under his fingernails as he checked his nose, but it didn't seem broken.

He ran his hands down his sides. More pain but nothing so bad it suggested his ribs had been broken or cracked. He wiggled his filthy toes – his trainers had also been removed on his arrival – and they obeyed his commands.

It wasn't the most comprehensive medical assessment, but Pike was satisfied that, all in all, he'd gotten off pretty lightly, and also got what he wanted – a return to some peace and quiet.

It lasted for another five minutes, until he heard two sets of footsteps approaching.

Pike brought his arms back, stifling a grunt as he propped himself up on his elbows and watched as a guard unlocked the section of the bars in front of him that were on hinges.

Before Pike had the chance to wonder if his old cellmate was being transferred to the morgue too in order to finish what he'd started, the guard stepped aside to reveal a woman Pike had never seen before. She was dressed in an immaculately pressed loosely tailored white linen suit, and had a perfectly symmetrical face framed by tight, jet-black finger-curled hair.

The woman stepped through the gap in the bars, looked Pike up and down, took in his surroundings and situation, and frowned.

Pike considered her more closely too and noticed that her suit sleeves and trouser legs were both turned up to just above her wrists and ankles. A style choice, a subtle admission of the heat, or a defence against the grime of the station holding cells? He wondered how much time this stranger spent in places like this.

'Who are you?' he asked, as she turned around and began to walk away, leaving him, the guard and the open door behind her.

After a few steps he heard her call back over her shoulder, 'Your fairy godmother.'

CHAPTER 3

Pike waited for the guard to shut the door behind the woman. When he didn't, Pike leapt up off his plinth, his pain suddenly faded, and walked out of the cell. However, he didn't bring himself up to his full height just yet, didn't take on the posture of the righteously free or throw a sarcastic smile the guard's way, because he wasn't certain where he was going next.

But more doors and corridors opened ahead of him and five minutes later he was outside. Ten minutes after that he was sitting in the open-air dining area of a roadside cafe with his mysterious benefactor, devouring two pad thais for the princely sum of three dollars.

He assessed at the woman opposite him. The theory of her looked out of place – too perfectly put together, too composed – yet the reality somehow seemed to fit – comfortable, relaxed, like she belonged. Her suit jacket had been removed and draped creaselessly over the back of an empty folding chair, and a glass of Bayon beer that was miraculously managing to retain its coolness in the afternoon heat rested on the table in front of her.

There was nothing of the stern prison visitor who could have been a warden about her now. But, having witnessed it first hand, Pike knew that version of her was still in there. He pondered how long it must have taken her to develop this skill of morphing and moulding herself to fit her surroundings, and if there was a true version underneath her effortless performances, or if she was all show.

They were the cafe's sole customers. The midday rush was long gone and the owner was busying herself inside, preparing for the evening flood of hungry mouths.

It was hot, but there was a breeze. Sea salt mingled with cooking oil, petrol, and the lime, tamarind and fish sauce Pike's large late lunch was doused in. He could just about smell all the heady aromas, and his other senses were working overtime to make up for what he might be missing. The sights, sounds and tastes of the outside world seemed more vivid after a couple of days locked up.

A cat with mottled brown fur lazily sunning itself stirred as it finally caught the scent of Pike's food. It rolled onto its legs, stretched and sauntered over. The woman gave it a look that made it clear she had nothing for it. The animal turned its attention to Pike, wrapping its tail around his ankles and sniffing at his bare feet – his trainers had not been returned to him.

Pike threw a piece of chicken over to a bit of shade a couple of tables away then went back to shovelling pad thai into his mouth. It didn't hurt to chew or swallow, which was good as he was doing both quickly.

The cat watched the chicken land, looked up at Pike and meowed. He threw another chunk into the shade. The cat seemed satisfied with that and began weaving its way between plastic and metal legs to feast on Pike's scraps.

'I need to know who you are to say thank you,' Pike said to the woman as he shifted his first, now finished plate to the side and got to work on his second.

'Melody Jones,' she replied.

Pike didn't believe for a second that that was her actual name. It belonged to the character she was playing. In fact, it sounded like the kind of pseudonym someone would come up with when they were so sure you'd never discover their real one that they didn't even need to try to make their alias convincing. It made him more curious about why she'd want to spring him, and it confirmed what had been obvious from the first moment he'd seen her in the police station: she was confident.

He lifted up chopsticks dangling with flat rice noodles in gratitude. She leaned forward, retrieved her glass and took a sip.

'You're welcome,' she said.

In total, Pike had heard her say precisely nine words since she'd materialised into his life (the other two had been 'a beer' when they'd arrived at the cafe) and he was sure that, like her name, her Mid-Atlantic accent flavoured with the softest twang of east coast America wasn't real. At least, it wasn't original. The lengths of her vowels had been evened out, her sharper consonants smoothed over years of buffing and polishing.

Pike could tell because he'd done the same thing himself. He was from Newcastle in the north-east of England but he'd removed any trace of that city's recognisable vocal inflections a long time ago, replacing it with the kind of neutral British accent that wasn't too regional or too posh, that subliminally communicated the best qualities ascribed to his nationality and none of the worst, and that gave away nothing about his personal history.

'So, Miss Jones,' he said between bites, 'I assume you're not part of some humanitarian mission going from town to town across Asia breaking people out of police stations. What do you want with me?'

She took another, longer swig of her beer, then replied, her directness matching his: 'I want you to steal something.'

Flashes of shock and confusion spread across Pike's face. He wondered if they looked convincing.

'I think you've mistaken me for someone else,' he said.

'I haven't,' she replied, the floodgates finally opening. 'You're Nathan Pike. British. Thirty-nine. You're a hacker. Except that's an understatement. Genius is a hyperbolic word, but it might be apt when it comes to you. You've never met a computer system or algorithm you couldn't bend to your will. You're a master of the digital world, the man who made Frankfurt airport disappear from every GPS and map on the planet for a whole week. Though you're not so hot with flesh and blood. You could be if you tried, but you've never been that interested in how other humans work. You're driven by curiosity, but not when it comes to other people. They're bugs you don't care about patching. Why is that? Laziness? Arrogance? A touch of the sociopath? The reason doesn't really matter, the result does. You're a loner, and you're alone a lot. Most of the time that suits you just fine, but sometimes it leaves you exposed and in need of rescuing.'

Pike had continued eating through Jones's speech, gathering up the final strands of noodle and chasing peanut crumbs across porcelain with his chopsticks, keeping his expression calm, neutral, with just a hint of bewilderment. He ate one last small mound of food, then balanced the two short lengths of bamboo next to each other on the edge of his plate.

'That's quite the assessment, and assassination. Begs the question, why?'

'Because I don't care about interpersonal failings or false modesty. You're very good at what you do, and now you owe me a favour.'

'A favour I didn't ask for.'

'Like I said, I'm your fairy godmother.'

'It's not altruism if you only do a nice thing for what you want in return. So, thanks for lunch, and for getting me back out on the streets, but I think I'll be heading off now.'

He tossed one last piece of chicken he'd been saving over to the cat, got up from the table, and started to walk away.

Jones took another swig of her beer and watched him go.

CHAPTER 4

Pike headed for his bungalow, via the beach. The pavement was hot on the soles of his feet. He knew the first few metres of sand would be worse, but once he crossed them he'd reach the cooling balm of the sea.

He kept his pace steady. He didn't want Jones or anyone she might have watching him to think he was spooked and about to try to make a run for it – at least not yet. And he didn't want to draw any more attention than he figured the state of him already would.

When Pike reached clear water and low-lapping waves he resisted the urge to plunge his whole body into them. He just reached cupped hands down to collect enough water to tip over his face and the rest of his head.

He started to follow the thin, shifting line of white bubbles that separated blue water and yellow sand, sauntering as if he didn't have a single care in the world.

He considered Jones's monologue about him. He didn't really think it had been a character assassination, because it was mostly accurate, if a little exaggerated. She'd clearly done her homework. Pike was a hacker, though he preferred the term cybersecurity specialist. It had fewer negative, clichéd connotations. Plus, Pike was just as good at building impenetrable digital defences as he was at taking them apart one line of corrupt code at a time. And, depending on how much a prospective client was willing to pay and what he could discover about their motives for hiring someone like him, he was happy to do both.

Sometimes he worked for free too, to entertain and test himself. Frankfurt had been both. He'd wanted to see if he could pull a digital version of an old magic trick: make something truly massive vanish into thin air. He managed it, and spent a couple of days enjoying the memes of people putting giant cats and flying saucers in the airport's place on Google Maps while air traffic control brushed up on some old pre-digital skills and the ESA and NASA tried to undo his work. When it became clear they couldn't, he spent a morning doing it for them and letting them take the credit. He'd left no trace, made no boasts, never used it as a calling card. In a few months most people had forgotten it had even happened – the cycle of unexplained news and technological glitches moved on. He was impressed Jones had pinned it on him, even if it had been a guess.

He was also impressed by how brazen her approach had been. Pike's customers usually solicited him via coded messages on unloved and esoteric subreddit threads or through dark web hacker market forums. Even the British government had been more circumspect when they'd tapped him to work for METIS, the joint GCHQ and Defence Intelligence white hat cyber security division, three years ago.

METIS's remit was to keep the United Kingdom one step ahead of the next generation of attacks coming out of China, Russia and the Middle East by constantly probing the nation's digital defences and shore them up before anyone else had a chance to exploit any weaknesses or widen any cracks in them.

They'd danced around Pike for weeks, leaving him little tests to find buried in the structural codes and meta data of websites for various quangos and arms-length government organisations, tempting him to do his bit for the good guys.

It had been a decent gig. Ok pay. Almost enough challenges to hold his interest most of the time. And, while he'd consulted for the odd global corporate, he'd never worked for a government before. He'd wanted to see how the levers of power worked from the inside in case he ever found himself needing to pull at them.

Still, though his contract had been for two years – such was the pace of evolution of cyber warfare, most people's time at the top of the game was short – it was terminated after one by mutual agreement. Pike had eventually lost patience with the combined inertia of civil service bureaucracy and military discipline, and they'd done the same with him.

A version of 'irreconcilable personality differences' was recorded on the confidential paperwork no one was supposed to ever see but which Pike, of course, had taken a peek at a few months after he'd had his security clearance revoked. The kind of phrase normally reserved for sparing both party's blushes when a marriage was cut short – neither side levelling fault on the other to avoid shouldering their own blame.

Pike had been a solo operator for fifteen years before METIS, and he went back to freelancing after it. Being his own boss meant more choice over the work he took on, more money for it, and fewer stakeholders or supposed superiors doling out orders they barely understood and overseeing wash-up reviews of incredible feats that were lightyears beyond their comprehension.

One implication Jones had made that Pike might have resented if his ego was fragile enough to be dented by a total stranger was that he was lazy. He was the opposite. He never stopped. His desire to understand how things worked – how they *really* worked – was insatiable and, without the occasional break he'd learned to force on himself, all-consuming. Hence, again if anyone had asked, the holiday.

He inwardly smirked whenever he overheard someone a couple of towels or bar tables over from him talking about digital detox. They were amateurs, casual users, still just dipping their toes in the shallows with their days spent staring at screens on desks and in the palms of their hands. Pike was a true addict. He had more ones and zeros coursing through his veins than blood cells. He knew how deep, vast, consuming and terrifying the digital realm could be.

And now, instead of another day or two in police custody before they got bored of watching and feeding him and let him go so he could get back to some sun and cocktails, someone was trying to cut his trip short.

He reached the cluster of triangle roofs stilted up the side of a surprisingly precipitous headland and cut back across the sand towards them.

Pike passed the small hut that functioned as check-in, silently retrieving his key from the man who had laughed at him when he'd first arrived – 'A big hut for one person, maybe you'll make friends' – and walked up the worn dirt path lined with palm trees to his bungalow.

The sound of two dogs attacking or loving each other emanated from the undergrowth off to his right, the saccharine, melodic rhythm that accompanied a massage somewhere on his left.

Pike climbed the steps up to his bungalow, his feet quietly begging him to put them back in some cool water or at least socks, unlocked the door and was enveloped by darkness and stale, damp heat.

He flicked the switch that turned on the cabin's electricity, a single bulb slowly glowed into life, and a three-blade fan started languidly cutting through the air above him. The initial buzz of power faded into a gentle background hum.

He looked the room over – mosquito netting surrounded his roughly made bed, another hanging knotted over the second one that was pushed up against the bathroom wall on the far side of the cabin. At first glance everything looked like he'd left it, which was good because he wasn't paying enough for daily housekeeping.

It was basic, but that had been the point. He'd wanted to switch off, disconnect, make his mind slow down by removing as much stimulus and opportunities to do rather than just be as possible. However, after the last couple of days of being able to do absolutely nothing, he was starting to ponder the virtues of air-conditioning, room service and WiFi. Maybe it was time to treat himself, and change location in case whatever bribe Jones had paid to secure his freedom had included a refund clause.

Pike walked carefully over to the double doors that framed a view of the Gulf of Thailand spreading out beyond tree-tops that he was happy to pay for and opened the shutters to let more light in. He could now see the thin layer of dust that had settled on every surface over the last three days, and the single track of footprints that had disturbed it. He opened the rickety wardrobe where he'd stashed a six pack of litre water bottles, broke the seal on one of them and drank almost the whole lukewarm thing.

Next, he went into the bathroom and finally took a look at himself in the small, lozenge-shaped mirror that hung between the dull grey metal sink and the flat orange of the vanity light.

He was, to put it mildly, a bit of a mess. His quick wash in the sea hadn't got rid of the blood that had caked his nostrils. It had turned it into a dual smear, running down the sides of his philtrum and into his fortnight-old moustache and beard. It was matched by a rust-coloured stain running down the middle of his t-shirt that he hadn't noticed.

His dark hair, which usually lay obediently in a natural side parting, stood in odd directions, the drying salt in it adding volume and structure a Camden punk would be proud of. The grey-green pupil of his left eye was threatened with red tendrils.

He ran his hands over his face like he had when he'd woken up in the morgue. The pain was already fainter. No broken cheekbones. No new kink in his thin, straight nose.

It could have been worse.

Pike sighed. It was echoed by a croak.

He turned to his right to see a frog staring up at him from the tray of the shower. He used the bucket next to the toilet to shepherd the amphibian back down the drain, then turned the water on and stood underneath it until the pressure started to give out.

Once he was dried and dressed in a cleaner t-shirt and pair of shorts, Pike knelt down next to his bed and inspected the dust that covered and surrounded his Arc'teryx Bora backpack. He'd shoved it under the bed frame out of the way, laying its long straps in a precise, overlapping lattice. He lifted each one in turn, checking they still matched their mirror pattern in the motes and specks that had accumulated on the floorboards.

Satisfied that no one had touched his luggage in his absence, he pulled the backpack out from under the bed, cradled it in crossed legs and reached a hand inside. His fingers felt its only contents – a thin flat oblong with a seam that ran round its sides.

Pike was about to pull the object out of its dark hiding place when he sensed that he was being watched.

Someone else was in the room with him.

Jones, standing just inside the door.

'No means no,' Pike said, his voice heavy with mock prudishness.

'You're at least three showers away from having to worry about anyone trying to seduce you,' Jones replied. Then she held up his passport, which should have been in the drawer next to Pike's bed underneath the two paperbacks he'd brought with him but still hadn't got round to reading. 'Looking for this?'

He hadn't been, but he nodded.

Jones turned and vanished down the steps, clearly expecting him to follow her a second time. He slipped the oblong into his shorts pocket, then did.

She guided him to another folding table, this time at a beachfront bar that was gearing up for the evening. Songs from the last five years played sped up and slowed down – Pike wasn't sure if either was on purpose – through tinny speakers, already luring people to its short stretch of sunset views.

'Shall we try this again,' Jones said, sitting down at one of the tables nearest the sea and furthest from the bar.

'You seem pretty good at acquiring things all by yourself,' Pike replied, choosing a chair to her side so he wouldn't have his back to the water. 'Why do you need my help?'

He didn't see any point in pretending he was someone else this time round.

'What I'm after is slightly harder to get than a poorly hidden passport.'

'It wasn't hidden.'

A waiter approached, pausing the conversation as Jones ordered another bottle of Bayon. Pike opted for the same.

'You could have asked nicely,' Pike said, once the drinks had been delivered.

'I prefer guarantees,' Jones replied.

'So, not a favour.'

'More of a debt.'

'You know passports aren't exactly that hard to come by.'

'No, but they take time to get, legitimately and otherwise. And you might still find getting out of dodge a bit tricky.'

'Your friends at the police station.'

'They're very accommodating when you're nice to them.'

'I could just pay them more.'

'True, but they prefer cash to bank transfers and the ATMs around here are running a little low at the moment. Plus, I think you'll find yourself very interested in what I'm proposing. In fact, I don't think you'll be able to resist it.'

Pike flicked the ring pull on his can and tasted his beer. It was considerably more refreshing than the water that had been stewing in his bungalow. 'So tell me about it.'

'When we're on our way.'

He wondered if she thought her vagueness was turning on his innate inquisitiveness, activating his deep, fundamental drive to solve a problem, take something apart and put it back together the way he wanted. It was, a little.

He could say no again. He could slip away from Sihanoukville, pay the British Embassy in Phnom Penh a visit or someone in a dark digital corner a few thousand pounds for a new passport. Fly back to London and the flat he'd rented off Holloway Road while he was with METIS and kept on afterwards even though he hardly spent any time there – he was a digital nomad as much as an addict but his post had to go somewhere – and wait for a job testing an app's security protocols or probing a start-up's transparency promises to come up. Or he could say yes to something that might be a lot more interesting.

Whoever Jones was, and whoever she was working for, she'd clearly come a long way and gone to a lot of trouble to try to secure Pike's services. And she was prepared to make things at least a bit uncomfortable for him if he refused her. He should have probably felt flattered, and wary, but mostly he wanted to know what the hell it was all for.

He shook his head. 'I only do things if I know what I'm getting into.'

'Which is how you ended up assaulting a gang of corrupt cops, one of whom also happens to be the local drug kingpin.'

He smiled. 'Fair point. At least give me a clue.'

'Central America.'

'Never been. Is it nice?'

Now she smiled. 'It has its charms.'

'First class?'

'Private jet.'

Pike's grin widened. 'Ok, Miss Jones, you're starting to win me over.'

CHAPTER 5

The sun was rising over Rwanda.

Lucius Gasana was normally up early enough to see the morning's first rays creep over the peaks and into the deep, verdant grooves of the Nyungwe National Park from his bed but most days he missed them because he would already be sitting behind the desk in his glass-walled office which faced in the opposite direction and offered a very different view.

Gasana's home straddled the ridge that separated two valleys, and was a building of two halves seamlessly brought together by Aziz Kabore, the Burkinabé architect renowned for fusing ultra-modern construction materials with traditional shapes and details, who personally designed the entire place.

The eastern side was for rest and pleasure: two levels of bedrooms, including his expansive own which took up almost half an entire storey, and an enormous open plan living, dining and kitchen area which did, with a wrap-around balcony off it for outdoor entertaining.

The western side was dedicated to work, given over to a large conference room, Gasana's office, and several others which all looked out over the second valley and the Mars colony-like structures of the latest and largest Gasana Mineral Extraction facility. This side also got the sunsets.

This house wasn't Gasana's only home but it was where he'd spent most of his time for the last six months, tucked in the southernmost corner of Rwanda near the borders with the Democratic Republic of the Congo and Burundi. And today he'd afforded himself the luxury of a little more time in his living quarters to enjoy the majesty of an African dawn as he decided what to wear for his first appointment.

He'd already showered and shaved, and was standing in the deep plush of his bedroom carpet, considering the wardrobe that stretched the length of the room's back wall behind tessellating mahogany slides.

He ignored the suits, smiled at the idea of picking out one of the brighter dashikis, and opted for a simple maroon t-shirt, deep navy wide-legged pleated Moses Turahirwa trousers and a pair of leather Kofi Ansah sandals. Suitable attire for being profiled as one of the leading members of Africa's new wave of entrepreneurs.

On any other continent he'd be called a magnate, a titan of industry for almost two decades, but the readers of *Lorgnette*, the European magazine that had dispatched their East African correspondent – a single reporter to cover six million square kilometres of land and two hundred and sixty million people – to interview him were apparently still trying to wrap their heads round the concept that people from Africa could be rich, established and successful.

He could have rejected the interview request that had come from *Lorgnette*'s headquarters in Amsterdam and pointed out how fundamentally offensive its phrasing was, but he knew better how to play the publicity game. So he'd settled for just making a few stipulations. The first was vetting the questions he'd be asked, the second was that he could only give them twenty minutes of his time before his work-day started, and the third was that they would have to come to him.

The conditions hadn't put the magazine off. The reporter had flown into Kigali yesterday morning. Another flight from the capital to Cyangugu on the DRC border in the evening was followed by a two-and-a-half-hour car ride and an early night in one of the guest suites beneath Gasana's.

He was slipping on the sandals when there was a knock at the door.

'Come in,' Gasana replied, summoning the person he knew would be standing out in the corridor.

It was Eric Dusabe, Gasana's *umuntu* – his assistant, bodyguard, enforcer. A man who had been at Gasana's right hand side for almost twenty-five years.

Gasana was well over six feet tall and built like he exercised every day, which he usually did, but Dusabe towered over him and most other people with a frame that, if you were standing in the right place, could block out the sun.

And while Gasana had spent years cultivating the kinds of mannerisms, expressions and appearance that put others at ease without revealing his true thoughts about them, Dusabe gave nothing away about himself by giving nothing at all to begin with. Everything about him was entirely utilitarian. His face was almost always set hard, his head kept shaved bald, and he rarely strayed from wearing a uniform of a black polo shirt tucked into black cargo pants.

'She's ready,' Dusabe announced.

Five minutes later, the two men strode into the conference room next to Gasana's office. A woman was waiting for them, standing at one of the full-height windows looking down at clusters of white geodesic domes of various sizes and snaking thick plastic tunnels. She turned at their arrival and offered a polite smile and a hand for Gasana to shake.

She looked young to Gasana, like a gap year student who had taken a wrong turn somewhere on their way to Bangkok, yet also professional. She had poise. Her white shirt and cream trousers were neatly pressed, her black hair tied back simply. Her tan was even and deep. Gasana wondered how long she'd been in Africa for.

She introduced herself as Beatrice Forte, the hard 'cheh' at the end of her first name revealing her Italian origins.

They sat down at one of the corners of the conference room's onyx-topped table, where a phone sat on top of a closed notebook. Dusabe stood by the door.

'Thank you for your hospitality,' Forte said.

'Thank you for accommodating my schedule,' Gasana replied. 'I hope the journey here wasn't too difficult.'

'More than worth it for the view when I woke up.' Forte gestured to the window and added, 'And that one.'

Gasana smiled at her smooth flattery.

He met his fair share of young Europeans when he did the rounds of embassy receptions in Kigali and they usually fell into one of two camps: the bewildered ones who were trying to get through their time in Africa by keeping their heads as close to the ground as possible, and the ones who thrived in the continent's chaos and contradictions. He was starting to think Forte belonged to that second group.

'I know I don't have a lot of your time, so shall we get down to it?' she asked.

Gasana nodded, still smiling, and Forte picked up the phone, opened a voice note app, and set it back down on the table between them.

'Did we insist on that?' Gasana asked, glancing towards Dusabe.

'I did,' Forte replied, opening the notebook. 'So we both have something to refer back to.'

Gasana nodded, his opinion of the woman across from him continuing to evolve quickly. He signalled that he was ready to begin the interview.

'Something easy to begin with,' she said. 'What do you think of people calling Rwanda the Singapore of Africa?'

'It's a nice sound bite, and not the worst comparison. Our financial sector isn't as big, and we do a lot less shipping obviously, but our streets are as clean and we're driven by the same desire for progress and a belief in hard work.'

Forte was apparently satisfied with Gasana's stock answer and moved on.

'Your official biography is quite brief,' she said. 'Born in 1979. Your father was a miner, and you followed him into the family business. First prospecting then building an empire that this year became the only African company outside South Africa to be on the list of the top fifty mining businesses in the world. Is there anything else you'd like to add to it?'

It was a potted history, and intentionally so. Even before he'd become a well-known figure within Rwanda, Gasana had been meticulous about the version of his life story people were allowed to know.

For example, no one apart from him knew that one of the things that had driven him most when he was starting out and had made sure he never gave up was the mixture of anger, frustration and shame he felt about his father.

Gasana's father had spent his whole working life employed by an international mining consortium, slowly clawing his way up from the lowest rung of the ladder and eventually reaching a position of some small responsibility and pride, which was cruelly and suddenly snatched away from him when his superiors decided to pause operations for six months at the mine where he was a shift manager and fire the whole staff to lower costs during the break.

When, after a slightly longer delay than planned, a representative from the consortium came to offer Gasana's father his job back a year later, Gasana showed the man the grave where he'd been buried three months ago after he'd committed suicide.

Two weeks before, Gasana had laid his mother to rest next to his father. She'd got sick and wasted away in front of his eyes faster than he could scrabble enough money together to take her to a city and hospital that might be able to do something to help her.

'No,' Gasana replied with another well-practised smile. 'Just that I don't like the word "mining". It implies quarries and open pits. We specialise in extraction, and no more so than here.'

Forte nodded. 'Tell me about the Nyungwe operation.'

'The techniques we've developed at GME mean that we actually put more into the ground than we take from it. And we're precise. Modern prospecting technology combines satellite imaging, geochemical surveying and ground penetrating radar to allow us to locate exactly where the minerals we want to remove are, and once we've retrieved them we tidy up after ourselves meticulously, including soil enrichment and replanting. A net positive for the planet, and a supply chain that's sustainable from its source.'

Forte made a few notes, though not so many that she was copying down his answer verbatim. Gasana guessed the recording was for that, and her notebook was for her personal impressions. She may have been sent to write a puff piece, but he sensed she had ambitions that stretched beyond writing profiles that could just as easily be drafted by her subject's PR team.

'Is that why you've been allowed to set up close to the national park?'

That national park wasn't on the approved subject list, but it was a natural next step in the conversation, so Gasana answered it.

'Exactly. We're helping protect it through our example.'

'Can others reach the bar you've set?'

Forte's tone was as warm and curious as it had been since the start of the interview, but Gasana detected the pointedness in the heart of that question.

'I'd say it's something to aim for, and that's not a bad thing,' he replied. 'Africa's resources have been raped and pillaged for hundreds of years. We must do better than the people who invaded our lands and took what was ours.'

If Forte registered the less than subtle attack on the legacy of European colonialism – and Gasana was sure she was well aware of her own country's less than noble past in East Africa – she didn't let it show.

'Let's talk about what you're extracting here,' she said. 'Tantalum.'

Tantalum was a highly dense, conductive, and corrosion-resistant elemental metal that was a key component of the electrolytic capacitors that made all mobile phones, computers, and almost every other piece of modern electronic equipment work. Until the early 2010s, most tantalum had come from Australia and Brazil, but since then far richer sources had been located in Africa and China.

The Nyungwe tantalum was a rare kind because it was pure rather than the more common columbite-tantalite ore, which required extracting first from the ground and then again from itself via industrial hydrometallurgy.

'We may be behind when it comes to covering ourselves in fibre optics and WiFi, but the things that will power the future? The minerals and raw materials? They will come from Africa. And we should all reap the benefits.'

'That's not what's happening in the coltan mines over the border in the DRC.'

Gasana was used to the comparison. Coltan ore was a major source of tantalum, and it was mined in barbaric, unregulated conditions all across the west and south of Rwanda's next door neighbour.

'And not every diamond company is Debswana,' Gasana replied. 'But the partnership between De Beers and the Botswana government is a better parallel for what we're doing. We also treat our staff better. They're well paid and their families are looked after.'

'On the topic of workers, you're a symbol of Rwandan success but you make no secret that your workforce contains a lot of migrants. Why is that?'

Gasana sensed Dusabe tense behind him. The interview was straying again, but Forte's twenty minutes were nearly up so, once more, Gasana answered.

'Take your pick,' he said. 'I'm not interested in the borders drawn over land by people who don't live on it. I believe it will take all of Africa working together to raise us up. I don't care where you're from if you're willing to put in the work for your pay-cheque.' He glanced round to Dusabe, who nodded at him, and added, 'But I'm afraid we're out of time, and I have to get to my next meeting.'

'Of course,' Forte said, closing her notebook and standing up to shake his hand again. 'I appreciate that you were able to see me at all.'

'The pleasure was all mine, and I look forward to reading your article,' he replied, then he nodded at the phone that was still recording their every word. 'Dusabe will arrange for our copy to be sent to us, and for you to get back to Kigali.'

'One more quick question, if you don't mind,' she said, giving him another large smile. 'What would happen if you found something even more valuable than tantalum?'

He grinned back, not missing a beat. 'That would be a great day for Rwanda, Miss Forte.'

Gasana said goodbye, then went next door into his office, a wood panelled space smaller and more intimate than either the boardroom or his bedroom – a sanctum very few people other than himself were ever allowed into.

He didn't have another meeting, but he did have a message to send.

He wasn't sure if Forte's last question was an innocent one, inspired by the trajectory of their conversation, or if their entire encounter had been building to it. But he needed to know which it was.

He woke his laptop up, unlocked it, and opened the secure email account he only used to contact two other people and typed out a short instruction to one of them: *Look into Beatrice Forte.*

CHAPTER 6

'*Otro espresso, por favor,*' Pike called out to the waiter leaning into the shade of the faded blue wall a couple of metres from him.

The man was slow to move inside and try to extract another shot of strong, black coffee from his geriatric and underused Gaggia.

Pike cast his eyes above where the man had been resting to a washed out blown-up photo of a night-time skyline, 'Dubai' scrawled in the corner in a cursive script. Rome was next to it, New York on the other side. Paris after that. It made the run-down cafe on the corner of Alameda Juan Pablo II and 17 Avenida look like a giant, international postcard stand.

It was a week since he'd left Cambodia, and five and a half days since he'd arrived in San Salvador, the capital of El Salvador, the smallest and most densely populated country in Central America on the eastern side of one of the bumps in the spine that connected the United States to Colombia.

As promised, Jones had had a plane waiting. A Gulfstream G650ER, one of the new generation of ultra-long-range, ultra-fast private jets. It took them from Sihanoukville to Sydney, then Santiago and San Salvador. All the S's.

The combined flight time of almost thirty-two hours had been spent in total luxury. Technically the plane was another cell that Pike was being held in by Jones and the laws of pressure differentials, but it was hard to think of it as anything other than a five-star hotel suite in the sky. The interior of the G650ER could be entirely configured to its owner's whims, and Jones's included separate, fully climate-controlled cabins for her and her prisoner, each with a double bed, sofa, desk, and bathroom, all covered in marble and mahogany veneers.

Pike slept, showered, ate like a king, and tried to guess each of their destinations by the spin of the view from his window. Then he came back down to Earth with a bump. When the jet touched down in San Salvador, Jones was escorted to a black Mercedes-Benz W220 and Pike was shepherded to a taxi with a flaking yellow paint job and told to go play tourist.

So he had.

He pounded the city's pavements. San Salvador wasn't a looker. Most of its buildings squatted low, hunkering down against the elements rather than opening up for them. But Jones had been right, there were some charms.

He ambled round Plaza Libertad with its colonnaded edges, wide paths and angular verges, and central monument of an angel reaching up into the sky clutching twin laurel wreaths. He gaped in wonder at the curved concrete and glass roof of the Iglesia El Rosario that streamed rainbows into its Brutalist innards.

He took a boat out on Lake Ilopango, an ancient volcano ringed by younger siblings, to where its waters were warmed by the magma that still bubbled away beneath its deep crater bed. He even booked onto a day trip that took him on a tour of the cluster of pre-Columbian Mayan sites that surrounded the town of Santa Ana, eighty kilometres north-west of the capital.

Pike hadn't noticed any tails on his various expeditions, but he sensed that if he'd tried to go to ground or go for the border they would have made themselves known.

He transformed himself to fit the role of a travelling businessman with some downtime. He shaved and got a haircut (the bright white skin of his scalp and chin matched his Cambodian tan after two days). He bought some new clothes, all linen, and became expert in applying just the right amount of concealer to cover up the yellowing bruises across his face that had started to appear midway across the Pacific.

He also spent some time quietly looking into Jones and getting up to speed on El Salvador's recent history.

Jones was a total enigma. Most people left at least some wake as they moved through the world. Even if they weren't on Facebook or Instagram, something would always turn up with enough digging and patience – a stray reference to an email address in an old pdf invoice archived somewhere, a forgotten photo with a half-blurred face in the background. But Pike couldn't find any trace of Jones anywhere, and he knew how to look everywhere.

People who managed to completely scrub themselves from all records of existence had to be extremely well resourced and equally well funded. Such an achievement also invited suspicion (another reason Pike kept his flat in London – it reassured GCHQ and DI that he hadn't gone completely over to the dark side, which meant they left him alone). So, either Melody Jones was a completely fake persona, or she was someone who really didn't want anyone to know anything about her or what she might get up to. Both possibilities intrigued Pike.

El Salvador was a lot easier to learn about.

It was a poor, exploited land that had been conquered and controlled by outside forces over and over throughout history, from ancient Mesoamerican civilisations to the Spanish, to the First Mexican Empire and the Federal Republic of Central America. It became a sovereign nation in 1841 and spent the remainder of the nineteenth century and nearly all the twentieth enduring instability, coups and revolts, which built up to a thirteen-year civil war between left-wing guerrillas and the American-backed, military-led government. Since then, left and right had alternated presidencies as each tried to stabilise and grow the country's tremulous economy and lift its people out of poverty.

Successive heads of state oversaw an incremental shift away from a long-term reliance on coffee production towards manufacturing and opening up international trade. Then the previous president, the right-wing populist Nestor Barrera, decided to try something completely different. He embraced cryptocurrency.

Bitcoin was declared legal tender alongside the US dollar, which Barrera claimed would give El Salvador 'the power to dictate our own destiny.' Suddenly Salvadorans had the choice of keeping their hard-earned money in bank accounts or a blockchain.

The basic concept of a blockchain might have appealed to people who were wary about what banks got up to with their money when they weren't looking.

At its core a blockchain was a long list of transactions that couldn't be edited, faked or cheated. It wasn't actually that different to how traditional banks had originally worked – your money stayed exactly where you put it instead of disappearing off into someone else's investment or house purchase, and your digital passbook kept an indelible, chronological record of all your deposits, transfers and withdrawals.

However, the cryptocurrencies that used the blockchain ecosystem were still in their early, volatile days, and unfortunately happened to take a considerable dip just as Barrera was trying to build trust in them.

An official, government-backed bitcoin payment app was released and sign-up bonuses were paid out to people who had phones smart enough to download it, and then everyone continued using their dollars and cents.

The bitcoin experiment became a millstone around the president's neck, chipping away at his authority until he had to call an election two years before his five-year term was up in an attempt to reassert some. He lost. But it was who he lost to that was really interesting.

Elena Rivas, daughter of the guerrilla legend Mauricio Rivas and firebrand of the left in her own right, defeated Barrera not by promising to dismantle his crypto obsession but by doubling down on it.

Like so much of politics, it came down to message and optics. Barrera had presented crypto as a tool of national destiny, Rivas framed it as a way to put food on the table. She didn't care what you used to buy a beer or pay for your groceries, she just wanted you to have enough to be able to do both. Voters responded positively.

Two days after her landslide victory, Rivas made a move that even Barrera had been too cautious to try after his own. She transferred half of El Salvador's international currency reserves into cryptocurrencies as the market bottomed out.

It was a gamble, and it paid off. Handsomely.

The $1.5billion she'd invested was now worth $4billion. The Ministry of Finance was able to syphon off money to pay for public works, infrastructure, education and health improvements, while still keeping a digital war chest large enough to withstand any ripples in the crypto market.

Salvadorans rejoiced. Other countries looked on enviously, suspiciously, or with thinly disguised terror. What would happen to the balance of geopolitics if governments at the bottom of the global pecking order could just magic fortunes out of thin air?

That was the question Jones asked Pike the one time he'd seen her in the last five days, over dinner in the chrome and onyx black restaurant of a hotel neither of them were staying in. A test of his new look and knowledge.

He answered: 'The biggest shift in economic power since the gold standard or dollarisation. The first of those made the UK the centre of the financial world, the second America. This could do the same for El Salvador and anyone that follows their example.'

'Do you think that's a good thing?'

'A globally distributed currency that can't be turned on or off by a single power to feed political whims or stoke trade wars? It might be,' he replied as he sliced through a steak that cut softer than butter. 'But I don't think you abducted me for my opinions on economic theory.'

Over dessert, she finally told him what she wanted him to do.

And now, downing his second espresso and double checking the time on the stainless steel Casio watch he'd bought along with the suit and rubber-soled brogues he was wearing, he was about to make it happen.

Pike reached into his jacket pocket, pulled out the long, matte black oblong he'd been so concerned about in his bungalow in Sihanoukville, and cracked its seam with his thumbnail.

To anyone apart from about ten other people on the planet, the device Pike had just opened up might look like a slightly outsized version of one of those folding phones that handset manufacturers kept hoping were going to become the next big thing. But it was more than that. A lot more.

It had become a well-worn joke told by executives at annual product launches that modern mobile phones were palm-sized supercomputers. By comparison, this one really was. It had almost fifty times the processing power of any flagship handset commercially available. It also had a few extra enhancements that were unlikely to ever make it into public hands. Most usefully, it was a digital skeleton key, capable of piggybacking on any kind of data network connection across every bandwidth.

Pike called it his PADD, a nod to his favourite science fiction television show.

He removed the knock-off Ray-Ban wayfarers he'd bought at a market stall two days ago, and brushed the bottom of the PADD's flexible OLED screen with his thumb, the sensor embedded within it using both the speed of the swipe and the patterns of his print and the veins behind them to unlock the first level of security.

The screen began to brighten, at which point micro cameras scanned Pike's face and irises, decided he was alive and wasn't under any form of immediate duress, and released full access. If it had concluded otherwise, it would have wiped itself. And if anyone other than Pike had tried to open it, it would have exploded.

Two windows appeared on the seamless screen. On the left, a web browser displaying the home page for the El Salvador Central Reserve Bank. On the right, a Command Prompt box half-filled with code.

A cursor blinked next to a Y/N request.

Pike shifted his gaze up, across the wide, quiet boulevard in front of him that had been built in anticipation of more traffic than it would ever see, towards the white concrete and blue glass building on the other side of it which matched the visual on the left of the PADD screen.

His hand hovered over the Command Prompt. The ghost outline of a semi-transparent keyboard appeared beneath it.

He pressed Y.

Then he closed the PADD, slipped it back into his suit pocket, got up, tucked a few dollar bills under his espresso cup, and crossed the road.

CHAPTER 7

The Central Reserve Bank of El Salvador didn't look like a bank. It had once, but its original thick stone walled and columned building in one of the better maintained streets of San Salvador's old town had long since been abandoned in favour of a multi-storey office block in the heart of the government district that looked simultaneously obvious and anonymous.

Pike strolled over Alameda Juan Pablo II and up the wide steps that led to its entrance – a bizarre Postmodernist throwback of a protruding Doric arch grafted onto the building, with all its gaps filled by plate glass.

He slowed slightly as he approached the automatic doors, checking that the open collar of his shirt was still sitting neatly inside the lapels of his jacket in his reflection, and stepped inside.

The entrance foyer was not busy. It was in the depths of a mid-afternoon lull.

Reception was directly ahead of him – a long desk pressed up against the back wall staffed by two women in matching maroon blazers with identical black hair scraped back across their scalps and bored looks on their faces.

They both looked up at Pike and then at each other. He guessed they were silently bartering over who would deal with him when he reached them. Before he did though, he had to pass security.

The building might not look like a bank, but it still was one, and with a lot more in its vaults than a regular high street branch, which meant that to get further than a few metres inside Pike and his belongings had to go through airport-style scanners.

A lone guard – male, old, also wearing a maroon blazer – got up off the stool he spent most of his eight-hour shifts perched on and picked up a small plastic grey tray for Pike to empty his pockets into. Pike dutifully complied, tipping in his PADD, wayfarers, wallet, and a few loose notes. Then he stepped through the metal detector and set it off.

He pantomimed an apology as he removed his Casio from his wrist, dropped it on top of his wallet and went through the tall, squared-off arch again. It was a simple distraction technique – a way of making sure the guard's attention stayed on him rather than the contents of the tray, and it worked.

Pike put his watch back on, glanced at the time, collected the rest of his things, and asked the guard in faltering Spanish where the nearest restroom was. He already knew there was one on the far left side of the foyer, past the waiting area of low, boxy white leather couches no one ever sat on, but he appreciated the guard pointing over to it for the two receptionists to see.

He might not have spent years learning how to plumb the depths of other people's emotions, but he was good at getting them to think and do what he wanted without them even realising they were.

'*Gracias*,' said Pike, and walked in the direction the guard had gestured towards, the rubber soles of his shoes carrying him out of the short term memories of all three members of staff with each near-silent step.

Then he disappeared from them entirely as he reached the door to the gents and every alarm the building was capable of making started to go off.

Sirens blared, unmoving lifts announced floor after floor, the automatic main doors swished open and closed, the security scanners announced phantom invaders, the receptionists' computer terminals sequenced through bright static-y squares, their phones rang and rang.

And it wasn't just the ground floor where every piece of technology was suddenly going completely haywire. Offices and conference rooms on every floor plunged into frigid darkness then baking illumination as the automated lighting and heating systems registered different temperatures and time of day every two seconds.

People tried to call for IT support only to find themselves speaking to other staff members in other parts of the bank trying to do exactly the same thing. Desktops went blank then burst to life as if they were trapped in an endless update loop. Printers reeled off toner test pages, photocopiers churned through paper. Mobile phones connected to WiFi launched all their apps at once, creating mini cacophonies of YouTube autoplay videos and Spotify playlists.

Pike had unleashed a distributed denial-of-service attack on the bank. The DDOS had launched a barrage of messages and connection requests that multiplied themselves over and over until they'd overwhelmed the bank's website and then moved on to the building itself's servers and anything linked to them. Pike had timed the digital assault to hit at the precise moment he should have been going to the toilet.

He didn't normally get to see the immediate impact of his work up close, and he reminded the adrenaline his heart was pumping round his body that everything was going to plan and he was supposed to be standing in the middle of a maelstrom.

He looked over his shoulder to check that the occupants of the foyer weren't paying any notice to him, and then walked past the two restroom doors and through a third one – a fire escape that led to a staircase that climbed all the way up the building and down to its four subterranean levels.

Emergency lights strobed in a rhythmic sequence, trying their best to do their job despite constant commands to the contrary.

Pike closed the door slowly behind him, the click of it shutting lost in the noise of the chaos. He paused, hearing more doors opening above him as bank staff either tried to work out if it was only their floors that were afflicted with technological problems or took the opportunity to knock off early.

Then he heard a succession of steps that belonged to several people moving in a single group coming from above. They sounded regimented, purposeful, and they were coming towards him.

The bank's real security detail: their afternoon break abruptly ended.

He only had a few seconds to decide what to do. Step back into the foyer, wait for the bodies rushing down to check on the vaults on the lowest basement level in case the problems afflicting the building's computer systems were a prelude to a robbery attempt to pass, and hope that his sudden reappearance in the foyer didn't draw any attention. Or make it to the floor he needed to reach two levels down ahead of them.

Pike chose the latter option. He took the stairs two at a time, keeping to the wall and out of any easy lines of sight, and tried to time his strides to match the impacts of boots that were getting closer and closer.

He ignored the first fire escape door, then pushed the next one open, slipping through and easing it shut again seconds before the security team raced past it.

The corridor Pike found himself in was dark, but a different kind to the one the stairwell was being repeatedly thrown into. It felt old, permanent, as if all power had been cut from this level of the bank a long time ago. The only light was the sporadic green glow of the flickering exit sign above him.

He walked slowly into the dimness, counting the doors he passed with his eyes and his palms until he reached the fifth one on the right hand side. There was a box bolted to the wall next to it at handle height. Pike slid the cover off it, revealing a modern 0-9 keypad. He retrieved his PADD, opened it and pulled up the sequencing programme that had been working its way through the bank's encrypted security code records for the last five minutes.

As he'd commanded, the program had hidden an algorithm within the DDOS attack that had gone searching for the one six-digit code that wasn't assigned to anything in the building. He tapped the six numbers it had found into the keypad and heard the subtle clicks and sighs of a pneumatic deadbolt lock releasing. Then he opened the door.

On the other side of it, haloed in the well of a single spotlight, was a dial combination safe that had to be at least forty years old.

CHAPTER 8

'Well, hello there,' Pike said to the reinforced steel box.

He didn't make a habit of talking to the equipment or technology he used, but when he came across something that was a lot older than he was, had seen a lot more than he had, and that he needed onside, it was good to show a little deference.

He checked over the rest of the room, just in case the safe was actually a distraction and not his true target, but it was bare. No tables, storage units or lockers, computer mainframes, or slits or grooves in the walls or floor that suggested hidden compartments. The ceiling too was flat and smooth, aside from three five-bulb strips of recessed lights that weren't on, and the single hanging lamp that was.

There was also, he registered, no noise apart from his own breathing. No siren blares seeping in from outside, no alarms ringing in his ears from inside. The room was soundproof.

He checked his watch – he'd been in the building for almost eight minutes – and then his PADD. It searched for a network connection and came up short. It wasn't just sound-waves the room was cut off from.

He stood in front of the safe and began assessing it for clues. It was slightly bluey grey, almost duck-egg, and pristine. It had a black dial, numbered every ten digits from 0 to 100 in crisp white, and a single, well-polished handle. There was no brand name or serial number he could have searched if he'd been able to get online. Though even if there was and he could, he'd probably only be able to track down a default code that would have been long-since changed.

Had Pike known this was going to be his target's last line of defence he might have tried to work out how to smuggle a titanium-tipped drill or a small, shaped charge of plastic explosive into the bank to quickly and forcibly open the safe. But, with a little luck and cooperation he still might be able to get to its contents, because years before he'd mastered how to penetrate digital security systems he'd apprenticed on analogue ones.

He didn't advertise the fact, and he hadn't picked a lock or cracked a safe in a long time, but they were both like riding bicycles – once you'd had the skills drummed into you through hours and hours of practice you didn't forget them.

'We're going to get along, aren't we?' he said, reaching out one palm to the dial and pressing the other against the steel front. It was joined by his right ear.

The first thing Pike needed to do was work out how many wheels were attached to the lock's drive-cam. Most safes had three. Some had five. Three he stood a chance with, five he probably didn't.

He closed his eyes and began to breathe lightly through his mouth, removing any visual distraction and quietening the sounds of his body. He slowly turned the dial, trying to sense where the contact area was on the drive-cam, the groove that the extended nose of the lock's lever would drop into once all the notches in the edges of the wheels were aligned correctly.

He believed in the old thief's adage that locks want to open, that what's hidden yearns to be found, that the nose craved nestling into the drive-cam more than anything else. So, even when a safe is fully secure, the lever will eventually give away the contact area.

He found it within the first full revolution of the dial, and once he knew the particular sensation hitting it created he was able to count the number of pick-ups until all the wheels in the mechanism were moving. Three pick-ups equalled three wheels.

So, now he had the basic parameters. He only had to find the right sequence of three numbers out of about a million possible combinations.

He spun the dial back in the opposite direction, parking all the wheels at zero before beginning his search for the notches in each wheel. These would be harder to find than the contact area but they would still reveal themselves with enough time and patience.

Pike checked his watch. He was twelve minutes in.

He moved the dial in small increments, feeling for the slightest imperfections in the edge of the first wheel that would tell him where its notch had been cut. It took him another three minutes of steady hands and even breathing to locate five possible notch sites and then shrink that shortlist to one: somewhere between 23 and 27 on the dial.

He mouthed, 'Thank you.'

If he had all the time in the world he'd repeat the same process with the remaining two wheels, methodically going round the whole dial to find their near-invisible flaws. But he didn't have that luxury. He needed to make some calculated guesses.

Even when people think they've come up with a completely random string of numbers there will be some unconscious bias at work. They'll avoid numbers that are too close together. Depending on their age they'll err towards making the last number the highest one (people born after the millennium go the other way). And if people pick an odd first number they'll pick an even second one, and vice versa.

Pike gave the high twenties a wide berth on the next spin. It paid off – he found the next notch around the low fifties. On the third spin he focused on the bottom and top of the dial, and settled around 80.

He glanced at his watch again, and wiped the sweat from the palm of his dial hand on his trousers. His gamble had saved him crucial minutes, and in a few more he had the three numbers he'd been searching for: 24-51-79.

Assuming he was right, he'd managed to shorten the possible combinations from six figures to six. He just had to reset the dial again and alternate left and right spins hitting 24, 51 and 79 in different orders until he found the right one.

But before he could, all the recessed ceiling lights suddenly flicked on and ten armed police officers in riot gear rushed into the room and encircled him, assault rifles raised.

Pike held both hands up next to his head, stood, and turned to face the doorway as three more people stepped through it: Elena Rivas, Jones, and a thin man with greying hair who Pike recognised from his online reconnaissance as Fernando Argueta, the head of the Central Reserve Bank.

All three of them were wearing suits. Argueta's was pin-striped, double-breasted and buttoned up. Jones's was a taupe version of the one Pike had first met her in, though with hems that grazed her wrists and ankles. And Rivas's was a bright pink that somehow didn't clash with her long, deep red hair or scarlet-stained lips.

Jones had her usual calm look about her, as if there was nothing remarkable at all about what was going on. The president appeared entertained by it. The bank chief seemed simultaneously furious and ecstatic.

Pike kept his hands up until Rivas nodded at one of the police and they lowered their weapons.

'Your man is good,' she said to Jones.

'We wanted to make sure it was a proper test,' she replied.

'Not good enough,' Argueta added.

Rivas gave the bank chief a sly grin. 'But almost.'

'The attack on our computer systems was contained. And reinforcements arrived quickly. Even without fully deploy-ing our internal security this more than proves our defences work.'

Pike didn't mention that his DDOS bombardment was one of the weakest weapons in his arsenal and had been programmed to peter out after twenty minutes. He also didn't point out how close he'd come to breaking into the safe.

He kept his expression neutral as he watched Rivas turn to him.

'Tell me,' she said. 'Could you have got away with your little heist if you'd really wanted to?'

'Even the most advanced security systems on the planet can be beaten eventually,' he replied.

Rivas let out a loud laugh that filled the room.

'Very diplomatic,' she said. Then added, 'Shall we see what you could have won?'

Argueta almost leapt forward as she reached past Pike for the dial.

'I don't think that's a good idea,' he said, drawing a single raised eyebrow from the president. 'There are too many people in the room.'

'That's not what you said a minute ago,' Rivas replied, mischief now in her voice. 'Unless you think these fine officers would jump at the chance to steal something they've sworn to protect.'

Argueta's face transformed again, a chagrined look spreading across it as he realised that the president had turned his instinctive implication into a direct accusation.

Rivas nodded at Jones.

'Clear the room,' she said. 'Everyone but myself, the president and our would-be thief.'

'I must protest,' Argueta stammered.

'You can pat us down yourself,' Jones replied. 'Outside.'

Reluctantly, Argueta gave in and stalked out of the room, along with the team of armed police who had come to his rescue and who he had just announced he didn't trust.

Another laugh emerged from somewhere deep in Rivas's stomach once it was just her, Jones and Pike.

'How can someone be so arrogant and so paranoid at the same time?' she asked, rhetorically.

Then she finally ushered Pike out of the way and spun the dial left and right, which Pike made a show of not watching, until the nose at last dropped into its groove and the safe unlocked.

She stepped back and let both Jones and Pike take a good look inside.

There were four USB sticks lying neatly next to each other on a single shelf. Four USB sticks that were each worth $1billion.

CHAPTER 9

Pike hadn't expected to be whisked straight from the Central Reserve Bank to the Casa Presidencial, or to find some kind of carnival in full swing in its grounds.

The Casa Presidencial looked like a country club, because it had once been one – a bastion for El Salvador's miniature upper class. Now, however, its ballroom was home to a ten-metre-long conference table, its staff quarters had been converted into the official presidential apartment, and the sand traps and artificial lakes of its five-hole golf course had been filled in to create rolling, tree-shaded lawns that were currently strewn with picnic blankets.

Rivas, Jones and Pike were chaperoned through the crowd – Rivas stopped for photos, hugs and handshakes – to a flat, open area of the gardens where a stage had been set up. People made space for them and the protection officers that had accompanied the president across the city in her car drifted away.

A troop of children in white and blue danced across the stage, spinning each other in circles, sending long, pleated skirts ballooning and rough-edged straw hats almost flying.

The audience whooped as the young dancers reached their climax and cheered as they took their wide-smiling bows.

Over the sound of her own clapping, Rivas turned to Jones and Pike and said, 'This is the true power of cryptocurrency. Culture thrives when bellies are full.'

'What are we celebrating?' Pike asked.

'Whatever people want to,' Rivas replied. 'San Salvador doesn't have many parks, so we made this one.'

The next act took the dancers' place: a trio of male acrobats stripped to the waistband of their knee-length shorts.

Cheers turned to gasps as the men cartwheeled and flipped, leaping through a basic repertoire of gymnastics moves. Pike snuck a glance at Rivas, who seemed to be completely enraptured by the performance, as if she was watching the greatest feats of human dexterity.

After a couple more adequately executed tumbles the three men lined up for what was apparently going to be their coup de grace.

The largest of them dropped into a low squat with arms stretched high. One of the others clambered up onto him, feet on his shoulders. Then they both raised up, swaying slightly before their bodies both settled and the third acrobat started to climb up them, his hands gripping at arms, knees and hips.

The audience began to whoop, their shouts of encouragement getting louder the higher the last man got. He began to smile, wink and wave at the crowd as it goaded him on. He made it all the way up the back of the second man, and started to fold himself almost in half, bringing his entire lower body up and over his comrade's shoulders.

A little more exertion, and the trio would have delivered something of an impressive spectacle. But then disaster struck. Too much sweat between bodies or an infinitesimal shift in weight and balance, and suddenly the third man was tumbling headfirst towards the stage.

It felt as if the entire city had fallen silent for a long second when he landed. The other acrobats froze in place, stunned at what had just happened to their friend. But then he sprang up, a sheepish look on his face and a hand going to his forehead.

Rivas was the first to applaud. The rest of the crowd followed, and the acrobats took it as a cue to end their performance.

'Another benefit,' she said, as the three men left the stage. 'We can pay our doctors a decent wage.'

Pike looked at the crowd, now everyone seemed to have one eye on the stage and one on their president, following her lead and watching to see what they should do next. He was impressed by the devotion her people seemed to show her. And he could understand why. Rivas was charming, charismatic, a natural leader of people. But she was a politician. It was her job to be all those things, and, like with Jones, he couldn't resist wondering how much of it was authentic and how much of it was a performance.

'With a currency you can't control,' Pike said.

Jones shot him a look, Rivas a grin.

'Crypto isn't a cure-all. There's nothing to stop people taking their money and running. I could end up collapsing our economy forever. I've heard the arguments.'

Pike had too. For centuries the distribution of wealth had been managed by governments and institutions as a way to maintain their power and control their populations. By removing money from those systems and structures through something like cryptocurrency, people might start questioning why they existed in the first place. In short, if you didn't need a head of state's face or a bank's logo on your currency, did you need them at all?

'And you disagree with them?' he said.

'El Salvador hasn't had its own currency since we got rid of the colón two decades ago. No one complained about our lack of sovereignty when it was only American dollars flowing in and out of our borders. They're only prophesying doom now because we're doing something they aren't in charge of. No one controls blockchains. It's a level playing field that can't be manipulated. They're scared we might become a beacon for other nations that have had their resources exploited and economies held under foreign thumbs.'

'You could just reintroduce the colón.'

'With foreign permission and recognition it would take too long to fight for. Cryptocurrencies are already here. The old powers can be as upset as they want about them but that's their problem. And to answer your first question. I have faith in people, and their ability to see that we all rise up further when we support each other.'

The acrobats were hovering in the shade of a nearby tree, the one who had fallen slowly rolling his neck as one of the others pressed into his shoulders, checking for damage. Rivas left Pike and Jones and went over to them, shaking their hands with a wide smile and reassuring eyes.

Jones took a step closer to Pike and lifted an eyebrow.

'I wanted to know if she believes what she's selling,' he said, in response to her silent question.

'And?'

Pike watched Rivas stroll back over, nodding at older generations and waving at children. He half-expected someone to hand her a baby to rock to sleep.

'She does,' he said. 'And more importantly it looks like her adoring voters do too.'

'Let's eat,' Rivas said, when she reached them, 'and talk business.'

*　*　*

Two layers of white lace cloth had been spread across one end of the conference table in the casa's old ballroom. Rivas sat on one side, Pike and Jones next to each other on the opposite one. There was no chair at the head of the table.

No sooner had they taken their seats than an old woman with grey hair tied back in a tight bun and a half-apron wrapped around her wheeled in a trolley piled with food.

Rivas leapt up, embraced the woman and kissed her forehead.

'*Mi abuela*,' she announced. 'And before you accuse me of nepotism I only get to borrow her on special occasions or when she decides I'm not eating enough.'

The president's grandmother withdrew after another hug and Rivas loaded up three plates and shared them round.

'*Pupusas, yuca frita* and *empanadas*. Simple food but you won't taste better,' she said, sitting back down. 'Now, I have faith in people, but I'm not naive. Argueta thinks our little escapade this afternoon proves that our private keys are safe exactly where they are. I disagree, which is why I hired Miss Jones to get me a second opinion. So, Mr Pike, what do you think?'

Pike took a bite of one of the three empanadas he'd been given. Firm yet flaky pastry dissolved on his tongue, revealing chunks of salty ham hock smothered in silky soft cheese. It was very good.

He looked at Jones. She nodded. He swallowed.

'Keeping your private keys in cold storage is sensible,' he said. 'Having them offline makes it harder for them to be copied or used by someone else to steal your money.'

For all the jargon and opaque terminology designed to confuse people and make them think cryptocurrency was some kind of illuminati magic, it was actually pretty straight-forward. Owning bitcoin or any other cryptocurrency really meant possessing two long strings of digits. One was known as a public key, essentially an account number. And the second was a private key, basically a password. They could both be kept online in a piece of software called a wallet, which made accessing and transferring cryptocurrency almost as easy as shifting funds between your current and savings account on any regular banking app. However, just like with traditional banking, if someone knew your password they could drain your account and you wouldn't be able to stop them. Keeping a private key offline and away from the blockchain in so-called cold storage was a secure precaution, though it also came with its own risks.

'But?' Rivas asked.

'But if someone wanted to do real damage they wouldn't need to steal your reserves. They could just flatten the bank or blow up the safe. If the private keys are destroyed when they're offline then there's no way to access the crypto, no online record of it on the blockchain that it could be recovered from. It effectively ceases to exist. And no matter how secret you keep the location of the keys, eventually it'll get out. Someone will let something slip, someone else will put two and two together, you'll have to ramp up security and that will just make the target more obvious.'

Rivas sliced a thick oblong of fried *yuca* in half, then half again.

'Then what do you suggest I do?' she asked as she raised the now bite-sized piece of tuber up to her mouth.

Another glance to Jones. Another nod.

'You have three options. First, take the keys out of cold storage and put them in an online vault. They'd be more susceptible to cyberattacks, but at least they'd cause less collateral damage. Second, you could make your own copies or keep some online and some off, but that would just compound your

security problems. Third, split them up. Spread the risk, hopefully without adding too much to it. It's not a perfect solution,
there isn't one, but it's probably the least worst.'

Rivas chuckled as she chewed.

'Least worst,' she said once she'd swallowed her *yuca*. 'I like
that. It's like you read my mind.'

Then she stood up, taking an *empanada* with her. Pike went
to get up too, assuming dinner was over, but Rivas waved at
him with her free hand to stay where he was as she began
walking towards the door.

'Enjoy the food,' she said. '*Mi abuela* will be upset if you
don't finish your plates. Then get some rest. We leave first
thing.'

CHAPTER 10

Pike waited until they'd left the Casa Presidencial before he asked Jones what was going on and where they were supposed to be headed in the morning.

They were walking north along the Avenida La Capilla, towards the cluster of hotels that surrounded the Museu de Arte de El Salvador.

'I've fulfilled my side of the bargain,' he said.

'You haven't stolen anything yet, and Rivas isn't my boss,' Jones replied. 'I thought you were supposed to be smart. Good work encouraging her to split the keys up though. That should make things easier.'

'That was just sensible advice. I've done what you wanted. Now I'm done.'

'No you're not. You're in this now and your only way out is seeing it through. Do I really need to give you the "you know too much" speech?'

She didn't. Ever since Jones had explained exactly what she wanted Pike to do he'd known that at some point that threat would be levelled at him either subtly or bluntly.

He made a show of sighing, resigning himself to his fate.

'Who do you really work for?' he asked. 'CIA? The Federal Reserve? Interpol?'

'Why would I give that away? I want to keep you fascinated with me.'

Pike wondered if she somehow knew that he'd tried – and failed – to look into her. He was confident his PADD hadn't been compromised, but he made a mental note to run a couple of diagnostics on it overnight.

They reached Pike's hotel. A decent enough three-star establishment with inoffensive interiors and just enough other customers to stop the staff from being too overly attentive.

Pike hadn't been able to work out where Jones was staying. Either she'd used an alias or wiped her details, or she'd chosen a hotel that kept its records with pen and paper. She might not even be staying in a hotel – the game she was playing with Rivas could be such a long one that she had an apartment somewhere in the city, rented under a random name or through a non-existent shell company.

'Now, do what the president says and get some rest,' Jones said, continuing on her way to wherever she would be spending the night. 'We have a long journey tomorrow.'

Pike went up to his room, changed out of his suit, which he hung up in the bathroom as he showered to steam out some of its creases and wrinkles, put on a fresh outfit and went back out.

He wanted a drink.

He traced his steps down Avenida La Capilla to the Plaza Italia roundabout where he took a right onto Avenida de la Revolucion, past the low, white semi-circle of the Sheraton –

he didn't spot Jones watching him from any of its balconies – and the art museum.

On Bulevar Del Hipodromo he found a place that was a cocktail bar, winery, and several other things as well according to the words stencilled in various languages across the lower halves of its windows.

Inside Pike found a counter laden with *pintxos* and lined with beer pumps, and floor-to-ceiling shelves filled with wine bottles. There was only one small table free at the very back. He gladly took it, ordered a beer, declined the offer of food, and set about trying to work out what had been niggling at him since Rivas had left him and Jones alone with her grandmother's cooking.

It wasn't Jones's threat – he'd known that was coming. And it wasn't that he hadn't managed to steal the private key sticks – the plan had always been to fail today. He realised, eventually, that it was Rivas. Her incisive optimism was infectious, and he was starting to feel it creep into him.

Pike knew he was no Robin Hood, and that even when he'd occasionally convinced himself that he was doing something good for someone it would inevitably be bad for someone else. However, right now he found himself struggling to see how anything positive could come from derailing El Salvador's little cryptocurrency experiment. He didn't see her big gamble cascading, spreading round the world and completely changing the nature of global economics. And even if it did, so what? As he'd told Jones, it had happened before and society had survived.

He had two more pints then strolled back to his hotel.

The evening had turned muggy and he had another shower when he reached his room – cold first, then hot for ten minutes to get rid of any last wrinkles in his suit while he scrolled through the latest uncomplimentary international news stories about Rivas on his PADD.

Then when he climbed into bed and switched the lights off he found something else sneaking into his head. It was the memory of how he'd learned to crack safes.

CHAPTER 11

THIRTY YEARS AGO

Nathan Pike stared at the world slowly spinning in front of him.

At just a few weeks over nine years old it was still impossible for him to fathom the totality of what he was looking at – the aeons of history, the rises and falls of civilisations, the tremendous achievements and advances that were forever being balanced against catastrophes and acts of unspeakable evil, a population so large and vast but that could be fitted shoulder to shoulder on a speck of land too small to be made out on a 1:20 million scale replica of the planet.

However, as his dad, Ken, looked at him from the other side of the room, he could tell his son thought something wasn't quite right.

'It's going the wrong way,' Nathan said.

'What?' Ken Pike replied, making his way over from the entrance door to the Harbrook Museum's permanent astronomy exhibit that he'd been checking was still locked.

'The Earth,' Nathan replied. 'It's going right to left, but it really goes left to right.'

Ken looked at the globe. It took him a few moments to realise that Nathan was correct. It was spinning clockwise.

Ken wondered how many times he'd walked past it without noticing, and why none of the museum's curators had either.

How long had the sun been rising and setting on the wrong side of this miniature Earth's sky?

'You're meant to be doing your homework,' he said.

Nathan pointed at the small pile of blue and maroon A5 card-backed jotters stacked on top of each other on a bench in the middle of the room. 'Done it.'

His son hadn't yet learned the mysterious art of lying well, but Ken still walked over to the notebooks and checked the most recently filled in pages of each of them. Nathan had done everything he was supposed to. Spelling, handwriting, multiplication and fractions, all completed in less than half the time it was supposed to take. And all, from what Ken could tell, correct.

Ken couldn't help being impressed, and feeling proud. Nathan was a fast learner. Much faster than him or his mum, Viv. But he was also worried, because at this rate it wouldn't be long before him and Viv wouldn't be able to tell if his work was right or not.

Nathan's teachers had taken to repeatedly telling Ken and Viv that their son was gifted, as if they hadn't already realised themselves. They might have left school with a only a couple of O-Levels between them but they weren't that dumb. Unfortunately, and despite repeated requests, no one at Nathan's school had told them what they should do about Nathan's rapidly developing mind. That was, apparently, something that could be dealt with when he reached high school.

However, more concerning than the unanswered question of how Ken and Viv could support their son's intelligence beyond taking him to the local council library a couple of streets away from their flat in Wallsend – the middle floor of a three-storey terrace owned by the council – for a few hours every Saturday, was the other point that had started to be included in every end of term report.

Nathan had been at the same school for five years and still hadn't made a single friend. Or any enemies for that matter. There were no lifelong bonds being formed with classmates, he hadn't joined any little gangs, bullied anyone or been bullied by anyone. It was almost as if he didn't even register the presence of the twenty-or-so other kids who were his constant companions. And they, in turn, seemed content to ignore him.

'I can fix it,' Nathan said, eyes gleaming at the prospect of a fresh challenge and something new to play with.

Tinkering with things was a recent development, and Nathan was not good at it yet.

'I don't want you touching anything,' Ken replied, his words coming out a little more strongly than he meant. 'We're here to look after stuff, not fiddle with it.'

The Harbrook was an intimidating, thick-walled sandstone manor house that had once been on the outskirts of Newcastle but then swallowed up by the city as it grew. According to the small plaque tucked under one of the two staircases that flanked its grand entrance-way, the Harbrook family had bequeathed it to the city in 1901, along with most of its contents which had been acquired by multiple adventurous generations, in a fit of generosity and debt-settling when they'd decided to retreat full-time to their enormous estate that covered most of the upper reaches of Northumberland near the Scottish border.

It had taken almost a decade to convert the family home into a museum – replacing bedrooms with offices, ballrooms with galleries, and writing desks with ticket ones – and it had been open to the public ever since.

Ken had been one of the night guards at the Harbrook for six months. He'd been lucky to get the job after the ship-yard he'd worked at down on the river finally finished going through its death throes. It had lasted longer than most of the others on the Tyne, but he'd still ended up in the job centre in the middle of Newcastle, Viv's words ringing in his ears about swallowing his pride and taking whatever work they had for him. He'd slowly got used to wearing a shirt every night.

Nathan could have pouted and sulked at his dad's instruc-tion, but this was his first trip to the Harbrook and there was more than enough other new stuff for him to discover and for his brain to gobble up. So, he simply shrugged and moved onto the next bit of the exhibit – a large, barren and utterly colourless moonscape that had a small see-through Perspex box in the centre of it which contained a single petri dish. If the spotlight hanging above the box had been turned on,

Nathan could have seen a few crumbs of dirt that a sign nearby claimed were actually from the moon. But they weren't, so he had to make do with peering into the gloom and imagining what they might look like for a couple of minutes before his dad shepherded him into the next room.

This one was full of deep shadows that made it impossible to tell how big the space was, how far back it went, how high its ceilings were, and what might be hiding in its dark recesses.

At least until Ken flicked on a light switch and revealed a double-height galleried room full of stuffed animals of all shapes and sizes, each looking as if they were about to burst out of the cases they were perched or hunkered in, smash the thin glass barriers between them and the two humans who had intruded on their collective lair, and attack.

Ken watched as the fear that flashed across his son's face transformed first into curiosity and then excitement as he noticed what was laid out on the bench in the middle of this room: dinner.

Nathan ran ahead and hopped up onto the wide, flat bench, crossing his legs and leaning over to inspect the picnic that had miraculously appeared in the middle of a closed museum.

It was just sandwiches – spam and tomato, three of the crusts cut off but the top one left one – and some crisps – ready salted. Basically what Ken ate for dinner whenever he was on shift doubled-up. But it seemed to satisfy Nathan.

Ken lingered over his food while his son began guzzling his way through everything in front of him, knowing that while their indoor picnic would distract Nathan for a few minutes eventually it would lead to more questions – probably about why he'd picked him up from school instead of Viv, brought him into town on the bus instead of taking him home, and made him wait in the dull autumn cold behind one of the bigger bushes in the grounds behind the Harbrook for ten minutes while the museum's day staff clocked off and left.

'When do we have to go home?' Nathan asked eventually, between crisp crunches.

'You're staying here tonight with me,' Ken replied, putting as broad a smile as he could muster on his face. 'Take-your-son-to-work day and a sleepover all in one. Most kids have to enter competitions or go to London to spend a night in a museum. You're getting it for free.'

'Wow, cool,' Nathan said. Then, after fishing the last few crumbs of deep-fried potato from the bag, he asked, 'Where's my sleeping bag?'

'You're going to have to rough it a bit,' Ken replied. 'Once you've finished stuffing your gob and helping me with my rounds.'

Nathan set a serious frown on his face, licked his forefinger and ran it round the inside of the crisp packet, then folded it up along with the rest of the remnants of their dinner, and stood to attention, ready to follow his dad round the rest of the Harbrook, checking everything was where it was supposed to be.

It took another hour of going gallery-to-gallery and office-to-office, unlocking and relocking doors and checking windows before they returned to the astronomy exhibit, each of them clutching their coat. Ken would repeat the long walk through the museum four more times over the course of the night – the Harbrook had a CCTV system, but it wasn't very good, and it had been a while since anyone had changed its tapes – but that'd all be by himself and without Nathan.

Ken laid out his coat as if it was an open sleeping bag, then balled up Nathan's as a pillow and beckoned his son to climb up into his makeshift bed. Nathan happily obliged, silently delighted that he was getting to go to bed without brushing his teeth.

'Sleeping under the stars,' Ken said, pointing up at the constellation that was painted on the room's ceiling.

'Shame Mum couldn't come too,' Nathan replied, as his dad zipped up his coat around him.

'She's tired. Needed a night off,' Ken replied. 'So you're stuck with me.'

That was true, but it was nowhere near the full story.

Viv wasn't just tired, she was sick. According to her, she'd had 'a bit of a funny turn' at the end of her shift on the till in Safeway this afternoon. Nothing more than a moment of dizziness and a stumble. According to her manager, who called Ken to come and get her home ok, she'd fainted and almost hit her head on the end of her till's conveyor belt just after she'd got up to go to the staff room to fetch her coat and bag. And it wasn't the first time she'd momentarily lost consciousness at the store – in fact it was the third in three months, and she hadn't told Ken about any of it.

'No point worrying over nothing,' she said, when Ken asked her about it after making her a cup of tea back in the flat.

But it didn't feel like nothing to Ken. It felt like something he should be worried about, and that they should book an appointment with the doctor for first thing in the morning. In the meantime, he'd take Nathan to work so she could get a full evening and night of uninterrupted rest. He wished he could have stayed home and looked after her himself, but that wasn't an option.

Thankfully, his answer seemed enough for his son, and he watched as Nathan squirmed a little in the oversized coat to get himself comfortable, then said, 'Night, Dad,' and closed his eyes.

'Night, lad,' Ken replied, then waited the minute or so he knew it would only take Nathan to fall into a deep sleep before he reached into his trouser pocket, removed the hip flask he kept in there, and took the first of the half-hourly sips of whisky he would use to get him through the night.

CHAPTER 12

NOW

Lucius Gasana stood at his office window, gazing down at the plastic tunnels in the valley beneath him. They were pulsing slowly as people moved between the hard-sided domes they stretched between and released gusts of cooled air into the sinuous passageways.

It was the middle of the afternoon. A shift change.

There were currently a hundred workers at Nyungwe. If everything went according to plan that number would quadruple within a month or two.

He felt a gentle buzz in his pocket and pulled out his phone to check the notification. The gentle pulse of a smartwatch would have been a subtler way to draw his attention from the view, but Gasana had never liked the feel of anything against his wrists. He didn't wear jewellery on them or own a collection of diamond-encrusted Rolexes or gold-plated Patek Philippes. Even the thin navy merino jumper he was currently wearing had had its sleeves immaculately tailored to three-quarter length.

The reason he hated the sensation of his wrists being restricted was wrapped up with the secrecy he shrouded his past with.

Four generations back, Gasana's heritage blended Hutu and Tutsi, the ethnic groups that unevenly made up ninety-nine per cent of the Rwandan population. Even as a young boy Gasana understood that this biological history was never to be spoken of outside the family home, and as he neared puberty he displayed none of the physical markers that some claimed distinguished the ethnicities from each other, just like neither of his parents had.

However, this didn't stop some of the children in his village from singling him out when the tensions between the two groups that had led to the outbreak of a civil war in 1990 exploded into a genocidal campaign by extremist Hutus to permanently rid Rwanda of Tutsis four years later.

Mimicking the stories they heard from their parents and older siblings, gangs of kids prowled Gasana's village looking for anyone they could label as different and dangerous. Gasana even joined in, quickly realising it was safer to be part of the action than not. But the rules of the game changed every day, and so did the punishment for being the person that everyone else turned against.

One day, Gasana became their target, and the victim of their worst torture. He was grabbed off the street with no warning, dragged to a barn on a farm outside the village, strung up from one of the structure's cross beams by his wrists, and left to shout uselessly for help for almost three hours as his hands turned purple from lack of blood circulation.

There was no way the other children could have known about Gasana's secret lineage, but as he hung increasingly limply, waiting for his wrists to break, all he could think about was that they didn't care if he was really a Tutsi, they'd just wanted an excuse to make him suffer.

He was found by the barn's owner and cut down before permanent physical damage could be done. But it took a long time for the deep marks that had been gouged into his wrists to fade. The ones in his psyche, however, never had. And he'd vowed to himself that he wouldn't let something like that happen to him ever again.

Obeying the notification's demand for attention, Gasana turned away from the window and crossed the short distance to his desk and laptop.

There was a single email waiting in his secure inbox. It contained two links. He pressed the touch-sensitive pad embedded in the millimetre-thin glass sheet that covered the top of his four-hundred-year-old baobab wood desk and locked his office door – out of habit more than caution, no one would dare try to enter without knocking and waiting – and clicked the first link.

A new browser window loaded up an online layout editor that contained the two-page spread that his interview with Beatrice Forte had been turned into.

He read through it. There was no trace of the subtle insinuations and suspicions he'd detected from the woman's questions, just the standard, fawning praise. She'd focused on his patriotism rather than his past, which was exactly what he'd wanted, and wrote about GME's extraction techniques with the enthusiasm of an eco-convert who had just discovered the future of the planet was in their hands.

The photos that had been selected from the Nyungwe press pack were good too – the more interesting, better angled ones newspapers tended to ignore, the shapes and structures of forest mirrored in the domes and tunnels.

The only thing he didn't like was the use of the phrase 'green mining' in a couple of the paragraphs after he'd made it explicitly clear that he didn't like the m-word. An editorial oversight or the only jab Forte thought she might be able to land after all her other punches had been pulled? If it was he could take it without flinching.

He smiled to himself, satisfied with how mostly positive the profile had ended up. Then he swapped over to the original window and clicked the second link. This one launched an encrypted video conferencing interface. It only took a few seconds for the call Gasana's click had started to be answered and another man appeared on his laptop screen.

Jean Kamanzi, Rwanda's finance minister.

Kamanzi was older than Gasana, more salt than pepper in the short hair that had receded almost to the top of his head, with several deep grooves stretching across his high forehead and from the corners of his eyes. He was also more formally dressed than the head of GME, wearing a pin-striped suit jacket with unfashionably wide lapels and a bright red silk tie. He looked stressed, but then he always did. He was a man unsatisfied with the power his position gave him and frustrated with the lack of reward his level of authority came with. Which was exactly why Gasana had chosen him to be his government ally.

There was a blue cast to his face, and a blank wall behind him, which told Gasana that Kamanzi was in his office in the Ministry of Finance and Economic Planning – one of the government buildings in Kigali that had been thrown up when its civic developers were obsessed with cladding their generic, multi-storey public works in coloured glass to make up for their lack of personality and architectural ambition.

'How much needed changing?' Gasana asked.

'Enough that I had to offer a favour to Muhire to exert some pressure on her counterpart in The Hague,' Kamanzi replied, his voice as irritated as his expression.

Ingabire Muhire was the Minister for Foreign Affairs, a recent and ambitious entrant to the Cabinet – a woman who, as far as Gasana had observed, well understood the push and pull as well as the give and take of backroom politics. Had she been a minister a year ago she might well have been on this call rather than Kamanzi.

He half-nodded, half-shrugged. 'I'm sure we can afford that.'

'It would have been easier if you just hadn't done the interview.'

'But then what would you do with your days?' Gasana said, then continued before the finance minister had a chance to answer. 'I'm joking. I know you're a very busy man. But you know how important building my profile is to this partnership.'

They weren't equal partners. No one in Rwanda could ever be with Gasana. The relationship he'd cultivated with the minister was a means to an end, but Gasana was equally sure that Kamanzi thought the same thing about him – which meant he could put up with the occasional barb and request to pull his weight or throw someone else's around a little.

'And in a few more weeks you can hire someone full-time to make sure I behave myself with the press.'

Kamanzi huffed. 'Are we still on schedule?'

'Of course,' Gasana replied, as another notification on his phone pulled his focus away from his laptop screen – it was a message from Dusabe about a problem that needed his immediate attention.

He stifled a frown and waved the phone at the laptop camera, his signal that the call was over.

* * *

The valley floor was accessed from the building above it via a four-person tinted glass gondola that rode up and down curved tracks that were held up above the treetops on a series of struts no thicker than a juvenile trunk. The system had been designed to be silent, unobtrusive, yet also command attention – another little futuristic touch that spoke of responsible progress and was both more efficient and dramatic than cutting an access road.

Gasana reached the dome the gondola connected to as more workers were making their way to and from their shifts – each of Nyungwe's five main shafts worked on a slightly different rota pattern in order to prevent rushes on the canteen and encourage a stronger sense of camaraderie within the teams that worked together, as well as a little healthy competition between the shafts.

People in an even mix of pristine and mud-smeared overalls stood to the side as Gasana approached them, some heads down in silent deference, others held high with pride, eyes focused on the top of the curve of the tunnel or dome they were in. A few gazed at him with unconstrained curiosity, seemingly fascinated that a man so much richer and more successful than they were and who had picked them out of whatever their life had been before and brought them here was suddenly walking among them. Anyone who smiled or nodded at Gasana received one in return, but no one plucked up the courage to actually say anything to him.

The rota system also meant that all the people he passed belonged to a single shaft – Shaft 3, as it happened – and that as soon as he diverted from the path that led directly from it to the accommodation and canteen blocks he'd be alone.

Nyungwe's five primary shafts were numbered in simple ascending order. Shaft B was different. There was no friendly rivalry between the people who worked in it and the other teams, because the other teams didn't know Shaft B was there. Only the people who spent their days in it, the scientists who analysed what was extracted from it, and Gasana and Dusabe knew it was there. And the workers had no idea they were engaged in work any different from the other shaft teams, and the scientists were sworn to secrecy.

Gasana reached the point where the polytunnel that led to Shaft B dipped beneath the Earth's surface and then, twenty metres later, where the plastic ended and the lights that would lead him even further underground were attached to posts and braces.

The sounds of excavation echoed around him as he descended, stooping slightly as the roof of the tunnel got closer and closer to the top of his head, until he reached a junction and found Dusabe almost entirely filling one of the turn-offs, looming over a shorter man in a pair of overalls whose eyes were fixed firmly on the steel-tipped toes of his own boots.

At Gasana's arrival, Dusabe raised one his hands, revealing a fist-sized chunk of silver metal whose jagged edges and sides glinted in the phosphorescence of the overhead lamp, sending tiny beams of reflected light bouncing around the shaft. It was not tantalum.

Gasana took the lump of metal from Dusabe and held it in front of the other man.

'Do you know what this is?' he asked.

The man shook his head, keeping his eyes pointed straight down.

Gasana sighed. 'So you threw the opportunity I've given you here away and you don't even know what for. What a shame. Where are you from?'

This question required a verbal answer.

'Nyangezi,' the man replied.

It was a town almost directly west from Nyungwe, over the border in the Democratic Republic of Congo.

'You're lucky you tried to steal from me and not someone in the DRC,' Gasana said. 'They'd have taken your hands on the spot. I like to think I'm more forgiving, but this betrayal can't go unpunished. You'll be home by nightfall.'

* * *

Gasana was right. The man was back in Nyangezi before sunset.

Once Gasana had been given enough of a head start out of the tunnel, clasping the large metal nugget behind his back between both of this hands, Dusabe nudged the man's shoulder, an order to start walking, and escorted him straight to his bunk, where he changed out of his overalls and into his only other clothes – the oversized shirt and faded jeans he'd arrived at Nyungwe in – and then to a Toyota Land Cruiser.

Dusabe drove the forty kilometres to the Ruzizi River, which traced the border between Rwanda and the DRC, and one of the unofficial ferry crossings where the water was wide and calm. The man sitting across from him in the passenger seat spent the whole journey in constant fear of his driver pulling over and dumping him at the side of the road, or slamming the edge of his palm into his face and his heel into his side.

However, none of that happened, and the land cruiser reached the crossing point as the single ferry – a wide, flat-bottomed boat just large enough to carry four vehicles – was about to leave the Rwandan side of the river.

It would be at least an hour's wait before the ferry returned.

The man had no interest in spending it in the Toyota with Dusabe, or finding out what punishment Gasana's *umuntu* might suddenly think about inflicting on him after all. And he knew there was no point in begging forgiveness for being tempted to try to keep a chunk of the precious, shiny material he'd spent weeks ripping out of the ground for himself.

So, he leapt out of the land cruiser and sprinted for the ferry, jumping on it at the last possible second and leaving Rwanda and Dusabe, who simply watched him get smaller through the windscreen as the boat got further away, behind.

Yet, despite his last-minute escape, the man's ultimate fate was still sealed.

Towns like Nyangezi that had little going for themselves and not enough work to spread around were fertile recruiting grounds for GME, so prospective employees needed to know how important it was to follow the rules. There also couldn't be any chance of the man talking about what he'd tried to steal from Shaft B, because even though he hadn't known what it was, someone else might, and the secret of Shaft B had to be maintained.

Sixty minutes after he'd jumped out of the Toyota's cabin and thirty since he'd hitched a ride on the other side of the Ruzizi the man was in Nyangezi.

And, as he lingered in the middle of the red dirt expanse that passed for the town's main square, looking for a familiar face to drown his sorrows and share stories from over the border with in a tin-roofed bar, another man who had received a text message on his battered old Nokia 3310 an hour earlier strolled across it towards him, pulled a Browning HP pistol from his waistband, and put a bullet in the back of his head.

CHAPTER 13

It turned out first thing really meant first thing. Pike got a wake-up call he hadn't asked for at six a.m. that told him to be ready to be picked up in twenty minutes.

After a quick shower and a bad coffee in his room, he found a blacked-out Jeep waiting for him in front of the hotel. Jones was already in the left-hand rear seat so he took the right one.

Pike had opted for a more casual look than yesterday – beige trousers and a blue Cuban collar shirt. Jones also seemed to be doing her own version of dressing down, today's suit more draped than tailored.

The Jeep took them east in silence. Even though they were starting their journey close to the Casa Presidencial it wasn't until they were near Lake Ilopango that they fell in behind a second Jeep that Pike guessed contained Rivas. It was a sensible precaution, avoiding an early morning motorcade being spotted leaving the capital.

The two vehicles continued east along CA-1, the Pan-American Highway, the central of the three roads that stretched across the width of El Salvador and connected it to Guatemala and the southern tip of Honduras.

Pike watched the scenery fly by – small roadside towns, river valleys, dormant volcanoes – subconsciously counting the major junctions and noting where road signs pointed. His PADD could have told him where he was in a second, and projected his likely destination in a handful more, but he didn't like people getting a closer look at it than absolutely necessary, including the person sat less than a metre away from him, so it stayed put in his trouser pocket.

Jones hadn't offered up any explanation about where they were going. In fact, she hadn't said a word since she'd nodded 'good morning' at him. Pike wondered if she knew and just wanted to keep it a secret from him, or if she was as much in the dark as he was.

After two hours on the road, Pike noticed a cluster of volcano peaks to the south, ringed with clouds that for a split-second made it look like they were all in the middle of slow-motion eruptions and, a few minutes later, a sign for a town called Berlin.

Pike was aware of all the rumours, myths and evidence of Nazis fleeing Europe for South America at the end of the Second World War, but he'd never come across anything that suggested they'd reached El Salvador. He guessed it was a prod-uct of some older conquest by a European adventurer seeking to make a nationalistic stamp on a foreign land. He was tempted to turn to Jones, who was staring out of her own window, and mention it to her, just to prove he was capable of small talk.

Another half-hour and they were starting to approach the outskirts of San Miguel, the country's third-largest city. But instead of driving into or through it, the two Jeeps took a left off CA-1 and started to head north along a smaller, quieter road.

Finally, after three hours on the road the motorcade stopped at a petrol station just south of the town of Chapeltique. The drivers and front passengers of both jeeps got out – one to fill their tanks with petrol, one to keep watch. Pike also got out, to stretch his legs, visit the bathroom and find something in the station's small shop that he could call his breakfast. Jones stayed where she was and, assuming she was in the front vehicle, so did Rivas.

Five minutes later they were moving again, letting a little distance creep between the vehicles so they wouldn't be so obviously together as they passed through Chapeltique. There was no radio chatter, and he'd noticed zero conversation between the drivers at the petrol station – either they'd had such precautions drilled into them before they'd left San Salvador, or they were a habit developed over multiple similar journeys.

They continued north, the ground rising up as they approached yet another volcano. This one was enormous. Pike guessed its ragged, ridged peak had to be at least a kilometre high. The Jeeps skirted round half of its circumference on an increasingly winding road, until they reached a junction with CA-3. Pike wasn't sure he'd call this road a highway – it didn't have lanes or even sides marked on it, but it was tarmacked and relatively wide.

Four hours after they'd left San Salvador, the motorcade reached the small town of Perquin, three kilometres from where the Honduran border wrapped round El Salvador. The drivers repeated their technique of falling a little apart and slowing down in the town, then they bunched up close together as they entered a road that was little more than two deep wheel tracks that climbed into steep mountain and dense jungle.

Pike heard both engines rev and branches smack into the windscreen in front of him and drag along his tinted window. He suddenly felt like one of those old KGB colonels from movies who were driven out to the forests outside Moscow once they were past their prime to have a bullet put through their heads in lieu of a pension. He told himself that there were plenty of places closer to San Salvador where he could have been dispatched, and, as Jones had reminded him last night, he still hadn't accomplished the task she'd broken him out of jail and flown him across the planet for.

The jungle began to thin out and both Jeeps pulled up to a halt. They'd reached their destination – a concrete bunker half-covered in vines that looked as if it had been chiselled out of the surrounding terrain.

'During the civil war this was a stronghold for the *Frente Farabundo Martí para la Liberación Nacional*,' Rivas said once the heavy, hidden doors to the bunker had been opened and she, Jones and Pike had gone inside. 'A command post, and final defence position. It was manned throughout all the fighting and false peaces. Even though there was so much fighting around Perquin this compound was never found. Its location was only revealed once the amnesty law was signed in 1993 and the FMLN was recognised as a political party instead of a guerrilla army.'

Pike latched onto the word *compound*. The bunker hadn't looked that large from the outside, maybe five metres by ten, one storey tall with a few slits cut into it thin enough to let in a little air and light but too narrow for a grenade or gas canister. But inside narrow, cool corridors had led to stairways and a series of large, open spaces strung with lights.

He hadn't seen anyone else inside since they'd arrived, and the architecture of the place managed to subdue all sounds rather than sending footsteps and voices echoing into its depths, but Pike could sense that it was inhabited. A hive of some kind of activity that meant the air was kept from getting stale or the floors dusty. He wondered how far underground and how far into the surrounding mountains the complex stretched, and how many people were in it.

They went down another short set of steps, turned another corner, and reached a door. There was an electronic keypad embedded in the wall at shoulder height, but it served no purpose because the door had been wedged open with a small stool.

Through the doorway was another wide room. This one was full of people.

Twenty-odd men and women in dark khaki uniforms or white shirts and suit trousers were busily packing up what seemed to be an enormous treasure trove. Ancient sculptures, carved panels, beaten metal cups, helmets, and weapons were being carefully packed away in rows of boxes, crates and climate-controlled containers. It looked like the most organised looting in history.

No heads turned in shock or adoration at the appearance of the president. Either they were all less enamoured with her toiling underground far from the capital, or they were simply used to seeing her on a regular basis.

Pike hadn't noticed any bunks or accommodation set up on the other levels they'd passed through. And there were no tents in the clearing or among the trees. Did a fleet of Jeeps or rickety old open-sided trucks ferry all these people up from Perquin every morning and back down every evening before it got dark?

He spied the near-perfect semi-circle of a ceremonial headdress balanced on a display stand in a hermetically sealed cube with glass sides and black metal top and bottom on a table a couple of rows over from them. It caught his eye not because of the shine of the gold it should have been hammered from, but because it was made of smooth white stone. It must have been gold once, but it had been petrified a long time ago, transformed by being submerged in mineral-rich water either on purpose or in some older hiding place that had accidentally flooded. He'd never seen anything like it, and he instinctively drifted towards it. Rivas and Jones followed.

'What do you think?' the president asked him as they all peered through the glass.

He looked at the curved, flowing pattern that had been carved along the rim of the semi-circle and was still visible in its stone form, and the pair of circles in its centre that had been an extra pair of eyes for its wearer.

'Pre-Columbian', Pike replied. 'Not geometric enough for Olmec, more abstract than Mayan. Probably not Mesoamerican at all. Incan?'

'Full marks,' Rivas said. 'This place had once been a symbol of resistance, then it became a monument to ego. For twenty years our corrupt leaders used it to hide away these things as insurance policies in case they needed to fund a flight from the country. My predecessor didn't know what to do about it once he'd been informed of its existence, so he ignored it. I have other plans.'

Pike asked the question the president was clearly waiting for. 'Which are?'

'I'm going to sell them.'

That wasn't the answer Pike was expecting. 'Not repatriate them?'

'People call me a socialist or a communist, but my concerns are more practical,' Rivas replied. 'The wellbeing of my people is more important to me than how another country feels about artefacts they haven't cared about missing for decades.' Her trademark smile spread across her face. 'And if they really want them back, they can buy them and help me build some hospitals.'

Pike looked around again at all the people cataloguing and carefully moving the relics and trinkets, and at the two security cameras suspended from the ceiling in opposite corners of the room. 'Do you need a second opinion on valuations?'

Rivas smiled, shook her head, and beckoned Pike and Jones to follow her down yet another staircase that led off the trove.

The trio descended another level into a smaller, lower-ceilinged space. This one only had one entrance and exit, no keypad and no camera. Rivas turned on a lamp and Pike noticed that the cable to it ran along the roof and back up the stairs they'd just descended. The air here was staler, too.

'Once the compound has been emptied out, the people who have come to know it's here will forget it again,' Rivas said. 'We're now almost ten metres underground, under several layers of reinforced concrete. A good place to store a couple of private keys, don't you think?'

Pike turned to Jones. The look on her face made it clear she'd known this was what the whole day had been leading up to, and explained why she hadn't said anything on the long journey.

'How long would it take you to make this room even more secure than the Central Reserve Bank's vault?' Rivas asked.

'Without assessing what's already in place, not knowing what kind of power or connections I'd be working with, and doing it around everything going on upstairs, two weeks,' Pike replied.

'The compound's power comes from its own generators with a geothermal back-up. It has no phone reception, and everyone else here is busy enough to ignore you. I was looking for something closer to five days. Let's split the difference and say ten, with the nation's eternal gratitude if you can get it done sooner.' Rivas held out a hand, 'Deal?'

Pike reached out and shook it. 'Deal. Just one problem, I didn't pack a change of clothes.'

CHAPTER 14

They went up to the treasure room and found it deserted.

'Lunchtime,' Rivas said, before guiding Pike and Jones back through the compound's winding corridors and out into the clearing, where more rows of long tables had been set out – these ones with benches along their sides and large dishes of stew and plates of unleavened bread on top of them.

The white shirts and khaki uniforms mixed together, all chatting and joking and none of them standing on any form of ceremony or sticking to any obvious hierarchy.

'Where did this come from?' Pike asked, as the three of them found a vacant spot at the end of one of the tables.

'Perquin,' Rivas replied, filling three bowls with a thick brown stew full of vegetables and what looked like chicken legs. 'No one ever found this place during the civil war, but the people of Perquin kept the FMLN forces operating in the areas well fed, including my grandfather. It's become a tradition.'

Pike spooned a large chunk of potato and what he hoped was a prune into his mouth. The stew was earthy, spicy and sweet all at the same time. Then he looked round – there were no new vehicles next to the two Jeeps.

'And they can keep a secret?'

A smile. 'Their generosity is being repaid.'

'How do they get up here? It's not exactly an easy drive.'

'It's quicker to walk, as long as you're only carrying a pot or two,' Rivas replied between her own mouthfuls. 'There are trails and paths running all through the jungle. Once you know which route to take, we're only about twenty minutes from the town.'

'Are they mined?'

Rivas shook her head. 'Mine clearance was one of the first tasks after the war that brought both sides together. Ex-military and guerrillas working on the same side to make the ground beneath us safe to walk on, so we could go back to just worrying about volcanic eruptions.'

Pike already knew about the joint effort in the early nineties to remove the four hundred-odd minefields that had been laid across the country. It had been officially declared mine-free for a long time, but official declarations and reality sometimes didn't tally. Pike wanted to check if it did this time, if Rivas would take the opportunity to give him a friendly warning before Jones gave him an unfriendly one about his immediate personal safety. He also wanted to sound engaged and curious. So he kept asking questions.

'How big is this place? How many ways in and out?'

'That's your first job. We don't have any blueprints. Some historians were sent to talk to the few living people who were based here, but after thirty years of trying to forget it their memories are vague.'

'Let's assume at least one more entrance, but I'll need to explore the whole place to see if there are any more and make up a proper map.'

'I'll arrange some paper and pencils, and tell the soldiers not to shoot at shadows. We don't want them thinking you're a looter.'

* * *

True to her word, half an hour later Rivas had magicked a pad of blank A3 paper and a tin of sketching pencils out of thin air, and a working space was set up for Pike on the ground floor of the compound in a small corner room. It had a single light and air slit high up one wall and a little desk in the middle of it. It felt like a prison cell masquerading as a one-person school.

He'd also been given a hurricane lamp, khaki fatigues and a pair of steel-toed boots, and handed free rein of the compound, the cover given to anyone who might ask that he was creating a map of it for posterity – totally reasonable and mostly true.

Rivas and Jones had disappeared somewhere together. Pike wondered how long it had taken Jones to establish her cover. Had she spent months acting as a legitimate consult-ant to the president in order to win her trust? Had she spent hours sitting in meetings and briefings and offering sage advice while she put her con in place? And what was the con for? Just to get the crypto, or to harm El Salvador? The result if she and Pike were successful would be both, but he was curious about which motive was the primary one.

Pike mulled over whether Jones was working to some larger personal agenda, one that matched the one that belonged to whoever her boss was, or if she'd just been offered a very sizeable cut as he descended back into the compound.

He had no idea how long mapping the place would take. If no one else had successfully managed it that might be because it really did go on forever, a Minotaur's labyrinth that stretched endlessly into the underworld, or it might actually be so easily navigable once you understood how it worked that the people who'd built it had never put its dimensions down on paper as a precaution.

Pike decided he had to treat it the same way he would a lock he needed to crack – because, really, that's what the whole place was. He had to be methodical, establish the basics, start with what he knew and work outwards from there.

He retraced the route from the main entrance down to the room Rivas wanted to make into the second private key vault and then began branching off that path. He went down every corridor, through every doorway, into every room, tracking double-backs, dead ends, and long-forgotten loops and shortcuts. He marked it all down on paper while his PADD also tracked his movements to create his own personal 3D digital map.

He found the half-floor between two larger levels that contained a large communal bathroom with multiple toilets and shower stalls – he had no idea how it was plumbed – and the rooms filled with bunks that were either made out of metal or cut into the walls.

Every so often, he came across a couple of security patrols and noted them down too for future reference, checking the times and routes they kept to.

And he also encountered a lot of corridors that ended abruptly and doorways that led to nothing but rock.

El Salvador had volcanoes, and it also had earthquakes – a result of the subduction of the Cocos tectonic plate beneath the Caribbean plate along the Pacific side of Central America. The country had averaged a 5 magnitude quake almost every year for the last decade, and had been hit by major seismic events in 2001 and 1986 that had each killed over a thousand people. Pike wondered how many bodies might have been buried in the parts of the compound that had caved in.

After six hours of walking and occasionally stumbling around every level of the complex, Pike had traced a comprehensive map and identified two extra exits. One of them was up a ladder at the end of a tunnel that extended far further than any others, implying a much larger original size to the place. The other was through a fissure that he'd almost missed in the deep gloom of a tiny, probable store room he'd had to clamber over fallen rocks in three other rooms to reach. The gap, just wide enough for him to slide through sideways, led out into a cave, the entrance of which was so thick with vines no outside light penetrated it. He guessed it wasn't an original secret escape route. He marked the ladder on his paper map, but omitted the crack.

Pike was making his way back up through the compound, along a corridor that hadn't been strung with lights, when a figure emerged from the dark ahead of him. Jones. She nodded towards a doorway off to her right and walked through. Pike followed her, put the lamp down in the middle of the completely bare space, then watched as she dragged the old door as close to shut as she could get it.

'So,' she said, wiping her hands together to rid them of whatever dust and grime had managed to cling to the door for however long until she'd disturbed it, 'how are we going to do this?'

'I have a couple of ideas,' Pike replied.

'And they would be?'

'What's keeping me alive and well, so I'm not about to give it all away.'

'You sound paranoid.'

'For good reason. I also think you've started to confuse me for a young Harrison Ford. This is not my natural environment.'

'I'm sure you'll adapt. And I need something to pass on to my superiors.'

'Where's your faith in me?'

'I renounced concepts like that a long time ago.'

Pike could have kept on with the verbal sparring, but decided to go fishing instead. 'The only way to make this work is for Rivas to have no idea it's happened at all until it's too late for her to do anything about it. That means not just getting the private keys out of here, but physically removing them from the country before uploading them anywhere near a blockchain. Unless you're just planning on destroying them.'

'I'm not,' Jones replied. 'And I only need one of the keys.'

Pike was shocked by Jones's restraint, at only wanting half a score when all of it would comfortably fit in a single hand. But it would be easier to disguise the theft if only one USB stick needed taking. He thought about the treasure room.

'How is she selling everything?'

Jones's mouth opened a fraction before it paused for a moment. Pike guessed she was trying to decide if she wanted her thief potentially distracted by the possibility of another score.

'Malak Ali,' she replied.

Pike nodded, impressed. 'That makes sense.'

Malak Ali, on the coast of Dubai, was one of the world's largest free zones. Almost sixty square kilometres of docks, offices and warehouses where anyone with enough money could do business without worrying about normal customs rules.

The marketing spin for free zones was usually all about trickle-down and spill-over local benefits – they encourage local manufacturing, boost employment, etcetera, etcetera – and since the middle of the last century they'd been used by countries whose governments thought making the ultra-rich pay even less tax was the best way to bolster their economies.

They also worked like Swiss banks writ large: no questions were asked about what came in, what left, and whose hands it might pass through in the interim. Which meant they had a habit of being used to launder money, traffick narcotics, and fence high-value items of uncertain ownership.

Pike was surprised that a previous premier of El Salvador hadn't established their own, or that Rivas was using one on the other side of the planet rather than a more local one in Panama, Colombia or The Bahamas. But Malak Ali was a smart move. And an opportunity.

'You have three days,' Jones said, bringing Pike's mind back to the task in hand. 'I'm heading back to San Salvador tonight. I'll come up with an excuse to check in on you. I expect progress, and for you to still be here.'

Pike detected a hint of irritation creeping into her voice. Was it because she was tired of being tethered to Rivas? Or just that she wasn't looking forward to another four-hour drive?

'I don't plan on getting lost in the jungle,' Pike said. 'But seeing as you're returning to civilisation you can pick up a few things for me.'

Jones rolled her shoulders, as if she was done with the conversation and already readying herself for her next task. 'What do you need?'

'A pair of running trainers, two small, identical backpacks, and a blank USB stick the same make as the ones the private keys are stored on.'

CHAPTER 15

THIRTY YEARS AGO

Viv's cancer was called lots of things by the doctors and nurses at the Royal Victoria Infirmary – malignant, aggressive, a bastard. Ken never quite got his head round the first term, but he understood the second two well enough.

But, what he really couldn't fathom was how his wife went from just having the odd fainting spell to needing regular trips across the city to the RVI so quickly once they finally managed to see their GP, Dr Finlay, a week after he'd taken her home from Safeway.

Even by then Viv was more tired, heavy and drained, and her appetite was almost gone, and they both felt their hopeful resolve that she'd just picked up an infection from a customer or a bad bit of fish from the discount aisle falter as they watched Dr Finlay's expression get more and more dour over the course of the ten minutes they had with him.

The two things seemed so far apart, so disconnected. The fainting, Finlay told them, was her body's way of saying something was wrong, but there was no way they could have had any clue just how bad Viv already was.

She put on a brave face, they both had to for Nathan, but they could both tell he knew something was up. Their son might have been forever distracted by some new thing to learn or take apart, but he was still observant.

After a month of bus trips and the odd taxi when money could stretch or Viv was feeling too exhausted to make it to the hospital on public transport, they agreed that they needed to tell Nathan what was going on. So, the next Saturday, Ken took him to the seaside.

They rode the Metro – a rare treat – that took them all the way along the river from Wallsend to Tynemouth.

'Why did the Romans build a wall across the whole country but stop before they reached the coast?' Nathan had once asked his dad, shortly after he'd learned why Wallsend was called Wallsend – he'd never been able to give him an answer despite promising to find out.

It was a glum day, the sky seemingly knowing that sad conversations shouldn't happen in dazzling sunlight, but Nathan didn't notice. He loved being by the beach whatever the weather, watching the waves rolling in and stretching out to nothing. He was too young to be able to comprehend or articulate that they soothed his racing mind, but that's what they did.

They walked a loop from Tynemouth Metro station, heading down to the fish quay that was half-full with trawlers, along the boardwalk that took them past the Black Middens, the rocks that filled the wide mouth of the river and only revealed the narrow, navigable path through them at low tide, round the headland that was home to a ruined priory, and back through the village to a bench that looked out over a small boating lake and, beyond that, the sea.

It was too cold for ice cream, so Nathan had a Mars Bar, and Ken took a couple of swigs from the flask that was now almost permanently kept in one of his pockets to build up the courage to talk to his son.

'Your mum's sick,' he finally said.

'I know,' Nathan replied.

The boy's voice was even, unsurprised, almost matter of fact. There were no tears or wails.

'And she's going to get worse before she gets better.'

'Ok.'

Nathan finished the chocolate bar and folded up the wrapper into a tight square. Then they both stared out at the North Sea in silence.

After a few minutes, Nathan turned to his dad and asked, with the littlest tremble in his words, 'Is she going to get better?'

'I hope so, lad,' Ken replied.

And she did, for a while.

The family fell into a strange nocturnal rhythm – on the evenings Viv felt ok, she and Nathan would stay in the flat looking after each other before they both went to bed early. When her chemotherapy had taken it out of her and she was already on the verge of unconsciousness before Ken left for

The Harbrook, he'd sneak Nathan in with him for another sleepover in the astronomy gallery.

The museum was the perfect distraction for Nathan. However it wasn't long until following his dad on his rounds and rereading all the signs he'd already learned by heart clearly wasn't enough and he demanded access to the secrets and knowledge locked away in the books and cupboards in the museum's behind-the-scenes offices. Ken, not wanting to upset his son, agreed, as long as he was careful and put everything back exactly where he found it.

His newly expanded intellectual playground seemed to make Nathan happy. It also tired him out, because he'd be up most of the night exploring ancient worlds and old scientific theories while Ken wandered the rest of the museum, swigging a little extra whisky with every shift.

Nathan's teachers noticed him becoming more withdrawn and disengaged in class but they'd all heard about what his mum was going through so they didn't say anything or kick up a fuss if he napped through break-time or lunch.

At no point did Nathan ever enquire what his mum was ill with, which was a relief to both his parents because they both knew that as soon as they told him what it was he'd want to go to the library and look it up on the one computer it had that was connected to the internet. Maybe, they thought, he also knew he wouldn't be able to resist the compulsion to understand, which is why he never asked.

They made it through Christmas, even all keeping up their tradition of going to see the festive window display at Fenwick's department store at the bottom of Northumberland Street in the middle of town to gawp at its twirling snowmen and optimistically wonder what next year's theme might be.

And then, suddenly, Viv wasn't ok.

It had been a long night at The Harbrook for Ken, because he'd run out of whisky and was a week away from payday and being able to buy some more. He'd got home to find Nathan washed, dressed and fed – all done by himself – and ready to go to school. He was getting to the age when he could probably make the short journey himself, but Ken still wanted to take him. So, after a quick check on Viv, who was still asleep in bed, and a kiss on her forehead, Ken and Nathan headed out. When Ken got back twenty minutes later and took a mug of tea into the bedroom, Viv wasn't breathing and her skin was cold.

The mug fell from Ken's grip, sending milky Earl Grey all over the bedspread and the carpet, as he collapsed onto the edge of the bed. Then slid off it onto the floor and started to cry.

He couldn't believe she was dead. He couldn't believe that he'd never get to hear her voice again. That he'd never get to curl up and fall asleep with her in his arms again. That she'd never get to be dragged round The Harbrook, Nathan pulling at her arm to show her something he already knew everything about. That she wouldn't get to see her son grow up.

She'd told him over and over to prepare for the worst, but not to worry because things would be ok as long as him and Nathan had each other. And he'd nodded along, said all the right things, and still maintained his desperate hope that everything would somehow miraculously turn out ok.

But they hadn't.

He was furious at himself for leaving the house instead of telling Nathan he could get to school on his own. Or that he'd not taken Nathan to work last night, but had dropped him off earlier, then rushed home to climb on top of the covers and snuggle Viv awake.

Could he have done something if he'd been home? Maybe not, but at least he'd have been with her, and she could have had someone to ask for help or say goodbye to.

In a moment of sudden, horrible clarity, he wondered if she'd waited until she was alone to slip away? Until she knew Ken was back to take care of Nathan? Then he realised there was no way for him to ever answer that question, and the not knowing almost drove him mad.

Ken had no idea what to do next. No idea who you were supposed to tell when someone had died.

He ended up phoning the number for the chemotherapy department at the RVI – the one phone number he now knew off by heart apart from the flat – and talking to a nurse there whose voice he recognised but whose name escaped him. She offered him some comforting words he didn't take in, then said she'd arrange for an ambulance to come out, which he did.

Then he called Nathan's school. The woman there was also a combination of sympathy and organisation. She asked if he wanted to come and get Nathan. He said yes, then no, when he remembered he'd need to stay in for the ambulance and leaving would mean leaving Viv alone, which he suddenly couldn't bear to do again. He asked if it would be ok if he collected Nathan at lunchtime, and if she could not mention anything to him before then. She said he could, and she wouldn't.

Once the ambulance arrived, lights and siren not blaring because there was no need for them, and Viv was taken out of the flat on a stretcher, wrapped in blankets, and Ken was given paperwork to sign and told there'd be more to come, he fetched Nathan from school.

Ken had planned to tell him what had happened back at the flat, but found his feet taking them both to the Metro and then to the bench by the pond next to the sea. They made the whole journey without a single word, Nathan mostly watching the cranes and roofs go by through the carriage windows and only stealing the occasional glance at his dad.

'I've got bad news,' Ken finally said, eyes fixed on the waves in front of them and arms wrapped round his stomach against the cold.

'Is it Mum?' Nathan asked, his gaze too staying straight ahead.

Ken didn't know how to phrase the next thing he had to say. 'Dead' seemed too cold, 'passed' too soft. He settled for, 'She's gone.'

Nathan nodded slowly, his eyes falling from the sea to the ground in front of him. Then he nestled up next to his dad, who pulled him in close to his side, and they both started to cry.

'You're going to have to be a big man now,' Ken said, once their tears had stopped. 'I need to trust you to be alone and take care of yourself when you have to.'

'I will,' Nathan replied, wiping the snot that had filled his nostrils away with the cuff of his coat.

The Harbrook gave Ken the week off to arrange the funeral and work out a new childcare routine. He managed the first, and Nathan took care of the second, getting himself up and out to school, then making basic dinners for both of them every night as Ken nursed whisky after whisky and grappled with the surprising amount of admin that came with unimaginable loss and the fear of how they were going to cope without Viv.

When he turned up for his first shift back, he found the museum's director, Malcolm Cornwell, waiting for him. It had taken a fair amount of Dutch courage to get himself to work, and he'd hoped to make it through the night without having to see or talk to anyone, but apparently that wasn't going to happen. Still, he told himself that if he could get through one short conversation and then one long shift ok then things might just turn out all right.

Cornwell was in his fifties, over ten years older than Ken, but he looked younger than him. Definitely healthier. He was a transplant from somewhere down south.

'How are you doing?' he asked, once they were in his office, a large corner room at the back of the building.

Ken had only met Cornwell once, on his first day. But he'd been inside his office a lot.

'As well as I can,' Ken replied.

'Good, that's good,' Cornwell replied as he sat down behind his desk.

Ken stayed standing in front of it, swaying ever so slightly.

'Now,' Cornwell continued, 'and I'm really sorry to have to do this, but we have a problem.'

Apprehension rushed through Ken, sobering him up a little.

'A problem?' he asked.

Had something happened while he was gone? A break in? A fire? Had the museum run out of funding?

'You know our CCTV has always been a bit funny,' Cornwell said.

Ken nodded.

'Well I guess you weren't told someone came and looked at it last month and got it working properly.'

Ken shook his head. Unfortunately the motion didn't clear it enough for him to realise what Cornwell was getting at. So the director had to spell it out.

'We've reviewed the footage from the last three weeks, and you've been consistently drinking on the job, and sneaking your son in overnight.' Cornwell said. 'I know times are tough, but we can't have inebriated staff or children on the premises after hours. I'm sorry, Ken, but we're going to have to let you go.'

CHAPTER 16

NOW

The next morning Pike woke up on the camp bed that had been set up for him in the room next to his makeshift office. It wasn't quite a return to cell-life, but it wasn't far off either. Just the bed, a small basin and cracked mirror in a corner, and a single, thin window. It was early again, but out in the jungle the day started at dawn and ended at nightfall, so he'd had a decent amount of sleep.

He got up, stretched, checked his PADD was still tucked under the thin mattress beneath his pillow, and washed his face and brushed his teeth with the army-issue toiletries that had been delivered along with his bed. He checked his face in the mirror – the yellow of the fading bruises had now merged with his tan – then he pulled on the khaki trousers and black vest he'd been given the previous day, along with his blue shirt, which he left unbuttoned.

Outside, tables were being set up for breakfast, care of the unending generosity of the residents of Perquin, and some of the compound's workers who preferred to spend the night with the stars were rolling up their sleeping bags and mats. But instead of helping lay things out or positioning himself to be at the head of the queue that would soon form, Pike wandered off into the jungle. He wanted people to get used to seeing him leaving the compound, and he was keen to check just how many possible escape routes led away from the complex, and where exactly they all led.

Pike didn't go far on his first stroll, and timed his return so he'd emerge from the undergrowth when most people would be fuelling themselves up for another morning of cataloguing and boxing-up. A couple of pairs of eyes noticed him and followed him to the end of a table where he cheerily scrounged three cold *empanadas* and washed them down with a metal mug of strong black coffee, but the vast majority of the compound's workers and their catering staff had already started to half-ignore him, content to let the foreigner get on with his morning exercise that was none of their business and job that was none of their concern.

He spent the rest of the morning making a show of double-checking the details of his draft map, adding in the paths of the compound's electrics and locations of its security cameras, and marking the best locations for things like reinforced doors and laser tripwires.

After lunch, which ended with him insisting – in faltering Spanish – on carrying two empty pots halfway to Perquin until their owner also insisted on him handing them back after he tripped over a hidden tree root, he took his A3 pad down to the treasure room, found a table in a corner no one else was using and set about producing a neater, cleaner version of his map for Rivas.

Again, this was a ploy to make people so used to him being around that they wouldn't pay attention to just how closely he was watching them and what they were doing. He studied the cataloguing process and how things were being packed up: what was being handled with care, what was less important, what was being buried in straw, what deserved something more high tech. He found his eyes lingering more than once on the petrified headdress in its hermetically sealed box, and pondering the journey it would be going on soon to Malak Ali.

On his second morning, he went for a longer hike in a different direction, reaching a steep and impassable ravine that had been created by a powerful torrent of water over thousands of years or a tectonic shift that had lasted seconds, possibly recently, possibly long ago.

He got back to the compound just in time to feast on the scraps left over after everyone else had finished breakfast. Then he went to see the ranking officer in charge of the compound, a captain called Martinez, who Pike put at roughly the same age as himself but half a foot shorter and with a considerably deeper tan, and started making demands.

Before she'd left, Rivas had informed Pike that Martinez was the only member of the permanent Perquin staff who knew his duties went beyond cartography. However, the captain wasn't privy to the full extent of them. According to the president, he'd been told Pike was there to create a comprehensive assessment of the complex's security systems, but not why or to what end.

It became immediately clear that he felt more than a little aggrieved about being kept in the dark on these points when Pike found the captain in his office, one storey below his own.

'You may be reviewing our security,' Martinez said. 'But I remind you that I am responsible for it.'

Pike played as acquiescent as he could without physically rolling over. 'I'm not here to get in your way, or make any judgements. Just observation and recommendation.'

Pike had managed a glimpse inside Martinez's office when they'd been introduced by Rivas. He could tell it had always been the compound's command centre. It was the only room that had more than the bare necessities of furniture: a small meeting table and old faded leather sofa alongside Martinez's desk. And it was home to the small server stack and computer terminal that the security cameras, locks and lights ran off, as well as the bank of slightly convex black and white monitors that showed a constant feed of what was happening in the treasure room, along a handful of corridors, and outside the main entrance.

'You are already doing enough observing,' Martinez said, revealing that he'd been paying attention to Pike's movements.

'I need to access the base's computer network.'

'Why?'

'Because the president told me to.'

It was a blunt reply, but Martinez's less than cooperative attitude had made Pike want to make it clear that he wasn't asking for the captain's permission because he was already working under a higher authority. It didn't win him a new friend, but it did work.

Martinez nodded to the computer terminal then went back to his desk and made a show of making his own meticulous assessment of whatever was written on the stack of papers that were in the middle of it.

Pike picked up one of the meeting table's chairs, put it down in front of the terminal and turned the monitor on. It asked him to input the passcode that had been written on a slip of paper and taped across the top of the screen.

As Rivas had promised, the small network was air-gapped, not connected to the outside world in any way. The equipment was old but in good condition, both physically and operationally. Like a middle of the range car that was only driven once a week, no exhausting demands had worn out any of its components, and it didn't have any bells or whistles that could cause problems or need more than the most basic maintenance and upkeep. It was a solid piece of technology. A perfect fit for its job, and for what Pike would eventually need to make it do.

On the third morning, Pike finally went looking for the entrance of the cave he'd found on his first exploration. The map of the compound was now firmly embedded in his mind as well as his PADD's memory so he was able to guess its general location, and after half an hour of pressing his hands against vines and leaves and feeling rock or dirt behind them, he pushed through into air that his fingers could tell was ever so slightly cooler than the ambient jungle temperature. He pulled apart a couple of strands of vine, careful not to shift them too far, and peered through the gap he'd created into his cave.

When Pike got back to the compound the first thing he noticed was the single black Jeep parked on one side of its entrance, the second was Jones standing on the other holding a plate and a runner's backpack.

As ever, she looked composed, near impossible to read, and not at all like she must have got up at something like two a.m. in order to make it to Perquin from San Salvador so early. Pike wondered if she'd dared to drop her constant guard and sleep on the journey. More likely she hadn't bothered going to bed.

'Come with me,' she said, handing him the plate, which he now saw contained three *pupusas*, and the backpack.

'Thanks,' Pike replied. 'And good morning to you too.'

She turned and strode into the compound. Pike followed her, swapping his gifts for his lamp as they passed his rooms. He was glad he did as he realised that she was taking them back to the room they'd had their last clandestine conversation in, and that she'd memorised the route to it as well as he had.

Two levels down they passed a couple of people in uniforms who were either late to breakfast or had found a reason to skip it this morning.

'How's your work progressing?' Jones said when they were still just in earshot, her tone carefully modulated to give the clear impression, even if the pair didn't speak English, that she didn't really care about Pike's answer, she just had to ask the question.

'Well,' he replied, sounding as academically enthusiastic as he could. 'I've completed my initial tracings and am ready to get stuck into the real detail today.'

Jones's tone changed as soon as they were back in the dark room and she'd dragged its door closed. For the first time, Pike sensed unbridled frustration in her words.

'We have a problem,' she said. 'Rivas has a fetish for old safes. She wants to use one here.'

Pike stifled a laugh.

'What's so funny?' Jones replied, the light of the lamp across her face making her look like some furious dystopian judge. 'You couldn't crack the other one.'

'Didn't, not couldn't,' Pike said. 'There's a big difference.'

CHAPTER 17

'You know how to break into safes?' Jones asked.

Pike nodded.

'Then why didn't you?' she said, before answering her own question. 'Because then Rivas would know too, and she'd want something even more secure for the private keys.'

Pike nodded again. 'And I don't like giving things away when I don't have to. But it seems we've reached the need-to-know stage.'

'Why should I believe you?'

Now Pike smiled. 'Because if you don't want to blow up the private keys or try to smuggle a whole safe out of here and the country without anyone noticing, I'm going to have to break into it. Would you like me to spend the morning explaining the principles of safecracking?'

An expression flickered across Jones's face that revealed for an instant just how much she didn't like not being in total control, and probably how much she'd like to wipe Pike's grin off his face, then she turned and left the room.

By the time they reached Pike's makeshift office she was back to being the cool, collected consultant.

'The president wasn't joking about wanting this place upgraded quickly,' she said. 'I need to go back with recommendations.'

'I'm way ahead of you,' Pike replied, moving the map he'd spent the previous afternoon finessing across his desk to reveal two lists of things he'd decided were needed to enhance the compound's security.

They were almost identical, structured in two parts – the first glossing the key points of weakness Pike had identified and marked on the map, the second his suggested materials for eradicating them. This part contained specifications for the thickness of the new steel door that should be installed at the entrance to the proposed safe room, the amount of concrete and brick that would be required to fill in the tunnel that led up to the secret escape hatch, the back-up computer it would be prudent to have on site in case the current one shorted out, and the number of new cameras and infrared sensors needed to blanket the whole compound.

The only difference was an extra inclusion on the second version of the list – the one that was for Jones – in the middle of the section detailing individual components: a square of matte black metal, precisely sixty by sixty centimetres, and one centimetre thick, its underside filled with black foam cut with a single short gash in the middle.

Jones looked at both lists and spotted the discrepancy immediately. She didn't say anything about it, but rolled up the first one with the map and folded the second one and slipped it inside her jacket. Then, with very few more words, she left.

* * *

Pike watched the Jeep enter the track that would eventually take Jones all the way back to San Salvador. She'd been in Perquin for less than an hour, and was already heading back on the road for another four. He almost felt sorry for her.

Once the Jeep had been swallowed by the trees, he returned to his office and checked over the delivery Jones had casually made when she'd arrived. Inside the backpack was exactly what he'd requested. A second, identical bag rolled up tightly in the bottom and a pair of trainers, one with a USB stick wedged in its toes. He transferred the stick into the second bag, which he re-rolled and stuffed back into the bottom of the first one.

Pike could have taken the rest of the day off. There wasn't anything he could really do at the compound until the materials he'd requested arrived other than potentially get in people's way, which he didn't want to do. He wanted to keep hovering in that sweet spot of being half-acknowledged and half-ignored.

So, he changed his boots for the trainers, slipped the backpack over his shoulders, and walked out into the clearing, eating his *pupusas*. He handed the plate to one of the Perquin locals who was stacking up the last of the post-breakfast dishes with a loud and enthusiastic '*gracias*' and strolled into the jungle.

To anyone who might have planted a GPS tracker on him, it looked like Pike was wandering aimlessly, taking turnings at random as he circled the compound and pushed further into the wilderness. But he was actually plotting out his possible escape routes, charting in his mind the spider's web of paths that led from the hidden cave to the town.

He walked for hours, his limbs loosening as they were stretched out then stiffening as they were overused, his clothes becoming patched with sweat then drenched by humidity. He skirted the edge of Perquin and headed back into the under-growth almost all the way back to the compound three times before he finally went into the town.

Pike could have kept going. Hitched a ride or even hiked over the border into Honduras. Left Jones to try to steal a billion dollars by herself before it was locked away in a vault that would be near impregnable to anyone but him. But if he did that, he doubted Jones would let it go. The cliché existed for a reason – knowing too much was an easy way to get your-self killed. But knowing more than everyone else was also the best way to keep you alive. They'd reached the point where the theft couldn't be pulled off without him, which made him safe. And he was happy to stay that way for as long as possible.

By now, most of the residents of the town had seen Pike or, he guessed, heard about him. And any that hadn't learned when, after a much needed drink under the shade of a faded parasol in front of a quiet cafe and a slow, respectful wander around the small civil war museum to stop his legs from completely seizing up, he insisted on accompanying the dinner crew back to the compound, carrying a cool box of beers and sodas for them as they showed him the most direct route in and out of the jungle.

* * *

Bright and early the next morning, trucks started to arrive at the compound. The noise of multiple hard-working engines over-revving woke Pike up before the light seeping into his bedroom had got bright enough to.

If this was Pike's next delivery from Jones, everything he needed must have been sourced in a matter of hours and dispatched overnight.

He pulled on some clothes, shook the tiredness from the previous day's exertions out of his limbs and went outside, where he found Martinez frowning at the new arrivals, one hand on his hip and the other resting on the butt of his SIG Sauer P227 pistol – Pike had seen a variety of weapons strung across the chests of the compound's military staff when they were on guard duty or patrol instead of shifting relics or assembling crates, but Martinez was the only soldier who seemed permanently armed.

The captain turned his unhappy gaze on Pike, clearly deciding that the four canvas-topped trucks parking exactly where the compound's open-air canteen was normally set up were his doing.

'They need to be moved,' he said.

'Of course,' Pike replied, as they watched three men climb out of the cabin of one of the trucks, open up its back and start to heave a six-by-three-feet slab of solid steel onto the grass.

'We have two days to finish packing up everything, before the president comes back,' Martinez said. 'I don't have time to deal with this.'

'It won't interfere with your work. It doesn't have anything to do with you.'

'How are you going to explain it?'

'I'm not,' Pike replied, the emphasis on the first word making it plain that that was the captain's responsibility. 'But the explanation is simple. The compound needs to be left secure once you're done.'

The captain huffed his response, still unsatisfied and angry with Pike. Pike was fine with that. His own experience made him pretty sure that the compound's residents would quickly learn to ignore the extra workers that would be briefly swelling their ranks, and the excuse they would be given would make perfect sense. However, if Martinez was going to spend the next two days being stressed, Pike wanted the man's frustration and attention directed squarely at him and no one else.

It became a race. An unspoken but fierce competition to see who could finish first. Martinez cajoled his staff to complete their cataloguing and have everything ready to be shipped out, while Pike oversaw the teams installing the security upgrades Rivas had approved and hooked it all up to the compound's self-contained computer network.

In the end, they both won. After forty-eight hours of hard slog, everyone was ready for their presidential inspection.

CHAPTER 18

Gasana was having a party, and none of his guests knew why. Of course, that didn't stop them from enjoying his hospitality, alcohol, and hors d'oeuvres. Some wondered why they'd been summoned to his mansion in Nyarutarama, Kigali's most affluent inner suburb, at less than twenty-four hours' notice, others feared asking in case it turned out they were supposed to know and their invitation had been a mistake which might lead to an embarrassing and swift departure. Plenty, however, didn't care and were more than content in their ignorance.

It was clear Gasana was celebrating something, but after two hours there'd been no announcement or speech explaining whatever that something might be. Perhaps it was simply a welcome home party after months away from the capital. Maybe he was just in a good mood after all and fancied spreading it around.

Gasana was happy, and it was the kind of happiness that came from knowing something that nobody else did. Of course, as he always thought, that wasn't a hard thing to achieve in Kigali. His wealth and position meant that he inhabited a version of Rwanda's capital that was a city of well-to-do sycophants who weren't as clever as they thought they were no matter how much their usually foreign education had cost. It wasn't that he'd rather spend his night in a run-down bar in a Gikondo backstreet or Mumena alleyway in the south of the city, drinking with people whose yearly salary roughly equated to a minute or two of his, but sometimes he was tempted.

Ingabire Muhire was certainly having fun. The fifty-year-old had spent almost the entire evening nestled between two young men on a secluded bench in the corner of the mansion's garden that was almost blocked from view from the back of the house by the tall, flowering amaranths that surrounded it.

Ostensibly the men were part of the catering crew that had been hired in a flurry of phone calls the previous afternoon when the house's staff were told to open the place up and get it cleaned and ready for the party. However, their job wasn't to make sure all the guests' drinks were topped up and bellies half-full with miniature South African wagyu beef brochettes and slivers of Lesotho smoked salmon – it was to show Muhire a good time.

How far that good time went was up to Muhire. The men had been chosen based on their lack of qualms about responding to the advances of a married woman who was known in certain circles for her casual relationship with the concept of monogamy, and paid enough to make sure they went through with whatever she might ask them to do as the night went on.

Gasana didn't want to interrupt Muhire for too long, but he also wanted to make sure she understood where her two admirers had come from so he excused himself from the couple he'd been talking to – an awkward fertiliser heir and his conspicuously younger wife – and strolled over the immaculately cut lawn to say good evening.

As he approached and came into full view of the bench, both men moved to get up, but Gasana waved at them with his champagne glass to stay where they were. One of them immediately turned his gaze back on Muhire, but the other suddenly seemed a little self-conscious and refastened a couple of the buttons on his shirt that had somehow come loose.

'Thank you for such a wonderful evening,' Muhire said, raising her own glass towards Gasana.

'My pleasure,' he replied.

'Will you be in Kigali long?' she asked.

'Only a couple of nights this time,' he replied. 'I just hate coming home to an empty house.'

Muhire took a long swig of champagne, her glass instantly refilled by the man to her left. 'Why such a short visit?'

'Too much to be getting on with in Nyungwe.'

Her lips spread into a conspiratorial smile. 'Ah, yes.'

'Thank you for your help with the *Lorgnette* profile, by the way.'

'Of course,' she replied. 'We can't have people being critical of our great nation, or our best and brightest. What you're doing down there sounds very exciting.'

Gasana grinned back. 'I must give you a tour sometime. Friends are always welcome. And so are theirs.'

Muhire's smile widened as she took another sip from her glass and Gasana nodded his goodbye, leaving her alone with her companions.

He sauntered back across the lawn, raising his glass and dipping his head towards more appreciative faces, until he saw one ahead of him that belonged to someone who looked like they weren't having fun at all.

Kamanzi.

He was standing in the middle of the wide entrance to the mansion's ground-floor living room that had been created by opening the concertina glass doors that usually framed the view of the garden. Unlike Muhire, who had apparently found time between leaving her ministry offices and arriving at the mansion to change into a long, plunging dress covered in orchid print, Kamanzi had come straight from work. He was wearing the same sombre suit he always did and appeared very much like a father who had just come home from a long day to discover his children in the middle of a house party. Irritation radiated from him.

Gasana scooped a glass of champagne from a nearby waiter and held it out for Kamanzi, who took it and promptly put it down on another passing tray.

'Not in the party mood?' Gasana asked.

'No,' Kamanzi replied. 'Why am I here?'

Gasana smirked and said, 'I guess not to relax.' Then he stepped into the living room, leaning close to the other man as he passed him and added, 'I've got something to show you.'

The mansion had been home to a succession of international ambassadors before Gasana bought it and had it renovated. It was an older building than the one that perched between the two valleys in Nyungwe, but it now obeyed the same fundamental architectural principle: one half was for pleasure, one was for work.

Decoration throughout the mansion was minimal, just a few sculptures here and there to complement the clean lines that had replaced the swirling, ornate ones that had been added when the property was first built, back when gaudy artifice and ornamentation had been used to communicate power, wealth and taste rather than the absence of them.

Gasana guided Kamanzi up the sweeping central staircase – hewn, to the casual eye, from a single long curve of marble that projected out of the wall without any obvious support – to the first floor, which was divided between the bedrooms that sat above the living room and the large office that was on top of the kitchen that catered more for parties than intimate dinners.

Subtle, recessed lights automatically turned on as Gasana opened the door to his office and Kamanzi closed it firmly shut behind them.

The room was soundproofed. As soon as the door was closed the background hum of conversation and Kwaito mixed with Afro-Pop that had followed them through the mansion ceased.

'I'm not funnelling you public money so you can spend it on champagne and snacks,' Kamanzi said as Gasana drained his glass.

'You aren't funnelling anything,' Gasana replied. 'You've given me contracts with paperwork that's completely legitimate. Contracts that will soon fill your ministry's coffers with more money than you can spend.'

'If your plan works. So far all you seem to be achieving is lowering the price for tantalum by flooding the market.'

'I'm realigning the market,' Gasana said, putting his now-empty glass down on his desk next to a ridged metal briefcase. 'It's basic economics, Finance Minister, or would you prefer we keep letting everyone else overcharge for theirs and put ours back in the ground?'

Kamanzi didn't answer that question. Instead, he repeated his earlier one. 'Why am I here?'

Gasana circled the desk, opened the briefcase, and lifted up a clear vial containing a small chunk of silver metal in it between his thumb and forefinger. His eyes brightened with glee as he shook the glass container, making the metal jump and bounce.

'I've seen that before,' Kamanzi said.

'No you haven't,' Gasana replied.

He returned the vial to the briefcase and turned it round, revealing a row of four identical vials containing small samples of metal, each more dazzling than the last.

Gasana pointed at them in turn, starting with the dullest. 'Tantalum, iridium, rhodium, and now, palladium.'

Kamanzi's unimpressed expression transformed into a mask of astonishment. 'How much have you found?'

'Enough to make Rwanda one of the most mineral rich countries on the planet.'

'All from Shaft B?'

'And its offshoot tunnels.'

A shadow of concern drifted across Kamanzi's face. 'How far into the park?'

'Only a few kilometres. And technically under it.'

These were the two secrets of Shaft B. The first, that it was where GME was extracting elements that were several times more valuable than tantalum. And the second, that they'd been found by excavating deep into the ground beneath the protected wilderness of Nyungwe National Park.

Kamanzi reached out, running his fingers across the four vials before picking up the last one and taking a closer look at the metal that was worth considerably more than its weight in gold.

'We've already refined enough of all of them to match the known supplies in Australia, Brazil, Russia, China and Canada,' Gasana said.

'They'll have more than their official data says,' Kamanzi replied, his voice suddenly quieter as he stared at the countless sharp facets of the palladium.

Gasana could tell the other man was already falling under the precious materials' spell. He saw the prospector's glint in his eyes. The look that drove people to trek for hundreds of miles to pan for flakes of gold in freezing rivers with their bare hands, or spend ten hours a day in almost pitch black just to catch a glimpse of something rare and sparkling.

'And so do we,' he said. 'What we've processed is just the tip. When we announce our discovery the whole world will be clamouring to put our elements in their capacitors, catalytic converters, and fuel cells. Apple, Samsung, Tesla, they'll all want to work with us. Even Tiffany and Cartier will come begging for our precious metals.'

Kamanzi finally put the vial back in the briefcase. 'Then we should go public now.'

Gasana shook his head.

'Why not?'

'There's no need to rush,' Gasana replied, closing the lid of the briefcase and tucking it under the desk. 'Don't worry, this will make you prime minister but we're still a year from the next election. We've always agreed timings are up to me. It's my reputation on the line, and stock value.'

'When?'

'Not long. But there's something else I need to do first. These elements will reshape the future. I don't just want Rwanda to build that future, I want it to belong to us. All of it. And I'm going to make sure it does.'

CHAPTER 19

TWENTY-FIVE YEARS AGO

Nathan couldn't remember the last time he'd had a conversation with his dad that had gone on longer than about four words each. A small part of him hoped what he was about to say might inspire a few extra words of praise, or even questions, but most of him knew it wouldn't.

'I passed my GCSEs,' Nathan said from the doorway to the living room, in which Ken was sitting in the big chair that was off limits to anyone but him (not that anyone other than Ken or Nathan had been in the flat for the last five years).

On the floor next to him, as ever, was a glass and a bottle of Netto own-brand whisky. It was ten thirty in the morning.

'Time to be getting a job then, lad,' Ken replied, reaching down for the glass without looking or turning his head away from the TV – always on, always on mute – to smile or frown at his first and only born.

Eight words. Twice as much as usual.

Nathan stifled the voice inside him that wanted to point out to his dad that after five years on the dole maybe he should be the one looking for work to support his son. But that was a subject they'd never spoken about out loud ever since Ken turned up back at home an hour after he'd left for his first shift at The Harbrook after Nathan's mum's funeral. Just like they'd never talked about the fact that Nathan hadn't stepped foot inside the high school he'd graduated to the summer after Viv died until the fortnight a few months ago when he'd sat all his GCSE exams a year early.

Nathan missed his mum. She would have been jumping round the flat right now, or running up and down the aisle of Safeway telling anyone who would listen how clever her not-so-little-any-more boy was. But she wasn't here any more. And he was barely allowed to speak her name in the flat. It was like his dad was the only one allowed to mourn her, and it was all he did. As if the loss only belonged to her husband and not her son. Nathan wanted to scream at his dad that he was hurting too, but that at least he was still doing stuff while his dad just wallowed in the pain.

And only wallowed in a single location. He hadn't even taken Nathan to visit Viv's grave in Hartlepool since her funeral – burying her in a cemetery thirty-odd miles south of Newcastle had been the sole condition Viv's sister, who lived in Hartlepool and who did not like Ken, had insisted on in exchange for paying for the funeral that Ken couldn't afford.

However, instead of bringing any of this up – or that he'd got straight A*s in all his subjects – Nathan just turned away from the living room door, went into his bedroom, shut the door, and turned on the computer that sat atop the blue ten-year-old's desk at the end of his single bed, next to the window covered by curtains printed with pictures of tank engines and turtles that were never opened.

The mongrel desktop was how Nathan had avoided going to school. He'd pieced it together from bits he'd salvaged over the summer holiday between primary and high school, when he was waiting for his dad to snap out of his slump and realise he wasn't the only one mourning the loss of the heart of their family.

The monitor came from a skip outside Wallsend Library, the tower from a pile of rubbish outside an internet cafe in a side street off the top end of Northumberland Street, near the university, the keyboard and mouse left outside a house in Heaton that looked like it had recently been vacated by students in a cardboard box marked 'Free – take me.' None of it matched, and to begin with it had barely worked. But, after a few research trips to the library and internet cafe, Nathan had managed to repair everything that was a bit broken. He also discovered how to get it online via a little tinkering with the phone lines that ran in and out of their terrace and piggy-backing off downstairs' internet connection.

The next thing he learned was the coding language he needed to know to be able to hack into the admittedly pretty basic digital records system that his future school, Birch Tree High, used. The school had too many students and too few teachers and support staff, which meant no one noticed that Nathan Pike had a perfect attendance and test record despite only ever having recently actually walked through its gates for the first time. He probably could have falsified his exam results too, but had decided that taking them was actually the easier option than hacking proper government systems. He also wanted to see how he'd do.

He loaded up MSN Messenger to see if anyone was around.

Messenger was the programme Nathan used most. He found it easier to deal with people through the mediums of screen and text rather than in person. It was a defensive barrier, but a bridge too. In the real world he could only engage with people whose whole lives were confined to a few miles' radius of his home. On Messenger he could talk to people who lived all over the world – or at least claimed to. And when he was on it, he wasn't Nathan Pike, he was ZAP3644.

None of his contacts were online, but he had a connection request waiting in his inbox from someone calling themselves ~~N£8F~~. Nathan clicked accept. A message appeared a few seconds later: *Every man's his own friend.*

He had no idea what it meant. But before he could respond asking who ~~N£8F~~ was, another message appeared: *It's a world of disappointment.*

Now he wondered if his mysterious messenger thought he was someone else, or if he was one of those people that just hung around the internet, spamming people with random stuff to confuse or get a reaction.

Nathan could have asked. But instead he got up from his little desk and went through to the kitchen. He'd skipped breakfast and was hungry. His dad hadn't moved from his chair, and Nathan didn't ask him if he wanted anything. Not that it turned out there was anything to have. There was no food in the cupboards. And, irritatingly, no cash left on the Formica worktop for Nathan to go buy any with. Food shopping, like almost everything else to do with running the household, had fallen to him since his mum died. The least, and only, thing his dad did to help was leave out some of his dole money to pay for it.

He left the flat, figuring he'd find something he could eat – a bakery on the high street with some of yesterday's bread left out the back, a food stall in the covered market with some bruised produce no one would buy.

But, as he walked towards the stretch of shops near the Metro station, his anger at his dad started to boil up. His dad, and the rest of the world. Why did he have to take care of himself? Why did he have to sort everything out? Why did he have to learn so much about the things that grown-ups were supposed to do for him?

He was sick of it. He didn't want to have to come up with a secret or clever way to get what he wanted. He just wanted to take it.

So, walking past the branch of Woolworths that had had closing-down signs in its windows for the last year and a half, he decided he would.

He doubled back on himself and went inside the store.

It was sad-looking, half of its lights out and more of its shelves empty. But it had customers, quietly shuffling up and down its aisle, working out what bits of its bones they might want to pick at. None of them paid him any attention. And neither did the staff, who seemed like they'd checked out of their jobs a long time ago. Even the recent growth spurt, which had made him feel awkward and gangly and stopped his clothes fitting quite right, didn't seem to single him out.

He went to the sweets aisle – the one that was still fully stocked – and relieved it of two Crunchie bars. One he kept in his hand, the other he slipped into his pocket while he considered what else was on offer. Then he put the bar he was still holding back and repeated the action with a couple of bags of chocolate buttons.

No one came dashing over or shouted at him over a tannoy.

He dared to do it again, this time slipping a Fry's Turkish Delight into his pocket. Then he moved away from the sweets section, and settled into a slow orbit of the rest of the store, as if he was browsing its remnants like everyone else. And still no one appeared in front of him, telling him to empty out his pockets.

He wanted to take something else, just to prove to himself that he could. A present for passing his exams, he told himself. He wandered over to the music section, but could tell from the first CD case that he picked up that it was empty. He tried the stationery but he didn't really need any pens.

He gave up and started towards the door, keeping his pace even and slow to avoid drawing attention. But just before he reached it, something caught his eye. A comic book cover emblazoned with cartoon men, women and beasts in bright blue and yellow costumes, looking weird and cool. He picked it up, pretending to flick through it while he glanced at the staff on the tills nearby. When they were all distracted by the customers they were serving, he stuffed the comic under his t-shirt and strode back out.

The comic and the sweets were the first real crime he'd ever committed – at least within the bounds of his quickly invented definition of what a 'real' crime was: taking something that definitely didn't belong to him, and that he couldn't say he should have. This wasn't like faking some school records or borrowing someone's internet connection when they weren't using it. This was actual theft. And the rush of it, combined with the sugar from the sweets he ate on the way home, was exhilarating.

When Nathan got back to the flat, he went straight into his room, flopped on his bed, pulled the comic out from under his t-shirt and read it cover to cover twice.

Once he was done reading the story of mutants fighting to save a country that didn't even want to admit they existed, he got up and checked Messenger again, which was when he noticed there was another message from ~~N£8F~~: *I know many who do worse things.*

That freaked Nathan out. The message was only eight minutes old. Was ~~N£8F~~ referring to the things he'd stolen? It was impossible. There was no way they could have known what he'd done. But then why else would they have said that? And the messages from before, that seemed like they were a direct response to how he was feeling after his non-celebration with his dad?

But, again, before he could decide how or if he wanted to respond, another message appeared on the monitor screen: *Please, sir, can I have some more?*

For all the time Nathan spent reading, he'd never bothered with much fiction. When he'd been younger he'd liked adventure stories set on alien planets or in space but he'd never been interested in major works of earthbound literature and had only skimmed the ones he'd had to read for his English exams. However, he recognised that last sentence his new digital pen pal had sent him.

He checked the time on the screen. It was quarter to one.

The library shut early on Thursdays, but if he raced he could get there before it closed for the afternoon.

Five minutes after sprinting out of the flat, he pushed the entry door of Wallsend Library open, almost barrelling straight through the member of staff who was already closing the narrow tilting panes that ran around the whole of the top of the single-storey building with a window pole.

Nathan went straight to the fiction section and ran his fingers along all the books with authors whose name began with D. When he couldn't find what he was looking for he went to the catalogue terminal that had recently replaced one of the two librarian's desks and searched for *Oliver Twist* by Charles Dickens. The library had two copies but they were both out on loan. The terminal asked him if he wanted to reserve one of them when they came back in, or one of the ones in Newcastle Central Library. He declined both suggestions but the second one prompted him where to try next.

He took the Metro five stops west to Monument, the station in the middle of the city named after the towering column that sat above it on the square where two of the city's main thoroughfares, Grainger and Grey Street, met. On the north side of the square was a branch of Waterstones in a carved sandstone and weathered copper building, and on the first floor of the bookshop was a very large classics section.

Nathan, dismissed by the counter staff by the entrance of the shop who noticed him come in as another one of the cadre of gothy teenagers who spent their summer holiday afternoons hanging out round the corner in Old Eldon Square goading each other to buy copies of *Mein Kampf* or *Das Kapital*, climbed up the first flight of the wide, central staircase and walked over to the shelves stacked with classic works of English literature.

There was only one other customer nearby, a man who Nathan might have guessed was in his late thirties or early forties, if he'd been paying attention to him. But he wasn't. He was focused entirely on finding a copy of *Oliver Twist* and checking that he was right about where he thought the messages ~~N£8F~~ had come from.

However, as Nathan found the shelf that was full of books by Dickens, and reached out a hand to retrieve a black-spined Penguin Classics edition of *Oliver Twist*, the other man suddenly appeared next to him, grabbed the book before Nathan could, and held it out for him, saying, 'About time you showed up.'

CHAPTER 20

NOW

Rivas was happy, which was good, because she hadn't only travelled all the way from San Salvador to check that everything she was planning on sending to Malak Ali had been properly prepared for the long journey there. She'd also brought a safe containing two billion-dollar private keys with her.

'How did you know we were ahead of schedule?' Pike had asked when she'd gleefully whispered this fact to him, nodding at the armoured truck that had emerged from the jungle behind the Jeep that had carried her and Jones.

'I have my sources,' she replied. 'Martinez has a satellite phone.'

So, Pike thought, the captain had been watching him even more conscientiously than the odd review of camera footage. Close enough to report on him, but hopefully not so closely that he'd sent any warnings or sounded a secret alarm.

Rivas was escorted on two tours of the compound. The first one was led by Martinez and she gave him all the congratulations and superlatives anyone could have wanted for his diligence and thoroughness in getting the secret trove packed up and ready to ship.

Though he would never admit it, and didn't volunteer it from the back of the small party that had accompanied Rivas down to the treasure room, Pike was impressed with what Martinez and his team had achieved. The cataloguing of the artefacts and relics, which Pike had taken a surreptitious look at the previous night, was meticulous, and their freight storage prepared to exact specifications with no corners cut or half measures. To deliver such uniformly high standards after months away from homes, families and comfortable beds took both an unwavering belief in what was being done, and extremely careful leadership. It was a testament to Rivas's persuasiveness and Martinez's management.

The second tour included just Rivas, Jones and Pike. Pike showed the two women the work he'd been in charge of, starting with the emergency exit that had been blocked off and filled in and had its opening in the dirt three hundred metres from the compound's main entrance welded shut for good measure. Then he led them on a circuit of each level, pointing out where new cameras and sensors had been installed, and then how to control them from the old computer terminal.

'You've built us our own Fort Knox,' Rivas said once Pike was done.

'Like I told you before, even the most advanced security system can be defeated with enough time and effort,' he replied. 'But this one will hold out more than long enough for reinforcements to arrive.'

The president turned to Jones. 'That doesn't sound like a money-back guarantee.'

'British modesty,' she replied to a laugh from Rivas.

They went above ground and found that all the trucks and the Jeep had been moved to the very edges of the clearing so that lunch tables could be set out. It was a repeat of Pike's first day at the compound, except the energy was different. People were happy, relieved, excited to be done with their long labour.

'You've done a great service for my country,' Rivas said to Pike as Jones walked over to speak with Rivas's driver who had been subtly waving at her since they'd reappeared.

'My pleasure,' Pike replied.

'Have you ever done the same for your own?'

Pike paused for a second, then gave her a reluctant nod.

'It didn't go well?'

'Let's just say I was better at asking questions than following orders. Eventually the people telling me what to do got tired of me not just obeying them.'

Rivas smiled.

'Like the child always asking why. Sometimes the only answer is why not,' she said

Then the president climbed up onto the bench she'd been sitting opposite Pike on and the whole clearing immediately fell silent, as if everyone in it had been waiting and watching for this exact moment.

Pike's Spanish was just about good enough for him to follow the gist of what she said to the crowd, and her tone, as usual, was abundantly clear. There were heartfelt thank yous, congratulations, and a request for one last push before the real celebrations tomorrow.

When she was done, cheers went up and people leapt to their feet and went back to work. The president's pep talk had done its job.

Jones returned as the tables cleared and Martinez, standing at the entrance of the compound, started barking orders.

'There's a problem with one of the lorries in Perquin,' she said. 'Nothing major, but I should go and deal with it.'

Rivas looked around at the activity that had erupted at her command and smiled again. 'I'm sure we can spare you a while.'

Jones nodded at the president, and Pike, and marched back over to the Jeep.

It took less than ten minutes for the first of the crates to start being wheeled out on platform and hand trucks, ready to be loaded up and ferried down to the town.

Once the operation was in full swing, Rivas gave a signal to the four men waiting next to the armoured truck and they unloaded the single crate in the back of it. Over the course of two very subtle hours, it was moved into the compound, through the treasure room like the crucial piece in one of those children's games where tiles were slid around a square to make up a complete picture, and then down into the new vault room without any of the people taking

boxes out noticing – or at least with none of them daring
to mention it.

The room looked very different to the last time the president had visited. The wiring for its lights had been made permanent, there were three cameras hanging from the ceiling,
two pointed at the floor in the centre of the room where the
crate was being manoeuvred to and one at the entrance, and
the entrance itself was now a thick steel door with a keypad
attached to the wall next to it at the bottom of the stairs.

As the crate was taken apart to reveal a safe that looked like
it was the same make and model as the one from the Central
Reserve Bank, Pike realised that Jones had never come back.

He briefly enjoyed picturing her caught in some drawn-out
argument with a local who hadn't seen any personal economic
benefit from the last couple of months and was now trying to
get their share by inventing parking charges or threatening
not to forget what had been going on at the compound. Or
maybe she was in the clearing, helping keep Martinez focused
on overseeing the loading up and not wondering where the
president had got to.

Either way it was better that for the next five minutes she
wasn't in the vault, as she would have just been another body
to be dismissed along with the four other men.

Once they were alone, Rivas gave the safe's dial a spin and
its sides a tap, then inspected the reinforced door.

'Can this be blown up?' she asked Pike.

'Not without bringing the ceiling down on you,' he replied,
then he pulled the door shut and pointed at the keypad. 'Six

digits of your choosing, followed by the star key to set it. Same to unlock it.'

Rivas gestured at him to turn around, which he did without protest, and five seconds later she gave him a pat on the back as she passed him and started up the stairs.

* * *

The sun's strength was just starting to fade when the last of the day's crates were leaving the compound. The treasure room was now two-thirds empty, only the most cumbersome and valuable pieces left behind for one more night of being guarded by the complex's staff and upgraded security systems.

It meant that tomorrow would be an easy morning, and most people would be on their way home, wherever that was, by the afternoon. It also meant that tonight was going to be their last night, so there were roars of appreciation when one truck made a last journey back up through the jungle to deliver several cases of beer, rum and tequila, care of the president.

Rivas opened one of the cases of tequila herself and handed Pike a bottle of *El Jimador Reposado*. 'I'd celebrate with you, but duty calls. Cabinet meeting in the morning.'

'We can trade places if you'd like,' he said, earning a chuckle.

'I think they'd notice,' Rivas replied.

Pike knew he wasn't going to be leaving with Rivas and Jones. He'd agreed with the former that he should stay to keep an eye on all his enhancements to make sure they were working as they were meant to. And he'd agreed with the latter that tonight would be the night he stole the private keys.

He waved along with everyone else as Rivas's Jeep left, then spent a couple of hours alternating between drinking shots and tipping them over his shoulders as people around him sang, danced, and competed to get the most drunk.

The only person who didn't seem to indulge at all, Pike noticed, was Martinez. The captain appeared content to stand on the sidelines like a parent at a school disco, making sure everyone was having fun but not too much fun.

Eventually, Pike slipped away to his bedroom without anyone noticing. He spent a few minutes checking everything he needed was where it was supposed to be, and then a couple more listening to the raucous sounds coming through the high window before they lulled him to sleep and dreams of robbery.

CHAPTER 21

The alarm on Pike's Casio woke him up at four a.m., an hour before dawn. He'd managed six solid hours, helped by just the right amount of tequila, and any tiredness he might have felt was quickly replaced by adrenaline.

He got dressed in his army-issue fatigues and double-checked that the rucksack he'd stuffed a change of clothes and the USB stick in was still inside the other bag then put it next to the door, along with his hurricane lamp and the black metal square Jones had slipped into his hands the day before which he'd hidden under his mattress. He retrieved his PADD from beneath his pillow, then briefly balanced on top of the camp bed, listening for anything louder than the occasional quiet snore coming through the high slit in the wall.

He slipped the rucksack over his shoulders, gathered up the lamp and metal slab, and made his way down towards the vault. There were no lights on anywhere, no cameras caught him in their lenses, and no alarms sounded as he passed through infrared beams. Which meant that the cascading worm he'd uploaded into the compound's computer system was doing exactly what it was supposed to.

The malware programme Pike had hidden in a tiny slaved part of the new back-up computer's hard drive had been timed to activate when it was least likely to be accidentally discovered, and selective in the targets it attacked as it crept, probed and corrupted its way through all the new connections that had been introduced to Perquin's self-contained digital network.

Pike needed most of the electrics knocked out, but not all of them. He didn't want anyone being disturbed from their drunken slumber, or being able to spot him easily if they went stumbling looking for a toilet. However, he had to keep a little bit of power eking through the compound otherwise the very large metal door he needed to get through would stay locked with no way of opening it beyond acquiring a few pounds of C4 from somewhere.

The treasure room was deserted, as it should have been, but he was still silent as he crossed over it. Even though the compound's acoustics dampened most human-made noise, he still knew some people slept nearby and didn't want to risk waking them. He paused momentarily to check the crate containing the petrified headdress was still with the other most valuable items, then continued on to the stairs that led down to the vault.

The glow of his lamp was joined first by the one that framed each of the buttons on the box embedded in the wall and second by his PADD as it revealed the code Rivas had inputted the day before – 695218. Pike had no idea if the digits meant anything significant in the president's history, or the nation's, but he didn't need to know. The bolts holding the door locked released.

Theoretically, he had much longer to crack this safe than the one in the Central Bank – the worm would keep the compound's security offline until both the back-up computer and the main one in Martinez's office were rebooted – but this part of Pike's plan was actually the easiest so he wanted to get through it as quickly as he could.

He put the lamp down in front of the safe, and the rucksack and metal square next to it, and got to work. He spun the safe's dial (black with white numbers, again) left several times to reset the drive-cam, then began slowly moving it right, counting the pickups with his free palm and ear.

It took him twenty minutes using the same mix of logic and guesses to find the three rough areas where the lock's combination was hiding, and another seven to settle on the exact digits: 05-14-83.

Pike tried them in ascending order, then swapped the first two and felt the lever drop into the notches of the three wheels and nestle into the notch on the drive-cam. He pulled open the door – it groaned on its hinges but not too much – and saw the two private keys inside. Then he reached into the first rucksack, opened the top of the second one, retrieved his dummy USB stick and placed it next to the ones inside the safe. They were a perfect match.

He smiled. The first stage of his little operation was complete.

One of the sticks remained in the safe, which he closed and locked again, one went into the inner rucksack, wrapped inside his Cuban collar shirt, and one was pressed into the thin slit that had been cut in the foam on the underside of the square of black matte metal.

Then Pike went upstairs, back into the treasure room, for the second stage.

This part of the plan required him to work completely silently and meticulously.

He kept the rucksack on his back, ready to make a run for it if needed, as he carried the black square over to the crate that contained the petrified headdress. He made a mental note of the shipping information that had already been stapled to the top and side of the large wooden box, then using a crow-bar borrowed from the tidied-away equipment rack he began slowly levering the lid off, easing the nails without bending them or the wood with the edges of the bar.

Pike went side by side, lifting the upper panel of wood a few millimetres on each until the lid was completely loose. He felt like he was Indiana Jones minus the whip and jacket, raiding an ancient temple or tomb. He removed the lid, and then the glass case containing the petrified headdress.

The thing still astounded Pike, even after looking at it and thinking about it so much over the last week. He could have stared at it for hours, but that was a luxury he didn't have. He was, however, going to get to touch it. He released the clasps that held the glass box's solid top – hoping he wasn't about to unleash some ancient curse – and removed it. Then he reached in, cradled the front of the headdress with one hand and gripped the styrofoam that had been moulded round its sides to hold it in place during transit, and gently lifted it out and put it on the floor.

So far, so good.

Next, he picked up the metal square with the USB stick tucked under its hard shell and lined it up with the glass box. It needed to be a perfect fit, and it was. Pike made sure it was completely level, let go, and watched as the air trapped beneath it slowly escaped and it sank to the bottom of the box, matching the metal that was already there and creating a false base no one would ever notice.

He let himself indulge in one last look at the headdress before he lifted it up, carefully placed it back in its container, lined up the nails in the crate lid with their holes and pushed it closed.

Pike had managed to complete the two most difficult parts of his plan flawlessly. Time to make it three for three.

He returned the crowbar to its hook, turned his lamp down to its lowest level, and began to creep his way towards the secret exit that would lead him to his hidden cave and out into the jungle.

He made it to the first corner out of the treasure room when an alarm started blaring. He froze and looked down at the bottom of the walls either side of his feet – he'd tripped an infrared sensor.

'Shit,' he muttered, the first words out of his mouth since he'd woken up.

He burst into a jog, as his brain raced to work out what had happened. Martinez must have reset the whole computer system. Maybe he'd simply risen early, realised the lights were down and needed rebooting. Maybe he'd never trusted Pike.

Pike heard confused mutterings and stirrings emanating from rooms that were suddenly being bathed in flickering light and noise. He turned off his lamp and kept his pace steady and his footsteps soft, hoping anyone who noticed him would assume he was as confused as they were and trying to find an explanation.

He needed to get as deep as he could into the complex before anyone realised he was heading the wrong way and was tempted to follow him.

A staircase took him to a darker corridor, only lit at its ends, and then another, smaller set of steps that descended into blackness. Pike kept his lamp off, but slowed his pace, navigating by memory. One doorway, then another, then the subtlest change in the humidity in the air that told him he'd reached the fissure that led to the cave.

He paused for a breathless moment. He couldn't hear anything, but that didn't mean a whole battalion of soldiers wasn't about to leap out of the gloom at him.

Dawn light was poking through the few gaps in foliage that covered the entrance to the cave – useful for helping Pike get through the jungle, but also for anyone hunting him.

He abandoned the lamp at last, pulled open a gap in the vines wide enough for him to fit through, and began a wide loop of the compound, navigating again from memory, towards the road that led north and south out of Perquin.

Pike's route involved cutting between multiple trails, never moving in anything close to a straight line for very long. He made it across the rutted grooves of the vehicle path, a green streak in mud-clad trainers, and over halfway to the road when a giant fern leaf next to his head shredded as he passed it and the bark of a tree in front of him exploded.

He'd been found, and someone was trying to stop him.

He'd left the treasure room in immaculate condition, the safe locked and behind a closed door. They couldn't know why he was fleeing, only that he was, and that was enough of an excuse to shoot. Martinez had definitely not trusted him.

As someone who spent most of his working life in cyberspace, Pike had been attacked before, but usually with code and binary digits. Occasionally with a fist or a foot. He'd never been shot at. He didn't like it at all. He hadn't minded playing at being the movie hero, or taking the odd punch if it got him what he wanted, but this was suddenly all too real.

Pike dodged to the side, plunging himself into the undergrowth and fighting his way through deep leaf mulch and spiky burrs before he reached another winding path. His heart pounded in his ears, but not loud enough to drown out the sound of more bullets.

He stayed on the new path for a few tens of metres until he heard shouts behind him replace the gunfire and he switched again, this time bounding through the undergrowth and raising his knees up to his chest with every rushed step.

Louder explosions sounded on all sides, and he wondered if Rivas had been lying about the lack of landmines around the compound, or if his pursuers were using grenades as well as weapons to try to flush him out.

The reality of running through a jungle as it blew up around him and soldiers hurled bullets at him was nothing like how Pike had imagined it'd be when he'd been plotting out scenarios for how this morning might turn out. He had to fight to stop it overwhelming him, keep his mind focused on all his possible routes out of the jungle, and remember that he wasn't just trying to escape but head somewhere very specific.

The voices began to fade, and not just because they were being drowned out by more booming noises. Pike was managing to put ground between himself and the people chasing him. But some of their shots still came dangerously close to his shoulders and head. He folded himself over as far as he could while still lifting his legs as high as possible to stop them getting tangled and tripping him up. He looked like some strange, long-legged crab working its way through a landscape it wasn't used to – trying desperately to escape while blending in.

The thought suddenly occurred to him that even if any bullets that came his way missed him they might still hit the backpack and slice straight through the billion-dollar private key. So, as he silently chastised himself for not considering this rather crucial point sooner, he yanked the pack off his back and strung it across his chest, turning himself into a long-legged pregnant crab.

He kept going, kept pushing on through the leaves and vines, alternating his glances ahead and behind him, trying to keep an eye on the people pursuing him while also making sure he wasn't losing himself.

Pike was almost at the road when he skidded to a halt next to a tree that had an unusually thick knot of intertwined roots wrapped around its base. He'd spotted it on his hike down to the town and etched it into his mental map. He couldn't say he was completely relieved to have stumbled on it – people were still trying to shoot and probably kill him – but he was glad he hadn't ended up too far off course.

He stepped off the path, knelt down, slipped the straps of the backpack off his shoulders, and shoved the second one which contained his change of clothes and the USB stick into a small cavity where two strands of root twisted over each other.

Then he slung the first rucksack back over his shoulders and, a minute later, emerged onto the tarmac looking like he was just out for a morning hike, and immediately saw that the road was blocked off twenty metres ahead of him by a Jeep and an armoured van that Rivas, Jones, and several soldiers with raised assault rifles were standing in front of.

He strolled towards them, trying to even out his breathing as quickly as possible and waving, a big smile on his face.

The president did not smile back. Neither did anyone else.

'I thought you were heading back to San Salvador yesterday?' he said to Rivas once he was five metres from the blockade.

'We decided to spend the night thanking the townspeople,' she replied. 'We were about to leave when we heard there was a problem at the compound.'

'That explains the shouting I could hear,' Pike said, keeping his voice light and mildly confused. 'I have to confess, I only got through a quarter of the reposado before I crashed on my bunk last night.'

'Why are you here?'

'I go for a stroll most mornings before breakfast. Keeps me out of everyone's way. Has something bad happened?'

Rivas didn't answer that question, she just gestured to one of the soldiers who stepped forward, lowered their weapon, and removed Pike's rucksack. They opened it and pulled out the only thing inside – a half-empty bottle of water with a torn label.

Pike was putting on a good act, and he might have gotten away with it if a second later Martinez hadn't appeared out of the jungle in the exact spot Pike had, carrying the other rucksack.

The captain, flanked by two other men, marched straight past Pike to Rivas and handed her the bag. The top was already unzipped and Pike, along with everyone else, watched as the president picked out the USB stick that had been wrapped in his blue shirt and let the bag fall, spilling the rest of his clothes onto the ground.

Everyone was silent, waiting for the president to speak. When she did, her voice was hard.

'You would take from us, after we opened our arms to you?'

Pike didn't say anything, but Jones stepped forward from the line and turned towards the other woman.

'Madam President—' was all she managed to get out before Rivas told her she was as guilty as Pike was of abusing her trust. A soldier took his silent cue and nudged Jones over next to Pike.

'Have the two of them escorted out of the country,' Rivas said to another uniform, and then to Pike and Jones, 'Consider your freedom extreme leniency for exposing holes in El Salvador's defences that will be plugged immediately.'

CHAPTER 22

TWENTY-FIVE YEARS AGO

Nathan stared dumbfounded at the man who had grabbed the copy of *Oliver Twist* before he could, taking him in properly.

He was about the same height as Nathan, but a heavier build, wearing a plain dark t-shirt, black jeans and black trainers. The only thing that was unusual about him was his shock of blond hair that was pushed back across his head and held in place by a hefty amount of gel. And, of course, what he'd just done.

The man half-smiled at Nathan, his grin stretching across the right side of his face without disturbing his left one at all, then spun round, carrying the book with him, and marched straight down the staircase and out of the shop.

Nathan, utterly confused, followed him. He'd read the word 'brazen' in books from the library and understood its definition, but this was the first time he'd seen it in action.

He kept his eyes fixed on the ground as he passed the till, expecting someone to call out at him, even though he'd done nothing wrong. But none of the shop assistants said anything – again, if they even noticed him they would have assumed he'd just bottled stumping up the eight pounds for whichever provocative-sounding but actually quite dull philosophical treatise he'd been dared to buy.

Nathan caught up with him on the other side of the monument, a few paces after the man had shoved the copy of *Oliver Twist* into the back pocket of his jeans, and they walked side-by-side, looking almost like father and son, down Grey Street. They took an abrupt left turn at the junction where it turned into Dean Street, heading along Mosley Street instead of descending down to the quayside.

They reached the big roundabout by the Unison union building, then went through a series of underpasses that brought them onto the eastern side of the Tyne Bridge. It occurred to Nathan that there were quicker ways to get to the bridge, but not that the circuitousness of the route they'd taken had been the point.

The eastern pavement of the bridge was as quiet as ever – there were plenty of faster ways across the river than walking over the most famous of the city's six bridges. The man stopped in the exact centre of the span, leaned against its dull green railing and looked out at the construction site that spanned the riverbanks, which would soon give the river its seventh crossing to celebrate the new millennium.

Nathan, uncertain what else to do, leaned against the railing a metre to the left of the man.

'Who are you?' he asked, once it became clear the other man wasn't going to speak first.

The man turned to him, half-smile back on his face and hand held out for him to shake. 'The name's Simon Delaney. Good to meet you, Nathan.'

Nathan looked at the proffered hand for a moment, then tentatively reached out to grasp it.

'How do you know who I am?'

'I like to get to know people who I think might be useful.'

That sounded, frankly, creepy. Yet, even though Nathan could have just turned around and walked away from the stranger, he found that he didn't want to. He wanted to know what was going on.

'What does that mean?' he asked.

'You're a smart boy, you show real promise.'

Nathan sensed the man was being sarcastic. But it was also the first time he'd been praised by anyone in five years. It felt good. And he wanted to prove it was true.

He retraced his steps, trying to find the man hiding somewhere in his memories. Had he been in the library, a brief glimpse of white hair through the book stacks? Had he been in Woolworths, another supposed shopper wandering the half-lit aisles? Or maybe outside the school? There had been a few parents lingering by the gates, but they all belonged to students. The man could have been masquerading as a teacher – Nathan didn't know what any of them looked like so wouldn't have registered an imposter – but he couldn't remember seeing the man who called himself Delaney anywhere before the bookshop.

'You've been watching me?'

'I've taken an interest,' the man said, turning back to look down at the river. 'As I said, you've got potential.'

Nathan realised that so far he'd only asked Delaney questions, but he couldn't stop himself from posing another one. 'What do you want with me?'

'I'm in the business of liberating things that people no longer need or maybe don't even remember they have, and finding them a home where they'll be appreciated.'

'You're a thief,' Nathan said. His first statement.

'Bingo. Told you you were smart.'

'That's not an answer,' Nathan said.

'Fair point,' Delaney said, turning back to him again. 'Sometimes my work is done to order. That's why I'm in town. I need to acquire something and I'm on a deadline. I could do it by myself but I think you'd make it a lot easier and faster.'

'Why would I help you?'

'The thrill of the illicit, which I bet is still pulsing through your veins a little after this morning. And revenge.'

Nathan's face contorted into a frown that mingled confusion, guilt and the realisation that maybe he was still riding the high of his trip to Woolworths a bit.

'The item I'm after is locked up in the depths of the Harbrook Museum's basement storage,' Delaney continued. 'Something everyone outside that venerable institution has forgotten even exists. Everyone but the person who wants me to get it for them.'

Nathan had blamed his dad for the Harbrook being taken away from him, but maybe Delaney was right. Maybe it was actually the museum's fault. His dad had made sure he always behaved himself when he was there, that everything was always put back where he'd found it. He hadn't caused any harm or done any damage. He'd been one of the museum's most loyal visitors, but as soon as the people in charge had found that out they'd effectively banned him from ever going back.

That wasn't a nice thing to do to someone, and maybe it did deserve a little revenge. And maybe his dad getting fired did too.

'You want me to hack their computer system?'

Delaney laughed at that. It was a garrulous laugh, like someone had just told him the funniest joke he'd ever heard. Nathan's frown deepened as irritation was added to the melting pot of emotions he'd been feeling ever since their conversation had started.

'You're still an amateur when it comes to computers,' Delaney said. 'But I bet you know the place better than the back of your hand. That's what I need to know. How it really works, its creaks and blind spots, the routines and habits that aren't stored on a hard drive.'

Nathan felt flattered again, like Delaney really did need him. But if he wanted to get revenge on the Harbrook – and he was increasingly convinced that he did – there were ways he could do it by himself. He might be an amateur, but he was still pretty sure he could work out how to take their payment systems online. Or just wait for a rainy night and smash a few windows and cause a mess whoever took his dad's job would have to clear up.

Delaney seemed to read Nathan's mind and added, 'And I'll throw in a little bit of the cut. Fair recompense for work done.'

Nathan liked the idea of having money of his own that he hadn't had to beg his dad for. But the man offering him some was a stranger and despite Nathan's teenage urge to rebel against childhood lessons and warnings he still knew he was supposed to be wary of strangers.

'I don't know you. Why should I trust you?'

'You already do. You followed me into the middle of a bridge I could tip you off the side of any second with no one else around.'

Nathan reflexively took a step back from the railing, which prompted another booming laugh from Delaney.

'I'm joking,' he said. 'And if it goes well there might be more in it for you. It's been a while since I had an apprentice, and I think you've got a gift.'

Before Nathan could ask him what exactly that meant, Delaney handed him the copy of *Oliver Twist* from his pocket and said, 'You ever read this?'

Nathan shook his head as he took the book.

'You should,' Delaney replied, as he started to stroll away over the bridge towards Gateshead on its south side. 'I'll drop you a line about meeting up again,' he called out behind him a few steps before he was out of Nathan's earshot.

CHAPTER 23

NOW

Pike waded out of the water, the whiter-than-white sand squeaking under his wet feet as he strolled up the shallow incline to the dry part of the beach. The Caribbean was calmer than the Bay of Thailand. And warmer too. So warm, in fact, that Pike had chuckled to himself when he'd first dipped his toes in it the previous afternoon and registered absolutely no difference to the high air temperature.

He raised his hand to shield his eyes and looked up to his left at the miniature stepped pyramid of the ancient Mayan fortress that stood on a headland above the town and beaches of Tulum.

It was a lot closer to him than it had been when he'd wandered down into the sea. It was a stunning sight, the grey stone surrounded by green trees, the white sand giving way to azure waters. Pike could easily understand why the Maya had chosen this specific location to worship the dawn from.

A few bright unnaturally coloured dots bobbed up and down in front of the pyramid's thick walls – the caps of day-tripping tourists who had come down from Cancun or Playa Del Carmen a couple of tens of kilometres north – but there weren't that many of them. The towels and parasols on the beach that seemed to stretch the entire Yucatan coast were also spaced far apart, occupied by the occasional couple or small group. The Riviera Maya was having a quiet week.

He turned away from the fortress, unbunched the swim shorts that had crept up his thighs as he'd floated along with the sea's gentle current, and started walking along the sand.

After ten minutes he reached the frayed umbrellas and unbrushed, overgrown paths of an old beachfront hotel that hadn't seen better days in a long time. And he walked straight past it, into the perfectly manicured grounds of the exclusive resort next door that Jones had checked them into the previous day and which, Pike guessed, was waiting for its neighbour to finally go out of business so it could put a few more villas and cabanas on its prime real estate.

A winding path and quiet, rhythmic music took him to a row of four-poster double-width day beds, facing the sea. Most of them were empty, their linen drapes tied back and side tables empty, but the one in the very middle of the line was occupied.

Jones was lounging in its centre, wearing a batik kaftan, large sunhat and tortoiseshell sunglasses, and holding a thin-stemmed glass containing a clear liquid Pike was sure wasn't water.

He perched on the edge of the bed, next to where he'd tucked a resort-branded tote bag an hour earlier, and followed Jones's gaze out towards the blue.

'Now I get why you do this,' he said.

'There are worse places to be exiled,' Jones replied.

The Gulfstream hadn't been waiting at San Salvador airport when Pike and Jones had been driven straight there from Perquin without any further words from Rivas or themselves once she'd ordered their expulsion from El Salvador. They'd been put on the next flight out of the country, which just happened to be going to Mexico City. But by the time they landed there a first-class transfer to the Yucatan peninsula had been miraculously arranged and they were whisked through their second airport of the day in considerably nicer fashion than the first one.

It was only when they were in the blacked-out Bentley Mulliner that pulled up at the arrivals zone at Cancun airport at the exact moment they strolled through its automatic exit doors that they discussed the events of the last twelve hours.

Jones had seemed uncharacteristically on edge to Pike since they'd left El Salvador, and the first words out of her mouth in the Bentley revealed why.

'Rivas shouldn't have let us go like that,' she said.

Pike shrugged. 'Maybe she meant what she said about being lenient.'

Jones gave him a look that made it clear she wasn't ready to buy that possibility, and that she thought Pike was being naively stupid if he did. 'Or she wanted us on foreign soil and away from her before she sent someone after us.'

'I haven't seen anything that suggests she even knows what really happened in Perquin. As far as she's concerned, we failed and have disappeared with our tails between our legs.'

Jones's expression changed from suspicious to quizzical, and Pike finally let her get a close-up look at his PADD – with a warning about its destructive defences – and played through a series of video feeds of the Perquin complex's security cameras.

They watched as Rivas stormed into the compound, down to the treasure room and through it to the vault. Then, a minute later, they followed her as she went to Captain Martinez's office, her strides less urgent but still purposeful, and had a short, silent conversation with him. After that, she left and Pike switched the feedback to the treasure room, where two armed guards took up position at the entrance to the staircase that led down to the vault as other soldiers continued removing the last of the crates, including the one that housed the petrified headdress and the second USB stick that Pike had hidden in the fake bottom of its hermetically sealed container.

'How do you have this?' Jones asked, as the Bentley sped past several signs offering the chance to swim with turtles at the next turning off the highway that was taking them down the coast to Tulum.

'The compound's computer network is a little less air gapped now,' Pike replied. 'Not a permanent connection, or a simple one from this distance, but there's enough of a digital dribble coming out of it that I can piggyback off nearby phones and on-board car computers to grab the odd data package. This was all downloaded before we left the country.'

Jones studied the screen, her eyes fixed on it even as the activity on the feed became more mundane and sporadic.

'No one's gone into the vault since Rivas?' she asked.

Pike shook his head. 'She'll change the code to the safe and the vault door at some point, and probably the ones in the central reserve bank too. But at the moment she and I are the only people that know both the Perquin codes and I doubt she'd let me back in the country and past her new guards before she sets new ones.'

'The headdress?'

Pike opened a new window, the PADD screen dividing in two to show the image of the near-empty treasure room on the left and a map of El Salvador on the right, with a red dot slowly pinging its way east, a few kilometres north of Lake Ilopango. This was a live feed showing the location of the truck carrying the shipment the headdress was on, the vehicle's Satnav system unwittingly feeding the PADD its real-time GPS information.

'En route, right on schedule with no diversions or delays.'

Jones seemed satisfied, though hardly elated.

He knew she would have preferred it if a tracker had been hidden in the headdress's container along with the private key. But, as he'd pointed out, even the most sophisticated trackers are, by their nature, designed to be traced, and for the plan to work, the headdress had to attract absolutely zero unwanted attention as it passed through airports or entered Malak Ali.

They couldn't afford a sudden signal spike or scan on an unexpected bandwidth to arouse anyone's curiosity. So, they had to make do with intuiting the progress of the delivery to Dubai by studying its data trail.

They'd arrived at the Tulum resort and were shown into adjoining suites with views out across its gardens and the beach.

Pike showered, ate alone in the hotel's restaurant, and then indulged in catching up on his sleep on an extremely comfortable and very large mattress. He didn't see Jones again until late the following morning when he'd wandered down for his dip in the Caribbean.

She'd seemed more relaxed to Pike in their brief exchanges of 'good morning' as he put the tote bag containing his PADD and balled-up t-shirt under her daybed, but still not entirely at ease.

Now, Pike reached down, retrieved the PADD, opened it up and scanned through the contents of the windows he'd last checked before leaving his room.

'Still no international arrest warrants issued for us, or bounties on our heads,' he said. 'And Rivas's emails and texts are all business as usual.'

In comparison to everything else he'd managed to achieve over the last week using just the most basic technology, gaining clandestine access to the official and personal communications accounts of the Salvadoran president had been a walk in the park.

He hadn't done it while they'd been in San Salvador building her trust, just in case they were protected by the kind of security that would have flagged an attempted hack. But as soon as they'd landed in Mexico City he'd put a couple of algorithms to work care of the free airport WiFi and discovered just the standard government-level protocols that were easy to overcome.

This made him all the more curious about the full extent of what was being planned with the private key. Because if stealing it was just about causing havoc and destabilising El Salvador there were much easier ways to achieve both of those things. A couple of emails from Rivas firing her entire government, declaring martial law, or announcing that she was the reincarnation of Jesus Christ would do the trick.

Pike silenced any qualms the less unethical parts of his brain might have voiced about invading Rivas's personal as well as presidential privacy by reminding himself that he'd rather have a head-start if she did decide to send a hit squad after them.

He scrolled through her inboxes and sent items, careful not to open any messages she hadn't looked at yet without immediately marking them as unread.

'Out of interest,' he continued, 'she won't be able to change the combinations on the two safes for a week. Turns out they were chosen specifically because they're difficult to reset so they've had to find a specialist.'

He smirked at Jones, but she only responded with a nod, a sip of her drink, and a question.

'Where's our stick?'

Pike's PADD had kept tracking the shipment that contained the headdress overnight, with instructions to wake him up with a very loud alarm if there was any delay or deviation to its journey. It hadn't. It had, however, monitored the departure records, flight paths of the cargo planes that had taken the headdress and everything else bound for Malak Ali to Panama City, then Istanbul. The shipment had started out on its final leg while he'd been in the water.

'Three hours from Dubai,' he said.

'And where are we headed?'

'That's taking a bit longer to figure out.'

Malak Ali was an auction house as well as an extremely high-end warehouse. But the trades, deals and exchanges that saw its contents moved between its oversized safety deposit boxes didn't happen on site or online. They were glamorous, in-person affairs, held in exclusive locations all around the globe. Invitations were only extended to people who already used Malak Ali, or who were being targeted as potential clients, and nothing about them was made public.

Pike would have needed digital trickery that he could unleash from a beach lounger to penetrate the free zone's own systems and work out where the upcoming auction Rivas had needed to get her loot to Dubai in time for was going to be. Instead, he'd sent a couple of emails containing a little light malware to a few high-net-worth names he guessed would be in attendance.

Not the most sophisticated approach, but he was willing to give it a little more time for it to work.

And a little more time was all that was needed. As soon as he moved over to the bed next to Jones's, rolled onto his back and clasped his hands behind his head, the PADD, now lying beside him, vibrated a notification.

Pike propped himself up, unlocked the screen, glanced at it and then lay back down again.

'Athens,' he said.

'When?' Jones asked.

'Two days,' he replied.

CHAPTER 24

Jones drained her glass and got up from her daybed.

'Don't go far,' she said as she walked away towards the main hotel building.

Pike took that to mean that while their time in Mexico might not last much longer they weren't in a rush to check out.

He stayed on his bed for a few minutes, feeling the heat of the day really start to build as the sun reached its zenith, then decided to go find some shade.

There were no rivers in the whole of the Yucatan. Its only source of freshwater were the cenotes dotted all over it – giant sinkholes and caves that had been created when the peninsula had been an ancient coral reef and then covered by jungle when sea levels fell.

The Maya had used the cenotes as a source of life-giving water and occasional sacrifice. Nowadays the more remote and mysterious ones attracted adventurous divers and the ones closer to towns and villages were treated pretty much like municipal swimming pools.

Some of the peninsula's best cenotes were on the outskirts of Tulum, an easy stroll or cycle on a hotel-branded rental bike away.

After dropping off his PADD in his suite, Pike went down to reception, consulted the map that was helpfully given to him by the man on reception, and picked Cenote Mariposa, the fourth furthest out of town.

The cycle was only about fifteen minutes in the bike he'd been given's lowest gear, but his gamble that the daytrippers and holidaymakers in Tulum would opt for nearer ones had been right – there were only a few other people enjoying the cool water and shade cast by the sinkhole's high sides.

He paid the modest entry fee, walked down the wood plank staircase that descended to the pontoon that ran round a quarter of the cenote's walls, shoved his t-shirt, towel and flip flops into a shelf box and dived into the water.

It was a lot colder than the sea, and Pike almost had to catch his breath as he broke the surface again and started moving his limbs to get them used to the change in temperature. But it only took a few strokes for his body to relax, and he turned over onto his back, letting the water lap over his ears as he gazed up at the tree-rimmed sky.

As he floated in slow, wide circles he wondered again about the extent of Jones's motives and when she or her bosses would consider their job complete – and who her bosses were.

He still hadn't been able to find anything about Jones on the internet, dark web, or in any old databases or records he could reach digital tentacles into that might give him a clear idea about her and her employer's true identity.

However, despite that they had still given him plenty of clues about the kind of organisation they were.

They weren't scared by high stakes but they also weren't greedy or purely interested in money – they could have taken more than one of El Salvador's private keys, maybe even tried for all of them. They played a long game – Jones had spent months ingratiating herself with Rivas as a seemingly legitimate security consultant before Pike came on the scene. And they were extremely well-resourced to have Gulfstreams and Bentleys on tap.

They also preferred to get disavowable third parties to do their dirty work – it was Pike who had been 'caught' stealing the private keys, and shot at for the privilege. And while they seemingly didn't want to risk injury themselves they were more than happy to use murder or at least the threat of death to get their way if needed.

Whoever they were, he thought they should be impressed with what he and Jones had achieved so far – and she should be a little more pleased about it too. They'd managed to get a billion-dollars-worth of cryptocurrency out of Perquin. A pretty incredible feat in and of itself. Yes, the USB stick wasn't in their hands yet and it was still, technically, in Salvadoran possession, but no one who had the power to stop its delivery to Malak Ali knew that.

Then, as he looked up at the rim of the cenote, he questioned whether that was true.

A figure, silhouetted against the sun, was looking down into the pool, staring at him.

For a few moments Pike wondered if the perspective was playing tricks with him and he'd anthropomorphised a stunted tree or plucky bush into a person, but as he continued his slow circuit of the water the light shifted and he became certain that it was a man wearing a wide-brimmed hat and bushy moustache, whose eyes were fixed on Pike.

Pike didn't consider himself an ugly sight. His face didn't inspire fascinated revulsion and his body was in reasonable condition and still had enough of a tan from Cambodia that he shouldn't look entirely ridiculous bobbing around in the deep blue water. But he'd also never been described as so strikingly handsome that it was impossible to take your eyes off him. And yet the man above him refused to look away.

Who was he? Had Rivas dispatched someone after him and Jones after all? Had Captain Martinez donned a disguise, slipped into the country to exact some revenge for being made a fool of? Had the Salvadorans warned the Centro Nacional de Inteligencia, and the Mexican version of the FBI had sent someone to spy on him and Jones? Or was this man working for Jones to keep an eye on him and make sure he really didn't go far?

Whoever he was, he wasn't being very subtle. Which either meant he was bad at his job or that Pike was supposed to know he was being watched.

Pike had the same choice as when he'd first turned Jones down in Sihanoukville – try to get away as quickly as possible, or pretend he hadn't noticed his admirer and play at everything being normal. He picked a third option. If the stranger was going to be obvious, he could be too.

He lifted his left arm up out of the water and waved at the other man, then twisted round onto his front and swam for the pontoon.

By the time Pike got up to ground level the stranger had vanished. Pike made a show of shrugging and looking round, just in case he was hiding behind a tree or bush still watching him, and went to his bike, which was still where he'd left it with no punctured tyres or bombs secreted about its frame.

The cycle back to the hotel was uneventful, no one tried to run him off the road or abduct him, but no sooner had he stepped back into his suite than Jones knocked at his door and told him they'd be leaving Mexico that evening.

CHAPTER 25

Gasana had cleared his schedule.

He was supposed to be taking meetings with wealth managers who believed they could secure him higher returns on the investments he made with the dividends he occasionally took out of GMA, and hearing the pitches of a group of young entrepreneurs looking for funding for some new venture. But they had only ever been pencils, and they were all happy to be moved if some flexibility meant the possibility of currying a little more favour. Instead, he'd been mostly locked away by himself in his office in the Kigali mansion, monitoring progress from Nyungwe remotely, and killing time.

Gasana was not a naturally patient person. He understood the importance and power of long-term planning, but he preferred to always be active in the present somehow – doing deals, planning new strategies, plotting the possible outcomes of any decision so that he could be prepared for whichever way the wind blew. However, he had learned that sometimes simply waiting was unavoidable.

The world didn't always spin as fast as he wanted it to, and there was a thin line between being the energetic voice driving things forward and a hectoring drone people eventually found a reason to tune out. Enthusiasm could be contagious but it could also be irritating. Force could inspire resistance as much as change.

Yet, even when he was waiting, he wasn't doing nothing. He was in a constant state of readiness – prepared to act and seize the initiative as soon as he could. Which meant it took all of an hour from him receiving the message from Mexico in his secure inbox and asking Dusabe to make some enquiries about office space in the Malak Ali free zone for the invitation to an extremely exclusive event in Athens to be sent to his official GME email address.

He appreciated the speed with which things were suddenly happening. It was bold, and flattering.

The invitation wasn't about lineage, influence, or being the right class of person. It was purely, simply, about money. He was someone who had it. How he acquired his wealth and what he used it for wasn't important. The only thing that mattered was that he might be persuaded to part with some of it in exchange for joining a private club of the equally rich.

Gasana forwarded the second email to Dusabe, telling him to RSVP on his behalf, then got to thinking about the kind of first impression he wanted to make when he made his entrance while he poured himself a glass of Martell XO cognac from the bar cabinet that was built into the wall behind his desk. He usually made a point of championing his mother continent's ability to craft luxuries on a par with anything the rest of the world could produce, but even he had to admit that

African spirits still had a way to go before they could compete with their European counterparts.

He decided he needed a jet.

He was normally happy to fly business or first-class on a regular commercial plane, but that wouldn't do for this occasion – and neither would any of the private airlines based at Kigali airport that exclusively flew second-hand planes in need of either a paint job or a retrofit or both. Something would need to be chartered from Nairobi or Cairo, or maybe even Cape Town.

Another thing for Dusabe to arrange.

Of course, he thought, as he tapped the briefcase that was still under his desk with his foot as he swirled the ice cube in his glass, if things went to plan he might treat himself to his own Learjet or Gulfstream.

How many people would he need to take with him? Gasana didn't like large entourages, and had never had one. He thought they were crass, obvious, wasteful, usually populated by hangers-on who did nothing useful and were liable to say things they shouldn't in order to steal a fraction of someone else's achievements to boost their own meagre ego.

Ever since the mansion had been tidied up after his 'welcome home' party its occupants had just been him, the security guard permanently stationed at the gate to its drive, and the cook who came and went every morning and evening.

No, just Dusabe would do. His *umuntu* was the only person he needed, and the only person he had ever completely trusted. Plus, seeing as he'd have arranged the trip it was only fair that he'd get to go on it too.

They'd only be out of Rwanda for a couple of days, but it would be the first time in months that at least one of him or Dusabe hadn't been in Nyungwe, overseeing operations and keeping everything running smoothly to the schedule that only they knew.

Things were at a critical juncture and both security and productivity had to be maintained. However, Gasana was confident that, thanks to the very clear messages that had been communicated to the facility's scientists, engineers and excavation crews after the recent unfortunate incident with the would-be thief, every single person working there realised that now was not the time to slack off or do any-thing stupid. They understood that now was not the time to jeopardise the triumph that they'd all worked so hard for and was so nearly within their collective grasp.

CHAPTER 26

After her profile on Lucius Gasana had finally been signed off following three rounds of edits that gouged any sense of authorial perspective from it, Beatrice Forte allowed herself exactly seventy-two hours of sulking.

She lived in the Parklands area of Nairobi. She'd chosen Nairobi as her base of operations because the Kenyan capital's airport was the busiest and most well connected in East Africa. And she'd picked Parklands because it was near the city centre but also next to the Karura Forest, which was a good place to go for a hike or run when she needed to clear her head or find a fresh angle on a story.

However, she did neither for three days. Instead, she stayed in her one-bedroom, twelfth-storey apartment, which she'd rented furnished six months ago and was still yet to decorate with anything other than plane tickets and newspapers, silently raging at the butchering of her work.

Then, once she'd burned through her anger, she allowed herself a further twenty-four hours to wallow.

Forte turned the blame on herself. Told herself that she should have just done the job right in the first place, swallowed her pride, written a thousand empty words of flattery and gotten on with her life. But she hadn't, and there were now probably several marks against her name in some digital database or next to a headshot of her on a pinboard in Amsterdam.

Lorgnette was a part-time job, one of three international correspondent gigs that just about paid her rent while she hunted for a big story that would make her career, and right now she couldn't afford to lose it. She really should have just paraphrased the contents of the Nyungwe press pack and added a few colourful lines about the sunrise over the national park.

On the fifth day, however, she felt her ego gradually start to rebuild itself, and her journalistic instincts begin to reignite.

Forte had anticipated some pushback on her profile. After all, very few articles ever reached publication without at least a few altered sentences, trimmed adjectives and other sub-editing tweaks. And any good writer knew to take grammatical changes on the chin. And she had, as she kept incessantly reminding herself, gone a little off-brief.

What had surprised her was just how many changes had been demanded, and not all at once. At the time she'd inter-preted the multiple demands for revisions as a sign that she'd fundamentally botched the assignment, and was continuing to botch it. But now she was curious about what else might be behind them.

Lorgnette worked to strict deadlines and was more likely to spike a story that wasn't working than drag out fixing it, which suggested some other power was at work here. Had Gasana been given approval of the article, or was someone else pulling on strings and favours to make sure the man was only painted in the most flattering light?

She decided that the first step to finding out the answer to that question was apologising.

Forte had eaten her way through the emergency bags of dried pasta she kept in her small kitchen and finally took herself out of her apartment in search of groceries. On her way to the local supermarket, she stopped at the coffee shop at the base of a residential building two junctions down from her that had become popular with the international young mothers crowd and ordered an espresso. While she waited for it to arrive, she pulled out her phone, found the website of a florist in Amsterdam that did next-day delivery, and ordered a bouquet of peonies to be sent to Clara Stoepker, her commissioning editor at *Lorgnette*.

The following morning, she kept her eyes glued to her laptop screen, refreshing her inbox every minute. Once she received the automated delivery note from the florist she watched for a thank you message from Stoepker. As soon as it arrived, almost an hour after the peonies had reached the *Lorgnette* offices, she snatched her phone up off the dining table-come-desk in front of her and dialled Stoepker's extension.

'You didn't have to,' Stoepker said in her Dutch-inflected English before Forte had the chance to confirm that she was the person calling from a number with a Kenyan country code at the front of it.

'I think I did,' Forte replied.

Forte had learned at the very beginning of her career that sometimes getting what you wanted out of a subject involved being sneaky or even borderline threatening, and sometimes it meant just being nice.

Clara Stoepker had worked for *Lorgnette* for as long as the magazine had been in business. She ran a tight ship and was respected throughout the industry for her professionalism. But she was also, if handled right, a bit of a gossip.

'I'm guessing I put you in the middle of something awkward,' Forte continued, already subtly steering the trajectory of the conversation in the direction she wanted it to go. 'I'm sorry for that. I promise I won't do it again.'

'Really, there's no need to apologise,' Stoepker replied. Then added, the volume of her voice dropping the slightest fraction, 'To be honest the whole thing was very weird. But then dealing with people like Gasana is always odd.'

The other woman's quick openness told Forte that the flowers had been the exact right move. And that the *Lorgnette* office, which was entirely open-plan, must have been quiet.

'Did he put up a fight?' Forte asked.

'I wish. We could have handled that. No matter how important millionaires think they are, unless they buy us it's our lawyers who have final say about what we print, not theirs.'

'Oh god, I haven't upset Dijkman, have I?' Forte said, pitching her voice up half an octave.

Nils Dijkman was the editor in chief of *Lorgnette* and he was feared as much as Stoepker was respected. He'd spent his career building high-end magazines, taking kickbacks from luxury advertisers and wielding his self-appointed position as a trend and tastemaker like a sword. Even people who hated Dijkman went to great pains to ensure they were never on his bad side. Forte didn't really suspect that she'd ended up there, but if she had it would pretty much mean the end of her career.

'The requests for changes came from an even higher power than Nils.'

Stoepker was one of the few people at *Lorgnette* and probably on the planet that called Dijkman by his first name.

'When the foreign ministry gets in touch,' she continued, 'it's usually about which city they want bumped up our best places to live list.'

'Great,' Forte said, now adding a little jovial lightness into her voice. 'So now I'm persona non grata in The Netherlands. How long does that last?'

Stoepker chuckled down the line and reassured her again not to worry about anything. They kept talking for a few more minutes before something else demanded the commissioning editor's attention, she thanked Forte for the peonies again and told her she needed to end the call.

Forte let the other woman go, glad that she hadn't soured their relationship, and that she'd been right about something strange having gone on.

Over lunch she wracked her brain and dove deeply into Google, trying to find some direct thread she could pull on between the Dutch government and Lucius Gasana or his company. There was none. No personal friendships, no prospective mining contracts, no quiet investment of Dutch public pension funds into African infrastructure projects. But that just meant that the connection had to be indirect.

Any request from Rwanda to The Netherlands would have gone between their respective foreign ministries. However, more research suggested that there was no particular closeness between Gasana and Ingabire Muhire, the Rwandan Minister for Foreign Affairs, or any of the more junior ministers that worked under her. So, there had to be another link in the chain.

Forte returned to another lesson that she'd learned when she'd been training as a journalist. An axiom that guided most stories when you got down to their real depths, and helped explain almost everything that had ever happened since the dawn of modern civilization: follow the money.

If public estimates of Gasana's finances were anywhere near accurate, he could have afforded to build his glass castle and the rest of the Nyungwe complex she'd seen in her brief visit by himself. But he'd needed government approval to build and mine there, and that approval would probably have come with some form of official or unofficial financial backing and an arrangement to split the proceeds that came from whatever he extracted from the ground.

This train of thought very quickly led her to Jean Kamanzi, the finance minister. Rwandan media was firmly controlled by the state – not openly regulated but very closely watched, and people did not criticise anything the government did if they wanted to keep their citizenship – so there was almost as little information about Kamanzi available online as there had been in the scant biography of Gasana she'd been sent ahead of her interview. However, reading between the lines, she could tell that Kamanzi had been prime minister-in-waiting for a long time and there was an underlying sense that his rumoured grab for power might finally be near. His name also had a habit of appearing in bylines that also featured Gasana.

She wanted to kick herself for not seeing it earlier. As soon as she'd received the brief about the profile of Gasana and started to look into him she'd suspected that something was off, both about him and what was happening in Nyungwe. But she'd focused on the wrong part of the story. She'd got caught up in Gasana's own spin instead of thinking about what it might be designed to distract people from.

This might not be a story of overblown egos and false messiahs of industry, she thought. It might just be one of good old corruption.

If it was, that would explain why her piece had ended up so neutered and pasteurised, and how it had been done. It would also make Kamanzi a thread she could pull on.

CHAPTER 27

TWENTY-FIVE YEARS AGO

Nathan read *Oliver Twist*, the story of a boy without a mother who becomes a thief before a couple of kind souls rescue him from a life of crime.

The parallels didn't match completely – Oliver was an orphan, and even if he wasn't paying any attention to him Nathan's dad was still alive – but there were enough for him to feel like Delaney was making a pretty obvious point by giving the book to him.

What he couldn't work out though, was who Delaney was meant to be. He was too old to be the Artful Dodger. But was he Fagin, the man who just wanted to use Oliver, or Mr Brownlow, the man who wanted to save him?

Whichever he might be, he was dangling the chance to learn something new in front of Nathan, and maybe a way to expand his horizons beyond the limits of Wallsend.

For almost two days, Nathan lay on his bed waiting for the promised next message. After countless screen refreshes and checks that the computer was still connected to downstairs' internet, he started to think it wasn't coming and that he'd actually just had a weird encounter with a strange man who liked giving people stolen books in the middle of bridges. But at nine p.m. on the second night a single line appeared in his MSN Messenger inbox below ~~N£8F~~'s other ones: *9 Etherley Road. Tomorrow. 12 p.m.*

Nathan didn't reply. But he did go into the living room, creep past his snoring dad to the shelf that had an old *A to Z* under an out-of-date *Yellow Pages* and looked up Etherley Road. It was in between Chillingham Road and Walkergate Metro stations, near the greyhound track, one of a few roads through what looked like industrial land by the colour shaded around it on the map. About a thirty-minute walk from the flat, or half that if he took the Metro.

He memorised the location, then put the *A to Z* back on the shelf and went to his room. He was tempted to go take a look at Etherley Road right away, but decided instead to poke around AltaVista and a couple of other less-public parts of the internet to see if he could find any mention of Simon Delaney anywhere. He couldn't. Which made him think there might have been some truth in what he'd said on the Tyne Bridge about Nathan still being an amateur.

The next day, Nathan ended up taking the Metro to Chillingham Road and walking back east the short distance to Etherley Road while he finished off the sausage roll he'd lifted from the Gregg's bakery by Wallsend Station. He was a bit shocked by how quickly he'd become comfortable with stealing, and how easy it was.

Etherley Road was an industrial area but, from the looks of it, an abandoned one. It was a row of single-storey garage lock-ups. Some of them had had their metal roller shutters caved in, others welded shut. Weeds sprang up between cracks of concrete and everything was covered in graffiti.

He reached number 9 and, with no door or bell in sight to knock or ring, banged on its red-painted shutter. Slowly, the hinged metal started to rise. Until it stopped at Nathan's waist.

He waited a few seconds in case its motor was struggling to finish its job before realising that if it did open all the way it would reveal whatever was inside to anyone that might be passing (not that he'd seen a single other person for the last ten minutes).

Nathan leaned over, shuffled through and stood up straight again as the roller began to descend back down to the ground. Inside, he found Delaney leaning against the side of a table, on top of which seven chunks of metal were arranged in a row.

'What's this?' Nathan asked.

'Your first lesson,' Delaney replied.

Nathan heard the shutters clatter against concrete behind him and for a moment thought he'd made a mistake – first for coming here at all and second for not telling anyone that he was. Delaney's comment about hurling him off the Tyne Bridge echoed through his mind, but then so did his follow-up about trusting him. Nathan still didn't really have any reason to, but what was the alternative? Spend the rest of the summer stuck in the flat, choosing between signing onto the dole or finding a sixth form college he could pretend to go to?

He stepped closer to the table, and realised he knew what the little angular blocks of metal were – they were all locks that had been removed from their doors.

'You've got to learn the basics,' Delaney said. 'Everything comes from mastering the basics.'

'But I can already break into computer systems.'

'And what happens when they go down and all the doors are still locked?'

Nathan shrugged. 'Smash it open.'

'With what?'

Nathan shrugged again.

'With something that'll make it blindingly obvious to any-one that you were there,' Delaney said. 'A good thief is a ghost who knows how to make the things that are there to stop him bend to his will.'

Nathan stepped closer to the table and picked up the lock on the left end of the row. It was a thick, hard-cornered barrel with a slit in one end of it. He turned it over in his hands, then looked at the other ones. They were all a slightly different shape, size and colour. He knew how they worked mechanically, in theory, but he'd never thought about how to open one without its key.

Delaney pulled something out of his pocket and put it down in the centre of the table. A rolled-up tube of fabric. He unfurled it, revealing its contents: a collection of small, scalpel-like metal picks. Some of them had jagged, pointy ends. Some had curved, bumpy ones. Some were dead straight right up until their tips, which were bent at a right angle.

'Try unlocking it,' Delaney said, gesturing at the tools.

Sceptically, Nathan picked up one of the curve-ended sticks and shoved it in the slit of the lock, feeling it rub against the notches of the mechanism that a key would normally push and hold into place. He reached the end of the narrow hole and nothing happened. So he pulled the pick out and tried a jagged one. Again, nothing. Nathan frowned. He didn't like failing.

'Come on,' Delaney said, a half-smile spreading across the right side of his face. 'You can do better than that.'

'I don't know how,' Nathan said, his voice ripe with petulance as he dropped the spiky pick on the table.

'Think about it. A key doesn't just move the pins out of the way, it stops them falling back down. So how do you do that?'

Nathan had a sudden flash of memory. To the last time he was in a classroom five years ago, listening to a teacher spoon-feed the other children answers to questions he already knew. He wondered if they'd felt as frustrated as he did now.

He thought in silence for a moment, then said, 'Tension.'

'Exactly,' Delaney replied. 'So how are you going to apply some?'

Nathan thought some more, about shifting the inner barrel of the lock just enough so that any pins he managed to move into place wouldn't slip back down. He reached out for one of the right-angled picks, placed it in the mouth of the slit, and put pressure on it while he tentatively nudged the first of the locks five pins up. It held in place. Then he did the second, the third, the fourth and the fifth, each one more slowly than the one before, out of fear that one wrong move could make all the pins fall back down. But they didn't, and, once they were all in place, he turned the right-angled pick all the way round, releasing the lock.

Delaney gave him a round of applause.

'Good work,' he said. 'Now do the next one.'

Spurred by his achievement, and desire to prove to his new tutor that it hadn't been a fluke, Nathan snatched up the second lock and got to work. This one was thicker and heavier than the first lock, but with a slightly narrower slit in it which required a different combination of tools to open. However, now Nathan understood the principles of what he was doing, it didn't put up much resistance. It took him less than three minutes. He shaved another ten seconds off his time with the third lock, and with all the rest until he'd conquered all seven.

Nathan put the final lock back in its original position on the table, and slotted the last pair of picks he'd used into the fabric pouch. He looked at Delaney, expecting another smile or more praise, but instead received the lock he'd just opened in one hand and the fabric pouch, rolled up, in the other.

'Now you've got the idea, you need to work on your speed. Come back tomorrow, and show me you can pick a lock in under thirty seconds.'

* * *

Nathan walked home, both hands gripping his gifts from Delaney stuffed in his pockets. If his dad wondered where his son had spent most of the afternoon he wasn't curious enough to actually ask. He had, however, remembered to put some money out for Nathan to go do a food shop with, which he did after stashing the lock and the picks in his room.

Nathan went to Netto. Safeway was closer, but obviously he wasn't going to go there. Once he'd got the groceries, made dinner, eaten his and left his dad's on the kitchen counter for him, he went to his room and got on with his homework.

After an hour he was down to two minutes. After another he made it to one. However, from that point the faster he got the slower his progress became. It took him until almost midnight to find the perfect balance of speed and patience, confidence and lightness. But, by the time he finally stopped and went to bed, he could open the lock in twenty seconds.

The next day he was back at the lock-up at midday, and this time he found Delaney leaning against something large, square, and covered in a sheet. On top of it was another tumbler lock.

Once Nathan was inside and the roller shutter had obeyed Delaney's invisible command to roll back down to the floor, Delaney tossed the lock to Nathan.

'Show me,' he said.

And Nathan did. He was a little slower than with the lock he'd practised with but he still got the new one open in under half a minute.

'Well done,' Delaney said, then he pulled away the sheet, like a magician about to show off the assistant they'd just sawn in half, to reveal a dull grey steel box with a small black enamel dial on the front of it. 'Lesson number two.'

*　*　*

It took a week for Delaney to teach Nathan how to crack a safe.

He couldn't take it home with him to practise, so Nathan spent almost every hour of every day in the lock-up, listening to Delaney explain the delicate, magical art of communicating with the cam, wheels and lever that were buried deep in the safe's reinforced steel. He listened to the man explain how to feel for the slightest change in resistance on the dial and hear the faintest sound that would lead him to discovering the combination.

For the first two days, Nathan did exactly what he was told, and achieved nothing. He just couldn't sense what Delaney was telling him to. There were no subtle shifts or subsonic sounds. And, if it wasn't for the fact that he had nothing else to do, he might have given up, thanked Delaney for teaching him how to pick a lock, and seen how many comics he could get away with stealing from Woolworths.

But then, on the third day, something changed. Maybe it was the familiarity that had developed after hours of having the side of his head pressed up against the safe, maybe it was cabin fever and lack of fresh air, but Nathan really started to believe he could feel and hear what the safe was trying to tell him.

'Deep down, every lock wants to be opened,' Delaney said.

Nathan believed him.

It took another two days of slowly spinning the dial left and right digit by digit searching for contact areas, but he narrowed down the options for the three numbers that made up the safe's combination. First to within ten, then five, then two.

He had six potential numbers.

Nathan didn't have a calculator, but even without one he knew that the possible combinations of six numbers ran into the thousands, and that was before factoring repetitions. He needed to get closer. He wanted to keep going, work through the night. However, Delaney sent him home.

'You can't force it. Push too hard and it'll push back,' he said.

That night Nathan dreamt of numbers, and the next day he told Delaney he knew which three he wanted to try.

Delaney, the half-smile back on his face, gestured at the dial on the front of the safe and told Nathan to give it a go.

Even with three numbers, there would still be several different combinations to run through, and no obvious one to start with. So Nathan picked an order at random. And, remarkably, the wheels inside the mechanism aligned, the lever fell into place, and the lock released.

Nathan pulled open the door to the safe.

Inside was a small oblong object about the length of Nathan's forefinger, wrapped in purple foil.

A bar of Fry's Turkish Delight.

Delaney reached into the safe, handed Nathan the chocolate bar and said, 'Now, let's talk about the Harbrook.'

CHAPTER 28

NOW

Another plane, another flight.

This time Pike and Jones were in the plush comfort of the Gulfstream again. They flew east across the midnight Atlantic for twelve hours to Europe, and Greece. They landed in Athens at eight p.m. the day after they'd left Mexico.

Their landing vector provided a dazzling view of the Saronic islands, the Piraeus port, and the Acropolis gleaming above the rest of the Greek capital, before they banked down towards the airport.

The private terminal was already busy with small jets parked alongside each other. Some of the planes would belong to the ranks of incredibly wealthy people who liked to spend a few weeks drifting around the Aegean or island hopping on their own mega-yacht, but it wasn't the height of sailing season just yet, and Pike guessed that a lot of the planes were here for the Malak Ali auction.

Once the Gulfstream was on the ground and taxiing over to the car that would take him and Jones into the city, he decided to check. He fired up his PADD, found an unsecure point on the airport's computer network and started to snoop through the arrivals list.

In the last four hours, planes from Moscow, Ankara, London, Zurich, Hong Kong and Kuala Lumpur had arrived. And more were due from all over the planet: Los Angeles, New York, Mumbai, Rihad, Cairo.

Two flights that were scheduled for the middle of the following day caught his eye.

The first was a plane that was on its way from Monterey on the California coast, the airport closest to Carmel-by-the-Sea, the town that had been a hippy enclave in the sixties and was now a playground for the mega-rich who were happy to pay a couple of million dollars per thousand square feet for their Big Sur weekend retreats.

The second would be coming from Kigali, but hadn't left yet because the plane was still on its way to the Rwandan capital from Cape Town in South Africa.

And then, once they'd walked down the Gulfstream's retractable stairs and straight into the open doors of the waiting car, they made their way to another hotel.

Pike had been to Athens for work once before, one of the first jobs he'd taken after METIS. A pharmaceutical company had been gearing up to launch a new ketamine-based analgesic gel and were terrified of the news leaking before their PR agency had the chance to shift public opinion on the safety and health benefits of the much-maligned and abused tranquilliser. It had taken Pike less than a day to identify the couple of legacy Windows programmes still running in the company's headquarters that could leave its data network vulnerable to someone snooping around. He'd also quietly taken a look at the personal digital correspondences of its various department heads and drawn up a shortlist of people who might be tempted to sell their employer out for the right amount of money.

In the end, someone responsible for signing off budget requests had decided that Pike's recommendations about updating the security of their computer systems was an expense they could get away with not paying, information about the ketamine gel got out, and the company ended up spending a lot more than Pike had suggested on reputation management and trying to convince the public that it hadn't been trying to turn people into drug addicts.

The city had surprised Pike in the few days he'd been there. He'd expected it to be like Rome, where eras of architecture and society bled politely into each other, creating a cohesive multigenerational landscape. It wasn't. It lurched from period to period. Ancient columns butted up against utilitarian office and apartment blocks. Wide, solemn boulevards clashed with chaotic, clogged side streets. It was a hectic mess, and he'd liked it.

That time, he'd Airbnb'd an apartment on the edge of Exarchia, an old anarchist neighbourhood in the north of the city that was covered in terrible graffiti and exceptional Cretan restaurants. However, it was clear from the turns the car took as they got closer to the centre of the capital that he wouldn't be staying in that part of the city again.

He considered asking Jones for a clue about their destination but decided not to bother. Her mood had remained as muted and distant as it had turned once they'd arrived in Mexico, and her words extremely few and far between since they'd left. He'd barely seen her the whole trip across the Atlantic after she'd disappeared into her cabin as soon as they'd boarded the Gulfstream in Cancun.

Eventually they turned into a large square that Pike recognised: Syntagma.

It was cut out of a slight natural incline, and stepped on one side, the thick, deep blocks of marble leading up to the wide, cream-coloured palace that housed the Hellenic parliament. The other three sides of the square were occupied by expensive hotels and tourist shops, and the roads that looped it swarmed with taxis and buses.

After a few sharp blasts of its deep horn to clear a path through some lingering bright yellow taxis that were hoping to pick up an evening fare, the car deposited Pike and Jones in front of the arched entrance to one of the square's grander hotels, the Marseille.

The Marseille was the inverse of the Tulum resort.

It was all brocade, plaster and curves with almost no straight lines in the entire place. A pungent, floral fragrance wafted through the entrance door held open by a man in a long wool jacket despite the warm summer's day. However, it seemed like it was there less to set the olfactory scene and more to act as a barrier against the petrol and diesel fumes that hung over Syntagma Square, trapped by the high pressure that kept the sky clear and the city hot into the night.

The auction was happening earlier than Pike had anticipated, though they'd still arrived in Athens a day before they'd needed to. They could have spent another evening and at least some of a morning enjoying Tulum's bright and calm vistas, but the early departure made sense to him.

Mexico was a useful stop off just in case Rivas came after them but there was no reason to stay so close to El Salvador longer than they really had to, lest it invited a little delayed retribution. He'd checked the president's emails again on the Gulfstream, and managed to download a data pack from Perquin. There were still no messages that suggested Rivas was after them, and only video footage of Captain Martinez sporadically stalking his now almost empty fiefdom and periodically checking on the guards still posted at the top of the vault staircase.

The next stage of the plan was – in principle – a lot more straightforward than the last one. They simply had to attend the auction and win the bid for the headdress.

It shouldn't be hard. Even though there was no official catalogue, there was also no way it was going to be a high-demand item. Few Mesoamerican artefacts had ever sold at auction for more than a couple of million dollars, and even amongst those collectors who cared more about owning a piece of the ancient past than how much they might have to shell out in order to achieve that goal, the Americas were not in fashion.

Yes, it was another cost on top of everything else, but not much compared to what had already been invested in securing the private key. And it would be worth it. Thanks to the secrecy and security that enveloped everything to do with Malak Ali, Rivas would also never know who had bought the headdress. The only problem would have been if they hadn't been able to arrange access to the auction, but apparently it hadn't taken much for Jones's boss to secure an invitation.

As Pike went up to his room on the hotel's fourth floor – no adjoining suites this time, but thick beige carpets and woven wall hangings that belonged halfway up an Alp rather than five kilometres from the sea, and only a side street view that gave him the slimmest glimpse of the pom-pom-footed guards outside the parliament building – he wondered if that was what was niggling away at Jones.

By her own admission, she was a woman who liked being in control. But she kept having to relinquish it – first to Pike and, shortly, to the boss he would finally meet – while still shouldering more than her share of the responsibility.

He reminded himself not to feel too sorry for her. She had, after all, threatened to kill him if he didn't do what she wanted. She'd made her bed and forced Pike to lie in it with her, but it was still hers.

* * *

Pike spent the following morning in his room getting on European time and drawing up profiles of the likely auction guests on top of the ones he'd already guessed. This was more for his benefit than Jones's – he wanted to know what kind of room he'd be walking into in a few hours, and he thought a more comprehensive list of the free zone's clientele might prove useful information at some point in the future.

After lunch, an elegantly deconstructed lamb souvlaki which arrived unordered just before two o'clock, there was another knock at his door from a man in an extremely sharply cut black suit carrying several more draped over his arms in bags with various designer names stencilled on them. He was accompanied by another man in a slightly looser fitting outfit cradling several shoe boxes in his arms.

Forty-five minutes later, they departed, leaving Pike dressed in a narrow-lapelled black Armani suit, a thin black silk tie, black dress shoes, crisp white shirt and matching silver tie pin and cufflinks. As soon as they'd gone, he changed out of the outfit and into something more comfortable for a few more hours until his room phone rang and Jones spoke to him for the first time that day, telling him to be ready in an hour.

He showered, shaved, went over the list of potential auction attendees again while he made himself a gin and tonic from the mini bar, then got dressed again.

After precisely an hour, Jones arrived to pick him up, wearing a floor-length emerald-coloured satin gown with gold bracelets on both her wrists and a twisted, multi-band gold choker round her neck.

They didn't leave the hotel. Instead, they took a lift up to its top floor and a corridor that stretched the length of the building but only had two doors leading off it, one on either side, halfway down and slightly off-set from each other.

Jones strolled to the right-hand door which, Pike guessed from the orientation of the corridor and the building, would lead to a suite that looked down over Syntagma Square and the parliament building, and knocked lightly on its glossy, white-painted wood.

The door was opened by a very tall and wide man in a dark suit, who gave Pike a once-over then stepped aside to reveal another man, smaller and thinner, behind him, standing in the middle of the suite's entrance hall.

Jones walked past the first man, who closed the door behind her and Pike. Then she introduced the second one.

'Nathan Pike, meet Lucius Gasana.'

CHAPTER 29

Pike recognised the name, and connected it to the flight that had been scheduled to arrive from Kigali an hour or so ago.

He'd clocked Gasana's profile bubbling up through the public and media consciousness over the last couple of years in various think-pieces and the line-ups for international back-slapping business conferences, but hadn't come across him or anything to do with his company, Gasana Mineral Extraction, in any professional capacity himself. No questions had been quietly asked on the dark web about the accuracy of his bottom line, the legality of his close relationship with the Rwandan government or how his workers were treated behind closed doors. At least none that Pike noticed.

From what Pike understood, the man was more or less what he presented to the world: a charismatic businessman who knew how to work a room, manage his image, and build a fortune through revolutionary green-mining techniques. However, there had to be more to him, because he'd gone to a lot of trouble to orchestrate a billion-dollar theft on the other side of the planet. This fact immediately made Pike question if he was the Svengali behind it all or just the next rung up from Jones on a longer ladder.

Gasana reached out a hand, which Pike noticed projected from a suit jacket sleeve that stopped midway down his fore-arm, and offered his new arrivals a broad smile.

'Welcome, Mr Pike,' he said. 'And thank you for all you've done to help.'

Pike couldn't stop himself saying 'Help what?' in reply, an almost natural unguarded curiosity in his voice.

'Fair, equitable progress,' the other man replied, a glint in his eye as he turned and led the small company into the suite's spacious main room.

Gasana certainly had the air of someone who was com-fortable being in charge, whether it was an illusion or not. He couldn't have been in the suite long but he walked through it as if it was his own living room and dropped casually into one of the two plush maroon sofas that had tassels along every edge and faced each other across a wide oblong gold and marble coffee table.

Pike briefly glanced around the rest of the room, which stretched away on either side, a twelve-seat dining table and another set of sofas in one direction, and a series of doors he guessed led to bedrooms, closets and bathrooms in the other. He'd been right about the view – all the tall, lace-draped windows faced the square.

Gasana beckoned for Pike and Jones to sit opposite him. The other man stayed looming in the arch between the seating area and the entranceway.

Once Pike and Jones were sitting at either end of the second sofa, Gasana leaned forward, his expression turning serious. The atmosphere in the room changed in an instant from relaxed and cordial to something closer to a headmaster on the verge of expelling a pair of underperforming students.

'This evening has already cost me two months of office rent in Dubai, private jet hire, and three hotel rooms. How much more am I going to be spending?'

Pike turned to Jones, expecting her to answer. She turned to him, clearly expecting him to. Did she simply want to shirk responsibility for whatever the answer to Gasana's question was, or was she testing Pike to see if his confidence in his own plan would evaporate under last-second scrutiny?

He wondered if they'd set this up – a little interrogation before their evening of champagne and canapes.

'We can't say for definite,' Pike said. 'But probably somewhere between one and two-point-five-million dollars. Maybe less depending on what else is on offer and the reserve price.'

The glint returned, the questioning apparently already over.

'I think I can manage that,' Gasana replied. Then he sprang back up to his feet and added, 'Well, let's not keep everyone waiting.'

*　*　*

Pike, Jones, Gasana and the tall man who curtly introduced himself to Pike as Dusabe rode the lift down to a limousine that had muscled its way through the ever-present scrum of taxis on Syntagma Square.

It was nearly seven o'clock, and Athens's roads were still clogged with evening commuter traffic, but it was only a short drive past the tree-lined paths of the National Garden and the ruins of Hadrian's Arch and the Temple of Olympian Zeus to their destination: the Acropolis Museum.

The museum was a modern architectural wonder, a parallel to the more ancient one that was the source of its permanent collection. It was also a symbol to the world, crafted in elegant lines of concrete, steel and glass, that the Greece of today was more than capable of caring for its past, and was ready to accept back every chunk or slab of it that had ended up in any other country's possession.

The entire place had been closed to the public all day so that every surface inside and outside it could be cleaned, buffed and polished. A small sign attached to its gates and a pop-up on its website apologised to disappointed tourists that it was shut for a private function. Most of its staff had also been given the day off, replaced by cleaners, caterers, guards and hosts heavily vetted and employed by a shell company owned by Malak Ali.

The limousine joined a queue of supercars and other beyond-top-of-the-line vehicles slowly making their way along the wide, cobbled boulevard between the museum and the ancient citadel that was usually reserved for pedestrians and tour groups, towards the museum's main entrance.

The vehicle directly in front of them was a ridiculous beast – a stretched matte-black Hummer on oversized wheels. It looked threatening, like it wanted people to be scared of it, and like it was ready to just drive right over the roofs of the couple of Rolls-Royces in front of it if they didn't keep moving.

When the Hummer reached the steps that led down to the museum's entrance it disgorged an enormous number of people.

Gasana and Jones seemed studiously uninterested in what was going on outside the limo, but Pike and Dusabe watched as more bodies than Pike would've thought could have fitted inside even the elongated vehicle piled out of it.

The mass of people orbited a central figure – a short, wide, bald Chinese man wearing a gold dinner jacket. Liu Qiang, the owner of the plane that had come all the way from Carmel on the west coast of America.

Once Liu's entourage was a few metres away from the Hummer, its horn sounded a single, low blare – a warning to the other vehicles slowly making their way away from the museum to get out of its way – and sped off.

The limo took a moment to pull up to the edge of the steps, the driver having been instructed before leaving the Marseille to wait until whoever ended up ahead of his passengers was far enough in front that they wouldn't overshadow Gasana's arrival.

Gasana led the way, flanked on either side by Dusabe and Jones, with Pike two steps behind.

The foursome strode through the museum's triple-height doors, opened by two greeters who promptly directed them through the elongated arch of a temporary metal detector – phones or any other electronic equipment were not welcome – and over to the wide, low information desk.

If Gasana had hoped for a dramatic entrance, heads turning and eyes widening in surprise and admiration at the latest member of this very exclusive club, he wasn't going to get it. At least not yet.

The only other people in the expansive foyer were Liu and his group of fifteen companions who were all almost as well built as Dusabe and were all dressed in identical boxy black suits.

Jones stepped ahead of the others to the information desk, where more staff were handing out the slate-grey computer tablets that contained the auction catalogue, and were about twice the size and half the thickness of Pike's PADD. However, before the young woman with the rigid, professional smile on the other side of the thick slab of white marble could give the one she'd just activated to Jones it was snatched from her hands by one of Liu's suits.

'We're doing a lot of shopping tonight,' he said as he turned away.

The woman didn't protest and her smile didn't falter. And, without skipping a beat, she handed Jones another tablet.

'Who is that?' Gasana asked quietly once Jones was back in step with them and they were slowly following Liu's group up the escalators that led up to the museum's main floors.

After a moment's silence where it became clear Jones and Dusabe weren't going to answer the question, Pike leaned forward to do it for them.

'Liu Qiang,' he said. 'A shipping magnate. Technically disgraced and exiled but he's got too much of a monopoly and his company structure is too international for the Chinese government to seize or dismantle it.'

Liu Qiang was, according to the latest edition of the *Forbes* list of the world's wealthiest people, the thirtieth richest person on the planet, with a personal fortune of around forty billion dollars. His company was almost exactly the same size as Maersk, the huge Danish freight and logistics conglomerate, and he was its sole shareholder. His eye-watering wealth, and the extravagance with which he flaunted it, had made him persona non grata in mainland China for over a decade, during which time he'd invested untold millions buying the largest properties in the most exclusive neighbourhoods in every time-zone.

'How do you know that?'

Pike glanced at Jones. 'I like to know what I'm getting into.'

She didn't react to his attempt at a private joke. Instead, she turned on the tablet's screen, which automatically loaded the auction catalogue.

'What does he like?' she asked.

'Spending money,' Pike replied. 'He's a magpie.'

They reached the top of the escalator where they were offered flutes of Laurent Perrier champagne. Pike, Jones and Dusabe all declined. Gasana didn't.

Pike noticed classical music politely echoing through the museum's cavernous interiors – a string quartet hidden away somewhere providing just enough rise and fall to obscure private conversations.

They stepped into a large gallery that was dotted with groups of people, towering statues of Grecian warriors and prophetesses hewn from stone several thousands of years ago, and some of the last millennium's finest examples of human creativity and achievement from other cultures and countries.

The items from this last category weren't really there, of course. They were perfect, life-sized holographic projections of the auction lots that were safely locked away in Malak Ali.

Pike knew just how far projection technology had come in the last few years, putting long-dead or retired stars on stage to entertain adoring crowds that didn't mind if they weren't seeing exactly the real thing. But the quality of the holograms he was strolling past now was far, far more advanced than anything the public got to see.

As he passed a painting of a swirling blue sky hanging in thin air above a narrow and softly glowing white plinth, he had to stop himself from reaching a hand out to the gilt frame to see if it was actually really there or whether a scientist working for Malak Ali had managed to crack the mystery of creating hard light – the concept of solidifying light so that it could be touched.

Pike had expected Gasana to want to mingle, enjoy the opportunity to chat with his equals and betters. But he made no effort to approach any of the other people surrounded by their guards, servants and hangers-on. Perhaps he was waiting for one of them to approach him? Or maybe he wasn't bothered about making new friends.

'Where is my headdress?' Gasana asked as he lingered in front of a Ming Dynasty vase festooned in brightly coloured fish which, according to Jones's tablet, had a guide price of around fifty million dollars.

Jones scrolled through the catalogue. And kept scrolling, confirming Pike's belief that the Incan artefact was not going to be one the evening's higher value items, and only briefly making him worry that there were so many more expensive pieces on offer it might have dropped off the list of lots entirely.

'Second floor, north-west side,' Jones said eventually, turning to Dusabe who, like Pike, had done his homework and was able to point the most direct way.

With another escalator and a few strides across a suspended clear-glass walkway, the foursome entered a gallery that wrapped all the way round the museum, replicating the shape and layout of the Parthenon. And, in a gap between two relief panels carved with men fighting centaurs, was the petrified headdress.

The group didn't rush over, but casually made their way to it, Gasana relieving a waiter of another glass of champagne as they passed a projection of a neon-pink four-metre-high dog made from balloons, which was attracting considerably more interest than the unrestricted view of the sweeping semi-circle of the Theatre of Dionysus at the base of the Acropolis hill and the angled upper portions of the temple to Athena atop it.

By a stroke of luck, or a ploy by the auction's organisers to increase interest and make it clear that it wasn't a minor part of the museum's collection, the hologram of the headdress – which was resting once more on its thin display stand – included its hermetic container. This meant that Pike was able to fulfil his sole duty of the evening: confirm with a subtle nod that the false base he'd installed was still in place and the winning bid on it would come with a billion-dollar bonus.

Gasana opened his mouth to say something, but before he could the quiet calm of the gallery was shattered by a high-pitched laugh, which was followed by several more that were louder and deeper.

Pike, Jones, Gasana and Dusabe all looked towards the other end of the room and the source of the noise – Liu was standing in front of the balloon dog, pretending to take it for a walk and telling it off for some imaginary, stinking excrement it had deposited on the floor.

The audience he was paying to adore him lapped up his performance, and the other clusters and pairs spread around the floor cast the kind of smile or nod towards him that suggested they were used to politely indulging this behaviour.

Pike reminded himself that for every potential buyer here this evening there must be a seller as well. Liu's pantomime might be gauche, but he had deep pockets. Better to put up with him than piss him off.

Gasana, however, had no interest in hiding his feelings about the other man's behaviour. An unimpressed sneer spread across his face, covering the whole of it just as Liu turned towards him.

Pike watched the two men lock eyes for a long moment, Gasana's frown deepening as Liu's childish grin set even firmer, until another sound rose above the laughing – a sudden, brief change in the music the invisible string quartet was playing.

It was the sign that the auction was beginning.

CHAPTER 30

It was a silent auction. As soon as the softer music returned a notification pop-up appeared on the tablet in Jones's hands informing her that bidding was now live for the next fifteen minutes.

Liu's group burst into activity, and it immediately became clear they had actually acquired four of the digital slates from the information desk. Gasana, who had continued staring at Liu even as the other man shifted his focus to the tablet that was held in front of him, finally turned away from him and the headdress and affected a cool saunter over to the vast glass wall, apparently in no rush to make any bids himself.

Dusabe followed his boss as soon as he started moving, and Jones and Pike both drifted over after a few seconds. Aside from the near-frantic tapping by the Chinese magnate's minions, Pike couldn't detect much of a change in the atmosphere of the museum – the evening was retaining its refined ambience by shifting all the excitement to the screens clutched by its guest's assistants.

After five minutes, Gasana turned his attention away from the steep slope opposite the museum and towards a frieze of a man with half a horse's body holding another with the normal human number of legs in a headlock. Then, after another five he nodded at Jones, a signal to put in the first bid.

Pike watched as she lowballed at eight hundred thousand dollars. The tablet rejected it. She upped to nine hundred. Another rejection. Then, after adding a further hundred thousand dollars it was accepted. A million-dollar reserve price for something that was actually worth a thousand times that amount.

Jones navigated to a new screen that was now live – a list of the items that had registered bids on them. Again, she had to scroll a long way, but the headdress was there, near the bottom. And then suddenly it jumped up a few spots, its price increased from one to one-point-two-five million dollars. Someone else had placed a bid.

She showed the tablet screen to Gasana and shrugged at the question that would have been easy for anyone nearby to read in his expression.

'One-point-five,' Gasana said.

An extra quarter of a million dollars.

Jones entered the new figure, and became the highest bidder again.

Then someone else somewhere in the building matched the increase, taking it up to one million, seven hundred and fifty thousand dollars.

'Two.'

Pike hovered behind Jones so he could see the screen. No one else had been near the headdress hologram while they'd been in the gallery, and no remote bidding was allowed, a security precaution against information about any of the lots leaking – if you wanted something, you had to come in person. It was possible someone had scoped out the headdress earlier in the evening and had decided that they wanted it after all with a few minutes to go before the auction ended, but Pike suspected that wasn't what was happening.

The highest bid changed again. This time to three million.

Not as little as Gasana probably wanted to pay, Pike thought, but also not so far beyond the ballpark he'd given him.

A small pop-up appeared in the corner of the screen informing them that there were two minutes left of bidding.

'Five million,' Gasana said, his tone getting more serious with every number that passed his lips.

The screen changed again, showing that Gasana was the new highest bid. It stayed in place long enough that Jones switched to the full auction list and saw that even though the headdress was still near the bottom it had made its way a little higher. As she scrolled Pike saw that the neon-pink dog had reached sixty million.

Jones navigated back to the main listing for the headdress. A minute left and it was still at five million dollars. But then, with forty-five seconds to go it leapt to ten. Pike saw Jones's knuckles grip the tablet tighter.

Gasana stared at the screen. Pike knew he was rich, but even millionaires needed to think about cash flow. Did he have enough funds readily available to keep going? Assets that could be liquidated fast enough to prove he could deliver on a higher bid and not face the embarrassment of winning but not being able to pay? Pike wondered how many calculations he was running in his head.

'Fifteen,' the man said, quietly and through very gritted teeth with thirty seconds left to go.

Thirty seconds became twenty, twenty became fifteen with no change. It was almost over. No more mystery counter bids. Until ten seconds left when the highest bid doubled again to thirty million dollars.

Thirty million dollars. Thirty times the reserve price. Incredible news for Elena Rivas and the people of El Salvador. And, from the fire burning in his eyes as he looked up from the tablet screen to Pike, a disaster for Lucius Gasana.

The countdown reached zero. The auction was over.

The same couple of bars of music the string quartet had played fifteen minutes ago reverberated through the building once more, followed by an increase in the background volume of conversations and number of crystal champagne flutes being tapped against each other.

Gasana and Jones both stared at Pike, and then past him, their faces set hard like they were trying with all their strength to not explode. Pike twisted round to follow their furious gazes and saw Liu looking back at them, giggling.

CHAPTER 31

Gasana wasn't used to being the butt of someone else's joke. It had been a long time since anyone had dared openly laugh at him, and he'd spent the last twenty years shutting up the condescending mouths that might want to make light of his accomplishments. But now he'd been belittled in a place he was supposed to belong, somewhere he'd spent a lifetime working to be welcomed into, by someone a needling voice in his head told him was very far beyond a peer.

Rage began to seethe through him. He wanted to march over to Liu and punch him square in the face while Dusabe hurled his cronies through one of the floor-to-ceiling windows, and Pike along with them.

Instead, he placed his champagne flute, which had remarkably not shattered in his tightening grip, onto a nearby ledge and stalked out of the gallery. The last thing his ears registered before the pounding of blood through them drowned everything else out was a high-pitched 'Better luck next time' drifting through the air behind him.

Jones was the first to follow Gasana, her composure restored and own strides relaxed and considerably more elegant than the man in front of her's. Then Pike, with one of Dusabe's hands latched onto his shoulder.

A few other guests were starting to drift towards the main foyer, ready to celebrate the wins or sales they'd made in more raucous surroundings or commiserate over the things they'd missed out on in private, but the evening's organisers had already intuited that Gasana wanted to get out of the museum as quickly as possible and the limousine was waiting at the top of the entrance steps even before Jones returned the tablet to the information desk.

The journey back to the Marseille was short, quiet and tense. Gasana sat at the rear of the limousine's elongated interior, eyes fixed on whatever passed the window next to him, while Jones, Pike and Dusabe bunched together at the front end.

When they reached the hotel, Dusabe's hand returned to Pike's shoulder as the group trooped up to Gasana's suite. Then, once they were back in its main room, it released its grip, balled into a fist, and slammed into Pike's stomach, sending him flying clear over one of the sofas and onto the coffee table.

Pike didn't have the chance to even work out what had just happened to him before Dusabe's elbow came hammering down on his chest, completely winding him and probably putting hairline fractures in at least two of his ribs and maybe even the table top as well.

Pike gasped for breath, trying to inflate his crushed lungs as Gasana leaned over him.

'You lied to me,' he spat in the British man's face, his anger finally boiling over.

'I didn't know,' Pike managed to stutter, his voice a hoarse whisper. 'No idea . . . Why did he?'

Gasana wasn't about to answer that question, because the same voice that had told him he was nothing more than a bug compared to Liu since they'd left the museum had also been whispering to him that this was all his fault. But it couldn't be. Someone else had to be responsible for this failure.

Jones watched, expression completely neutral, as Dusabe picked Pike up with seemingly no effort at all and dropped his flailing body on the edge of the sofa he'd already been hurled over. His back hit the padded edge, not hard enough to break his spine but with enough force to send a lot of pain shooting up it. Jones didn't step in to call for restraint as he collapsed on the carpet, his mouth forming silent groans.

Now Gasana took over from his *umuntu*, landing a kick in Pike's side – another strike that would leave a deep mark nowhere anyone would see without stripping him.

'You've cost me a billion dollars,' he said by way of explanation, in case any was needed, for the violence being visited on the other man.

Pike wheezed in pain as he began shuffling across the floor towards the nearest wall.

'Does that matter?' he managed to say between breaths. 'I thought getting it out of El Salvador was the most important thing.'

It was, but it also wasn't.

Gasana could have had Jones and maybe even Kamanzi quietly spread word that El Salvador's cryptocurrency gamble wasn't the fairytale its president claimed it to be. He could manoeuvre the global press into ever more sceptical attacks on Rivas until even ardent trust faltered and she was compelled to defend herself and discover how much had been taken from her precious reserves. But he knew that wouldn't be enough. He didn't just want Rivas to lose, he wanted to beat her, and everyone else who had embraced crypto as a quick fix to an exploitative system that had been broken for centuries.

And he wanted to be the one to prove that it was an illusion.

'It's not enough,' he said, his tone shifting from rageful to righteous. 'The world needs to learn that you can't just invent wealth like that. And that crypto isn't some egalitarian future. It still exploits the people whose lives and land have been pillaged to build its brave new digital world that they're excluded from. It can't just fail, it has to come crashing down.'

His impromptu speech delivered, Gasana took a step back and Dusabe moved towards Pike, ready to haul him up into the air again and do even more damage to his body.

But Pike reached the wall before he could, pressed himself up against it and said, 'You can still get the private key.'

Dusabe paused, turning to Gasana for permission to ignore the desperate plea and keep beating the crap out of Pike. Gasana waved at him to stay.

'How?' he said.

'We'll steal it. We've already done it once, we can do it again.'

Jones finally spoke. 'You said Malak Ali was impenetrable.'

Pike shifted into a sitting position, knees defensively pulled up against his bruised trunk. 'The place is one giant safe. And every safe can be cracked eventually. We just have to get inside.'

Gasana repeated his last question. 'How?'

'A zero-day.'

'A what?'

'A zero-day exploit. A vulnerability in Malak Ali's security they don't know is there that we can use to breach it. Their outer security and firewalls are the problem. Once we're through them we can manipulate their internal systems like any normal network. Plus we know where the headdress is going to be, at least short-term.'

Gasana had to concede that the man on the floor in front of him was right about that. The headdress would be transferred to Liu's storage unit in the free zone, along with the private key. But would it stay there? Had Liu gone shopping at the Acropolis Museum just to flaunt his money, or was he collecting things to show off in his countless homes?

The idea of taking the private key from under the obnoxious billionaire's nose appealed to Gasana. Liu might never even know it had happened, but he would, and it'd go a long way to making up for the embarrassment the other man had caused him.

'How long would it take to find a zero-day exploit?'

'I'd need a few weeks,' Pike said, his tone turning sheepish again, like he knew he was bargaining for his life and the next few words might seal his fate. 'But I know somewhere we might be able to get one a lot faster.'

'Where?' This time the question came from Jones.

'Morocco,' Pike replied. 'Marrakech.'

Jones turned to Gasana, as did Pike and Dusabe. It was up to him. Could he settle for orchestrating a slow-burn collapse of faith in cryptocurrency? Could he risk Liu stumbling over the private key and adding another billion dollars to his vast fortune he'd barely notice until he wasted it? No, he couldn't, he decided, to both. The private key had slipped from his grasp, but while it was still within reach he had to try to grab it. He'd come too far to give up now.

Gasana walked over to Pike, who was still crouched against the wall, and loomed over him.

'If this fails,' he said, 'I'll take you back to Rwanda with us, put you to work underground until your hands become bloody stumps and you forget what the sun looks like, starve you until you lose your mind and you barely have enough energy to breathe, then cut off all your limbs and show them to you before I throw your armless and legless body in the Ruzizi River to drown in the rapids.'

CHAPTER 32

TWENTY-FIVE YEARS AGO

Nathan slurped at the dregs of his third milkshake in a booth at the back of the McDonald's on Northumberland Street. He hadn't known which flavour to pick when he'd reached the counter, so he'd started with a small vanilla one, then went back up for chocolate, and finally strawberry.

The same teenager, maybe a year older than him working their Saturday job, served him every time with the same blank, unregistering expression as Nathan slid successively smaller notes and coins across the counter to him.

Delaney had given him the money half an hour ago and told him to wait in McDonald's for him while he went to pick up some more shopping.

They'd come from JD Sports, a couple of doors up Northumberland Street's gently sloping hill, where they'd spent half an hour searching aisles and hangers for a new tracksuit for Nathan. There had been plenty of options, but only one that satisfied Delaney's strict list of requirements: no patterns, no colour other than black, no big logos, no pockets without zips.

Luckily, the one they found was also Nathan's size. Delaney had paid for that with cash too.

The bag was currently balled up between Nathan's feet, and he'd taken it with him every time he'd gone up to the counter. He couldn't remember the last time he'd had new clothes bought for him, and he didn't want to accidentally lose them.

Nathan finished the milkshake and was wondering what he might shovel into his mouth next with his remaining funds and how much longer Delaney was going to be when he appeared in front of Nathan's half-hexagon-shaped table carrying another two bags, one large, one small. Nathan looked at them as Delaney slid into the booth: Mountain Warehouse (large) and Cotswold (small) – both outdoors shops.

'Keeping out of trouble?' Delaney asked.

Nathan nodded at Delaney and then at the bags. Delaney shoved them across the plastic-moulded bench so he could look inside them. The larger bag contained two black rucksacks. Just like his tracksuit, there was nothing flashy about them – no reflective strips or big logos. In the smaller bag he could see the other things Delaney had told him he was going to buy: two short lengths of thin metal tubing balanced on top of a wad of woven black fabric. Hiking torches and balaclavas.

'Right,' Delaney said, reaching for the bags as he sidled back out of the booth. 'Still a couple more bits to get.'

They left McDonald's and crossed over Northumberland Street to the covered shopping centre that plugged a gap between three of Newcastle's wider boulevards and wrapped a U around the neatly clipped grass and weathered bronze war memorial of Old Eldon Square.

As they walked into the centre's gaping maw of an entrance, Delaney drifted over to the right, cutting through a wave of shoppers exiting. Nathan, realising Delaney was no longer next to him after a few seconds, scuttled over and fell into step by his side again.

'Time for another lesson,' Delaney said, leaning in close to Nathan's ear. 'Pick one.'

Nathan glanced at the older man, a quizzical arch to his left eyebrow until he realised that Delaney meant for him to choose a mark. He looked around, sizing up the middle-aged couples and gangs of young friends. Then he noticed a solo man on the other side of the wide corridor meandering ahead of them. It was a warm, dry day, but he was wearing an anorak and a flat cap. From the man's posture, gait and clothes, Nathan put him somewhere in his late sixties.

He gestured his choice, which seemed to please Delaney. And then they followed him. And just followed him.

'Keep your eyes soft,' Delaney said as they passed an information booth at a junction and slowed slightly, seemingly trying to decide which row of shops they wanted to head down next as the man a few metres ahead and across from them did the same. 'Don't dart around but don't stay fixed on him either. Keep his hat in your peripheral.'

Delaney was no longer leaning close to Nathan, he simply spoke light and soft enough so only his shopping companion could hear him and anyone passing them would ignore both them and their conversation.

The man took a sudden sharp left into a branch of Boots and Nathan paused too, ready to spin round and continue shadowing him, only to feel something smack into the back of his legs just above his ankles and Delaney grab his shoulder and yank him to the side.

A young woman with long, scraped-back hair and a push-chair containing a sleeping toddler passed them, her hard face glaring at him.

'Don't make sudden movements. They can give you away,' Delaney said once she'd turned her attention back to the way she was going. 'And watch out for young mothers. They think the whole world is out to get their little darling.'

They continued up on their way through the shopping centre, passing more stores and occasionally falling into step behind unsuspecting members of the public until they reached a wide, square space with a middle dominated by a set of foun-tains surrounded by clusters of seats.

Delaney guided them over to the shoe shop that lined its western flank and stopped in front of a display of boots that ranged from patent leather dress ones to mesh and fabric hik-ing ones. Delaney seemed to consider each one in turn before pointing to the ones Nathan had already guessed he would – the all-black, logo-less chukka boots with rubber soles.

'Those,' Delaney said, reaching into his jeans pocket and pulling out three twenty-pound notes, which he handed to Nathan.

Ten minutes later, Nathan left the show shop carrying a second bag containing his new boots. He saw Delaney, slouching inconspicuously next to the fountains like a bored father waiting for his family to be done with wasting their afternoon spending money. When he saw Nathan, he got up and started strolling towards Bainbridge's, the city's other big department store opposite the shoe shop.

Nathan caught up with him and they went up to the third floor to finish their shopping with a matching pair of black leather golf gloves.

'Thin enough to let you feel everything,' Delaney said as Nathan flexed his fingers in the ones that had been picked out for him, before another pair of notes were handed over to the assistant working the sports section till. 'And they don't leave marks,' he added as they left.

Walking back out of the department store, Nathan reflected on the strangeness of the afternoon. Shopping was not something he normally did on a Saturday, and neither was being taught how to follow people without being noticed or learning what were the best clothing choices for midnight break-ins.

They headed west out of the shopping centre along Grainger Street towards the central train station where they parked up on another bench, this time looking like father and son waiting for their platform to be called.

Nathan had been told what he needed to wear for a robbery, but was still in the dark about what exactly they were going to steal, and the specifics of how they were going to do it. He wanted to prove to Delaney that he was capable, that he'd make a worthy apprentice. But the lack of details was niggling at him.

Two trains arrived in quick succession and disgorged thick streams of passengers into the station. Nathan sensed that when the next one came in Delaney would slip away into the disembarking crowd, so he seized the brief lull that followed after both trains departed again.

'What happens if something goes wrong?' he asked.

'You don't think you're up to it?' Delaney replied, letting the pressure of what he'd just said register on Nathan's face before he nudged his shoulder to let him know he was joking.

'I mean if the police show up or something,' Nathan said.

'If it happens before, then you scarper. If it happens after and you can't run, you keep your mouth shut and let me sort everything out.'

Nathan nodded, taking more reassurance from those last few words than he'd realised he was after.

'You're sure there's no alarm?'

Delaney shook his head, watching a large intercity train snake into the nearest through-platform to them. 'Just the guard, who you're going to make sure we avoid.'

'What if they don't do what I think they will?'

'We plan as much as we can,' Delaney said, his voice becoming serious as he stood up. 'But in the end you have to act as the situation dictates.'

'What does that mean?'

Now Delaney's voice turned hard. 'It means I'm leaving with what I'm going in there for.'

CHAPTER 33

NOW

The medina of Marrakech was crushingly busy. Wafts of turmeric, apricot, tanning leather and raw meat floated through its tight passages and bustling souks. Sounds of people haggling, tired donkeys pulling squeaky carts and poorly maintained moped engines tumbled over each other.

It was just after three o'clock in the afternoon, and it seemed like everyone was in a rush to get whatever they needed to do done before the call for Salat al-'asr – afternoon prayer – was broadcast from old speakers on roofs and the occasional flesh and blood muezzin with a microphone perched on top of a mosque's minaret.

It would have been the perfect place for Pike to slip away, to duck down an unseen alleyway or between stalls piled high with rugs and shawls, if it hadn't been for the squat tip of the pistol barrel that Dusabe dug into the exact spot on his side where Gasana had kicked him in his suite in the Marseille whenever the pressing of bodies around them gave him sufficient cover.

257

Pike had had no idea the other man had been carrying a weapon until he'd felt it pressing into him. He wondered if he'd somehow acquired it without him noticing on their arrival in Morocco, but the single glance Dusabe let him get of it made him realise Gasana's bodyguard might have had the weapon in his possession all along.

Pike wasn't an expert on firearms but he was one on technology, and he could tell from just the snatched look at its odd, angular shape that it was a 3D printed carbon fibre pistol – as deadly as a traditional steel-made firearm but much lighter in weight and which, when taken apart, would go completely unnoticed by most normal scanners and detectors.

The one thing that should have given Pike some reassurance – but didn't – was that the weapon could only be loaded with a single fluorocarbon resin bullet at a time. So, if he could put some distance between them and Dusabe's first shot went wide or into something or someone else, Pike would stand a chance of getting away before he reloaded. However, at such close quarters he couldn't imagine the other man missing.

And, while he'd tried to explain to Dusabe that verbal threat of the handgun's existence was enough to make sure Pike wouldn't try to flee, it was clear from the repeated jab-bings of the short barrel into his ribs that the other man's faith in his good behaviour was lacking.

After he'd been threatened with dismemberment, Pike had been taken up to his room and locked inside it. He'd spent the rest of the evening processing the information Gasana had revealed about his plans for the private key, as well as checking his body for lasting injuries, soaking it in a bath as cold as he could run to ease the pain, and slowly squirming on top of the duvet on his bed, trying to find the least uncomfortable position to sleep in.

This morning, he'd been woken with a room-service breakfast of piled-high pastries and a large freddo espresso, which almost made him forget he was being held captive until the first swallow of *pain au raisin* sent a jab of pain through his chest.

Once he'd showered – again, cold – and got dressed in a loose shirt and linen trousers he was collected by Jones and Dusabe and taken downstairs. Gasana was waiting in the lobby, and the same limousine from last night was on the kerb-side.

The jet Gasana had chartered wasn't as plush as the one that had taken Pike across the Pacific and the Atlantic, but it would do for the four-hour hop over the width of the Mediterranean. There were no private cabins, but the seats were wide and soft enough for him to avoid accidentally putting too much pressure on any of the bruises that covered his midriff.

He spent most of the flight focused on the screen of his PADD – the only luggage he'd brought with him – making sure they'd find everything he needed in Morocco and ignoring the constant, unblinking stares of Dusabe from the backwards-facing chair diagonally opposite his. This mainly involved sending a long stream of messages to an anonymous profile on Signal, the encrypted mobile chat platform that was currently enjoying its yearly three months of popularity before users migrated to Tor, then Telegram, then Threema, then back to Signal again.

Now, he was guiding Gasana, Jones and Dusabe through the knot-like junctions and switchbacks of the ancient pink-walled city which seemed like they'd been specifically designed by its first residents to confuse and disorient visitors.

The foursome had been deposited on the edge of Jemaa el-Fna Square, the wide, open expanse that wouldn't get busy with food stalls, musicians and magicians until the sun started to go down. From there, they'd traversed almost the whole medina from south to north.

They were mostly ignored, dismissed as glum-faced tourists who had come into the old city from one of the large resorts that filled the gap between Marrakech and the Atlas Mountains. Even the rug sellers who spent their days convincing holidaymakers to buy traditional Moroccan floor coverings that might, if they were extremely lucky, eventually reach their home via an international courier the seller just happened to know, seemed to sense that it wasn't worth trying to get a sale out of them.

Like Athens, Marrakech was somewhere Pike had been before. But, while his most recent trip to Greece had exposed him to a rarefied side of its capital that belonged to the super rich and which he would never normally get – or particularly want – to experience, this time things were reversed. He was going to show his companions a different kind of hidden version of a place most people didn't know existed.

Pike had chosen a deliberately circuitous route to their destination that took them through more near-identical squares and almost-dead-ends than was necessary, in part to give the recipients of the messages he'd sent from the jet a little more time to get things prepared for his arrival, and also to put Gasana on edge.

'If we don't get there soon I'll have Dusabe beat the address out of you,' Gasana said as they passed maybe the tenth make-shift corner cafe huddled with old men in *djellabas* sipping small, gold-stencilled glasses of sweetened mint tea.

'Just a little further,' Pike replied, his tone intentionally and annoyingly bright.

Then he pulled Gasana against a wall, smearing brick dust across the other man's shoulder and pressing Dusabe's pistol deeper into his own side as three mopeds sped past them, each one belching out acrid petrol fumes and covering the sandal-wrapped feet of the men at the cafe with dirt.

Gasana did not thank Pike for getting him out of their way.

Pike had told Gasana as the jet was taxiing off the runway at Marrakech airport that he didn't need to trouble himself with accompanying him, Jones and Dusabe on this part of the expedition; that he might prefer to wait in the comfort of the jet, knowing full well it was the best way to make sure he did come.

Gasana's psychology wasn't hard to read. Pike could tell how much the man had hated becoming powerless at the auction, and how much he wanted to feel in charge again. And he planned to use that deep, desperate need to manipulate him.

After some more twists and turns, which took them into streets that were wider, quieter, and occupied by increasingly foetid smells and suspicious faces, they reached a big, old metal door covered in faded paint and rust marks set into a high, long, windowless wall.

Pike gave the door three hard bangs with the edge of this fist. A few seconds later it swung open a few centimetres and a face appeared from the darkness on the other side of the thick metal. It considered the four people in the light of the street for several more seconds before, lingering on Pike, there was what looked like the flicker of recognition and the door was pulled back far enough for them to pass through in single file.

It was shut as soon as they were through, and it took them a few moments to adjust their eyes and realise they hadn't entered a tannery or metalwork factory.

The first detail they picked out were the thick cables that ran along the ground and suspended above them, emerging from and disappearing into the gloom of the building's depths. Then they started to make out the edges of partitions made of wood, corrugated iron sheets and chicken wire, which also stretched off into the dark seemingly without end and gave the place the impression of being a long-abandoned and shut-up souk, its stalls given up on trading. Finally, they noticed the sole sources of light in the cavernous space: computer screens.

Each alcove was illuminated by at least one widescreen monitor, and some had as many as five, displaying cascading streams of code, live video feeds from security cameras and TV studios in faraway cities, stock market trackers and RPG playthroughs.

'What is this place?' Gasana asked, not hiding the surprise and confusion in his voice.

'A hacker market,' Pike replied. 'If you're after a particularly nasty piece of malware or something like a zero-day, this is the best place to come looking.'

Trading lines of code and algorithms was a big global business. It was also a surprisingly analogue one – though perhaps not that surprising given it was an industry built on the principle of messing with the digital world. Day to day deals might be done via the dark web or encrypted messaging platforms that auto-erased communications once they'd been read, but for real high-value items and ones-of-a-kind, sales were done at a market like this one, either in person or via a broker.

It was also a highly competitive industry. Each continent's hackers always wanted to be the fastest to find a weakness in a new operating or security system, come up with the most destructive worms, and plumb the deepest depths of the most sensitive information secretive nations and organisations wanted kept hidden.

Some governments tried to bring their hackers onside, like METIS had done with Pike. The United States even hosted a yearly hacking conference in Las Vegas, called DEF CON, where federal law enforcement departments spent a week wining and dining the people they spent the other fifty-one of the year trying to arrest. However, the smartest hackers kept their wares for markets like this one.

Pike took a step forward, glad that the change of environment had resulted in the pistol barrel being removed from his side. It was almost immediately replaced by the arms of a man in a black and grey-striped *djellaba* with a thick beard that reached his chest who appeared before him and gave him a tight bear hug.

Pike winced as the man bellowed, 'Nathan, it's good to see you.'

'Hello, Alif,' Pike replied, once he'd been let go. 'How's business?'

'Booming, of course,' the other man said, a broad smile spreading from ear to ear. 'And you've made some friends at last,' he added, gesturing at Gasana, Jones, and Dusabe, who had stashed his pistol under the light jacket he was wearing over his ever-present polo shirt.

'Associates,' Pike said, turning to the other three. 'Meet Alif, this is his market.'

'Should we know that?' Jones asked.

'I won't tell if you won't,' Alif said, winking at her.

Alif held out his hand for them all to bemusedly shake in turn, revealing the mint condition vintage Jaeger-LeCoultre Reverso wrapped round his wrist.

'Do you have what we need?' Pike asked, drawing Alif's attention back to him.

The other man nodded. 'Yes, yes. The broker's waiting for you.'

Alif had been the anonymous recipient of Pike's messages from the plane.

He took them further into the market, past booths whose occupants looked them all up and down, and others where prospective buyers and sellers conspicuously averted their gazes from the newcomers.

'Come here often?' Jones asked Pike as they turned a corner which, like so many in the medina, had a cafe serving sweet tea on small beaten-metal tables.

The only difference between this one and ones outside the market were the wires that snaked up each table's legs to the small screens and jailbroken old games consoles resting on top of them.

Pike shrugged. 'They know me.'

Pike had first come to Marrakech a decade ago. Back then the market was still in its infancy, more cables than booths and internet connections that were only slightly more reliable than you might get in the business centre of one of the then-new resort hotels. He'd revisited regularly since, either to refresh his network of contacts or clear out some of his inventory of older and weaker viruses.

Alif had latched onto him on his very first trip and, for once, Pike hadn't felt an instinctive responsive urge to flinch away from the unexpected human contact he offered. So, while the market owner managed his irregular stream of customers carrying bags of cash, gold or precious stones, he also shared his vision of the future of the market with Pike over endless teas. A future that had taken several large steps towards becoming reality since Pike had last visited a month before he'd joined METIS.

But Pike wasn't going to tell Jones any of that.

Pike's time in the city meant he also knew the best places in the medina to get a *hammam*, which restaurants sold alcohol, and where to find secret gardens and oases of calm in the middle of the ancient metropolis. He had no plans to share any of that information either.

He glanced behind him at Gasana and Dusabe. The latter's eyes were constantly moving, searching for threats that might be waiting to leap out of the shadows. The former, however, had a dual expression on his face – like he still wasn't completely sure of what he was seeing but was also trying to work out how he might be able to use it beyond his immediate need.

Pike couldn't help seeing the parallels between Gasana's story and ambitions, as much as he now understood them, and the market. And also, actually, what Rivas was trying to do too.

Morocco, El Salvador, Rwanda, and countless other of the world's developing nations wanted to leap into the future as quickly as its more developed ones. But without decades of digital investment and school curriculums that skewed towards computer science more and more year by year, they'd had to improvise. They'd learned how to make systems that had been designed by other people bend to their will.

Generations of resourceful kids worked out how to reverse engineer technologies almost as soon as they'd been created. They manipulated codebases to listen to the latest releases on Spotify or watch Netflix's newest film as easily as people in the developed world logged into their accounts.

For some, hacking into the most secure corners of the world's cyber infrastructure wasn't a very challenging next step, and it was worth the occasional threat of extradition to feel like they were getting a taste of the kind of life other people took for granted.

Alif finally stopped in front of a booth that had a single, large computer display bolted to a wall on the far side of a desk, behind which was a high-backed chair, turned towards the screen.

After a few moments of watching letters, digits and symbols race across the LED panel faster than any of them could keep up with, Alif let out a loud cough. An instant later, the display switched from the lines of code to a picture of Scarlett Johansson dressed as Black Widow, in the middle of a fight with a four-armed alien, and the high-backed chair slowly turned round to reveal the broker.

He was, at a very generous push, sixteen years old.

CHAPTER 34

His customers delivered, Alif retreated from the booth as Pike took a couple of steps forward. He nodded deferentially at the teenager, who was continuing the superhero theme with the oversized Hulk t-shirt that hung off his adolescent frame.

'Thank you for seeing us,' Pike said.

The broker shrugged. 'I'm busy. Let's get on with this.'

'Do you have the zero-day exploit we're after?'

'You wouldn't be here if I didn't,' the broker replied, his voice heavy with a mix of boredom and irritation at being disturbed. 'Five million dollars.'

Pike nodded and retreated to the others.

'It's a good deal,' he said to Gasana.

'I'm not giving that boy five million dollars,' he replied.

'He's just the middleman,' Pike said. Then he lowered his voice and added, 'It's less than you were ready to pay yesterday.'

'There's no guarantee it'll even work,' Gasana hissed in response.

'Don't question the quality of my merchandise,' the merchant said, leaning across the desk and raising his voice. 'Six million.'

Pike's eyes widened and he had to stifle a cough of surprise.

'I apologise on my associate's behalf,' he said, turning back towards the desk. 'He's not familiar with your work. Could we agree on the original price?'

'How about I don't agree to sell it at all?' the broker replied, now sounding every inch the petulant teenager. 'I can find a new buyer. You need this more than I do.'

He was right. The question was: after the events of the last twenty-four hours, would Gasana be able to swallow his pride and put up the cash? Pike was willing to bet that even though his ego was as bruised as his own body was, Gasana could take another couple of punches.

He swivelled his head towards Gasana just as Jones was whispering in his ear. Pike couldn't hear what she was saying, but whatever it was seemed to be enough to persuade him, if he'd been wavering, that he'd come too far to walk away now.

Gasana nodded at Pike. Pike nodded at the broker, adding the quickest, slightest wink that only the teenager caught.

A second later two bodies even younger than the one sitting behind the desk appeared on either side of it. One of them was holding a USB stick that they plugged into a portable screen, giving Pike a preview of the lines of code that made up the zero-day.

The other was clutching a second screen that was ready to accept an untraceable transfer for funds into a numbered Swiss bank account. Dusabe did the honours with that one and, as soon as he had, he took the USB stick that had been given to Pike and nudged him to follow Gasana and Jones, who were already striding towards the exit.

They were almost back at the door when Alif re-materialised and embraced Pike in another over-exaggerated hug, which was intended to distract everyone else from seeing him slip something into the other man's pocket.

'Get everything you came for?' he asked as he thrust Pike away from him, hands on his shoulders.

'We did, thanks,' Pike replied, feeling sharp edges against his thigh. 'You're doing bank transfers now?'

Alif chuckled. 'Had to move with the times. And everyone was getting bored of diamonds.'

He shook Pike's hand. He didn't offer one to Gasana, Jones or Dusabe, but he did tell them they were welcome back anytime. Then he bid them all farewell.

Outside, Pike could tell Gasana was keen to get as far away from the market and Marrakech as quickly as possible. He stormed off ahead of the others, and made it three turns – one more than Pike had guessed he'd manage – before he slowed down so Pike, without admission or instruction, could take over navigating them back across the medina.

Pike took them on a different route towards Jemaa el-Fna this time, and with no gun barrel digging into his side – just Dusabe looming half a foot behind him.

He was enjoying Gasana's frustration – every huff that came from his mouth and sudden dodge he had to take to avoid some mound of something unpleasant on the ground was a balm to the pain Pike still felt with each step – and he wanted to keep all of them confused and extremely unlikely to ever find their way back to the market again.

However, as they passed through the deep shadow of a long, tight arch between two buildings, he realised his companions weren't quite as unobservant as he'd thought.

Just as he'd reached the darkest part of the cut-through he sensed Dusabe step past him, then felt the other man's tree trunk of a forearm press against his neck and force him against the wall.

Dusabe's other hand went straight for Pike's trouser pocket, retrieved what Alif had slipped inside, and held them up for everyone to see in the low ambient light.

Four hexagonal disks, about the size of fifty-pence pieces, completely blank on the front and with slim tie-pin clasps on the back.

Pike didn't bother trying to reach out to grab them as Dusabe handed them over to Gasana.

'And what are these?' Gasana asked, picking up one of the disks from his palm and rolling it between the fingers of his other hand.

'Smart tags,' Pike croaked, Dusabe's arm stopping him from fully forming the words.

'Why do you have them?' This question came from Jones, and was followed by a minuscule loosening of the pressure on Pike's neck.

'The zero-day will get us into Malak Ali's systems. These are how we make sure no one knows we were ever there.'

'Explain.'

'Ask nicely.'

'Do it,' Gasana said, signalling Dusabe to reapply some force against Pike's jugular.

'You can't just knock out security somewhere like Malak Ali. There are too many back-ups and redundancies. We have to become invisible.'

'Why were you hiding them?' Gasana asked.

'I was being discreet. So it wasn't entirely bloody obvious to everyone in the market why we were really there. You're welcome,' Pike replied, his tone making it clear that he resented the implication in Gasana's question, and having to explain himself.

The other man opened his mouth, but Pike continued before he had a chance to say anything.

'Look, can we shortcut this? I know what will happen to me if we can't pull this off, and I just want to get it done. But you're more than welcome to go back and ask Alif if he knows anyone else who you can threaten into breaking into one of the most secure places on Earth for free.'

He stopped himself before he pointed out that it wasn't his sneering at Liu Qiang that had ended up costing them an extra day and a five-million-dollar trip to Marrakech.

Gasana mulled over Pike's outburst for a long moment, then nodded at Dusabe to release him as he pocketed the disks.

Rubbing his neck, Pike took up his position as point man again and led them back out into the light. By the time they reached Jemaa el-Fna, afternoon prayer was long done and the temporary stalls that spread out from the permanent bank of orange juice sellers on the square's northern side every afternoon and evening were starting to go up.

There were two cars waiting for them in the distance – one a gleaming dark blue town car, the other a slightly less impressive-looking mauve-coloured people carrier. Their presence seemed to cheer Gasana and he picked up his pace across the square, overtaking the others.

'I'm going home,' Gasana announced once they reached the cars. He handed three of the smart tags to Dusabe and gestured at the people carrier. 'You're all going to Dubai.'

Pike looked at Jones and Dusabe. If either of them hadn't been expecting this command they didn't show their surprise.

'Then what?' he asked Gasana, feeling compelled to point out to the other man once more that he wasn't a permanent member of his staff, despite how much the nature of their professional relationship had evolved since Jones had liberated him from Sihanoukville.

'If everything goes to plan,' Gasana replied, rolling the remaining smart tag between his thumb and fingers, 'we'll never see each other again.'

*　*　*

Sitting in the back of the people carrier, with Dusabe next to him, Jones in front, and the driver shouting abuse through his open window at the two carts that had jack-knifed while trying to avoid each other in the road ahead, Pike reviewed how he'd played the day.

Alif, who could joke about Pike making friends because he knew he was one of the few people close to actually being one, had acted his part brilliantly. As had his son, Elaid, in the role of the broker. The boy, who had spent his days picking pockets out in the souks or glued to an old Gameboy screen when Pike had first come to Marrakech, had grown into a natural performer – and a tough negotiator.

Pike's deference towards Elaid had been fake. His surprise when he upped the price of the zero-day was real. The move hadn't been part of the plan Pike had sent to Alif from the plane, and it could have turned Gasana sour. But it hadn't, and Pike couldn't blame the kid for trying to increase the value of the cut he'd get if the deal went through.

In its own way, the hard bargaining pandered to Gasana's ego, just like the entire trip to Morocco, which had been one big way for him to feel like he was regaining some control of the situation, that he still held power over people, and that his money could get him what he wanted after all.

It had also been, for Pike, a way to remove a variable from the situation. Having levelled his threats, thrown his weight around, and opened his wallet, Gasana was now on his way back to Rwanda. Which meant that Pike no longer needed to worry so much about the man's whims and moods derailing his plans. Of course, Jones and Dusabe would still be following Gasana's orders but there would be fewer impulses and outbursts to respond to.

And that should make what needed to happen next a lot easier.

CHAPTER 35

TWENTY-FIVE YEARS AGO

It was strange being back at the Harbrook. Nathan wanted to hate it, keep blaming it for what it had done to his dad. But he couldn't, at least not completely. The adrenaline bubbling up inside him was a mix of anticipation for what was about to happen and excitement about his very delayed return.

It was just after one a.m., and Nathan and Delaney were crouched behind one of the larger bushes near the staff entrance on the western side of the building.

Nathan was wearing the tracksuit Delaney had bought for him, along with his balaclava and golf gloves. He had his rucksack on his back, which contained the new Clarks Chukkas and one of the miniature hiking torches.

Delaney was also dressed head-to-toe in black, including gloves, balaclava pulled across his face, and his own rucksack. In their get-ups they looked near-identical – no one would have guessed there were several decades between them, and the only real difference between the two of them was that one was a bit thicker round the middle than the other.

Delaney peeled down the cuff of one of his gloves and checked the time.

'One more minute,' he whispered to Nathan.

They'd spent the last two days in the lock-up going over the plan Delaney had devised over a set of blown-up floor plans he'd somehow managed to acquire of the Harbrook.

Nathan had traced every route the museum's night guard could possibly take through its exhibition rooms and galleries, using the path his dad used to take as a basis for calculating the most probable one his most recent replacement would follow, along with some likely deviations and variations.

Delaney still hadn't told him what their target was, but he had shown Nathan where it would be, in a basement level of old kitchens, laundries, pantries and wine cellars that had been converted into storage for the items in the Harbrook's collection that weren't on public display.

It made sense to Nathan that the Harbrook would have had a subterranean level where all the menial jobs of making a grand old landed gentry house work were done. But he was irritated that it hadn't occurred to him when he'd had relative free rein of the place – had his dad kept it secret, or had he not known it was there? – and he'd missed out on exploring it.

Delaney had also explained to Nathan that human attention subliminally peaks at set time intervals. After a couple of hundred years of formalised work days, school times, lunch breaks and kick-offs, most people's senses naturally heightened roughly every fifteen minutes. The trick to not being noticed was to operate between these moments, when minds were wandering and distracted or completely focused on a task. Which was why they were going to break into the Harbrook at precisely 1:07 a.m.

Nathan silently counted the seconds down in his head, and at the exact moment he reached zero Delaney half stood up from his crouch and scuttled the short, exposed distance to the door.

There were no visible CCTV cameras bolted to the outside of the building pointing at the staff entrance, but Delaney had made it clear they shouldn't linger out in the open, even in the pitch black of night.

It took him less than twenty seconds to unlock the door. He opened it a crack, checking the night guard wasn't waiting on the other side, then pushed it wide enough for them both to slip through.

They both stilled, adjusting themselves to their new environment.

Inside was as dark as outside had been. Nathan's dad had always left at least some of the lights on throughout the building, but apparently the current guard preferred to keep the place shrouded in gloom. Maybe he had no fear of looming shadows, or maybe he'd been given orders to keep the electricity bill down.

Through the narrow slit of his balaclava, Nathan saw Delaney's brow crease into a frown, and it took him a few seconds to understand why.

On the one hand, having all the lights out meant they didn't need to waste time finding and cutting off the museum's internal security cameras. On the other it meant they might not know where the guard was until they were suddenly lit up in the middle of a gallery they were creeping through. And the only way to get to the one door that still led down to the basement was to go through several rooms that wouldn't offer them much more cover beyond a few benches to roll under or squeeze behind.

'Over there,' Nathan whispered, pointing at a little nook under the staircase which he remembered led up to one of the entrances to the taxidermy gallery.

The space was tight, but they just managed to fit. And their caution was rewarded when the staircase light suddenly flicked on and the security guard wandered through the small hallway a few moments later.

Nathan caught a quick glimpse of him before he turned the lights off again and continued on his way. He looked exactly like his dad. Well, how his dad used to look: a middle-aged man simultaneously uncomfortable in his uniform but glad that he had one to wear.

Once the guard was away from their immediate vicinity, they both slipped their rucksacks off their backs and changed into their fresh shoes, packing away the ones they'd worn outside. They tested the new soles with a couple of a arrhythmic bounds in the hallway – they made no sound and left no mark.

A game of cat-and-mouse-meets-follow-the-leader ensued as Nathan and Delaney trailed the guard on his rounds of the ground floor. They traced an identical path to the other man on a miniscule delay, darting between points of cover and unlocking and relocking the same doors the guard did, all in pitch blackness and total silence.

It worked. Nathan and Delaney made it the whole way to the basement door without the guard having any clue they were in the building with him.

Again, Delaney picked the lock and, once they were inside and the door closed, he reached into his rucksack and retrieved his torch. He slipped the short loop of paracord attached to one end of the torch around his wrist, then swivelled the other end of the short tube, turning it on and pointing it at the worn stone slabs that would lead them down under the museum. Nathan did the same.

Nathan's pulse, which had been getting faster and faster the closer they got to their destination, evened out, only to start pounding again as they reached the bottom of the stairs and he shone the narrow beam of light emanating from his tight fist at the seemingly endless rows of shelves of things that the museum's curators had seen fit to hide away from the world.

Some of the items he briefly illuminated looked fascinating and tantalising – mediaeval beaten-metal cups, carved wooden masks painted in flaking, gaudy colours – some of them looked like chunks of dirt-encrusted rocks, and some were exactly that.

They all had little yellowed paper tags hung round or draped over them on knotted lengths of string, and Nathan had to stop himself from disobeying Delaney's instructions not to touch anything that he absolutely didn't have to and pausing to inspect each one of them in turn.

They moved deeper and deeper into the museum's store, eventually reaching the far side of the basement and a large cage that had been bolted to the floor, ceiling and rear wall, and which the map in Nathan's mind told him was more or less directly under the scale model of Jupiter from the solar system exhibit.

Inside was a single shelf which Nathan could tell from a quick, cursory count contained eight items. They didn't look all that different from everything else in the store, but this was clearly where the Harbrook kept its most precious possessions.

Nathan went to step towards the cage but Delaney held his arm out in front of him, silently telling him to pause, before he pulled his rucksack off his back again and took a camera out of it. It was a Polaroid, with some sort of filter clipped onto its flash.

Delaney took a series of photos of the cage and the padlock that hung in front of it, placing the pictures on the floor to develop and stashing the film covers in the rucksack. Then he pointed his torch at the exact middle of the shelf, illuminating a small carved statue, a primitive representation of a person, Nathan thought, with one semi-formed arm raised up.

It was smooth and soft edged, like it had been carved from bone or ivory rather than stone, and the only detail etched into its surface was a geometric pattern that wrapped around the middle of it suggesting some form of clothing.

'What is it?' Nathan whispered before he realised there was a little cardboard sign next to it and dipped his torch beam to reveal the statue's name: *The Armstrong Hunter*.

'What we've come for,' Delaney replied. Then he tilted his torch down towards the padlock hanging off the front of the cage and added, 'Not going to lie, I was expecting a safe. Want to do the honours?'

Nathan didn't recognise the figurine's name from any of the books of notes about the museum's possessions he'd once pored over. Either it was a recent acquisition or it was so valuable it had to be kept completely secret. He felt a pang of guilt for helping remove it, but not enough to stop him from nodding eagerly as Delaney held out the picks he'd used to get them this far.

Nathan had been keeping count and the older man had averaged about fifteen seconds per lock. Nathan knew tonight was a test, and he wanted to impress Delaney. He was determined to get as close to his time as he could, and he managed to spring the padlock in eighteen. Not as good as his teacher, but close.

He slowly swung the cage door open, checking its hinges didn't grind or squeak, then stood back and watched as Delaney took another set of photos and let them develop before reaching in to remove the statue.

Then another set of pictures, compared to the ones from a few moments before to ensure the only thing that had been moved in the cage was the figurine.

Once Delaney was satisfied, he nodded to Nathan to shut the door and relock it again as he gathered up all the photos and put them in his rucksack along with the camera. After a last check that the cage was exactly as it had been before they'd arrived, minus one item, and that Nathan had fitted the padlock the same way round as they'd found it – he had – they made their way back over to the stairs.

Delaney had warned Nathan that getting out unnoticed was actually the hardest part of a theft, and that they needed to stay completely focused and alert until they were well away from the Harbrook. Yet, Nathan couldn't stop himself from relaxing just a little.

'Why does someone want that?' he asked Delaney, his voice still low.

Delaney shrugged. 'There are some people in this world who have so much money or power that they can just take whatever they fancy. Well, they pay people like me to take them for them.'

'People like us,' Nathan replied.

He couldn't tell for certain, but he was pretty sure Delaney half-smiled under his balaclava.

They reached the top of the stairs and Delaney leaned over to open the door. It was another quick job and a moment later he opened it onto the corridor they'd only left about fifteen minutes ago.

They should have had a straight run at leaving now. The guard had only just finished his rounds and wouldn't be bothering to leave wherever he spent most of his shift trying to stay awake any time soon. But, just after they passed a set of doors that led into a gallery they heard something behind them – a key in a lock – and froze as the security guard stepped into the corridor, shut the door behind him and turned on the light.

Nathan glanced at Delaney, looking for a sign of what he should do next – which bench or plinth he should dive for or which door he should sprint towards. But the other man stayed standing stock still.

Nathan's eyes darted to the ceiling, checking for security cameras that might explain Delaney's lack of movement. Then he watched as the guard's face transformed first into a look of complete surprise as he registered the two black figures in the corridor with him, and then a mask of shock and pain as one of them lurched forward and threw a vicious kick into the middle of his stomach.

The man staggered backwards, arms flailing, trying to grab at something to steady himself, then tilted all the way over. His body crashed onto the floor and his head made a horrible bone-breaking noise as it missed the carpet runner that ran down the middle of the corridor and bounced off the exposed stone floor next to the wall.

There was a long, awful moment of silence until Nathan glanced at Delaney and saw him turning away from the fallen man.

'Why did you do that?' Nathan asked, his words quiet from fear and shock.

'Whatever the situation dictates,' Delaney replied, his voice suddenly harder than Nathan had ever heard.

'We can't leave him,' Nathan said, now no longer whispering.

'He's not my problem. His fault for getting in the way.'

'He needs help.'

'I'm not calling an ambulance and explaining what we're doing in a museum in the middle of the night. You want to play good Samaritan then go right ahead, but I'm getting out of here. If you don't want to come with me I don't have a problem with leaving you behind.'

Nathan looked down at the man. His chest was still rising and falling pretty evenly, but his eyes were also still rolled back in their sockets and he could make out a thin smear of dark maroon creeping out across the floor from underneath the back of his head.

He couldn't process Delaney's sudden callousness. Was this what the world he'd indoctrinated Nathan into really involved? Stealing things was one thing. But hurting people and leaving them, possibly for dead, was completely different. There had to be something they could do, a way to help the man and make sure he was ok without getting caught.

He looked back up to continue his argument with Delaney, but there was just empty air where he was supposed to be.

Delaney had already gone.

Nathan stayed stuck in place for a few long breaths as he attempted to process what had happened. Then, not knowing any first aid but feeling like he needed to do something about the guard's prone position, gently pulled him over to the wall and propped him up against it. He wasn't sure if it was the right or safest thing to do, but he figured it would at least stop the man from choking on his tongue.

Once the guard was semi-upright, Nathan tried to decide what to do next.

It took a few more seconds of running options through his mind before he realised that there was no way to completely guarantee that the guard would be taken care of without incriminating himself. But there was something he could do that gave the man a decent chance and still let him make a cowardly escape.

He walked over to the nearest fire alarm and smashed his elbow through the little glass window in the middle of it, setting its siren blaring and sending a message to the Fire Brigade that something was very wrong at the Harbrook.

He went back to the guard, sat next to him, silently counted down five minutes. Then he picked up the set of keys the guard had dropped when he'd stumbled backwards from Delaney's kick and ran for the staff entrance.

CHAPTER 36

NOW

Forte was taking a risk returning to Kigali. She hadn't been sent by *Lorgnette* or any of the other publications she worked for. She was there purely of her own volition, under no instructions and without the protection of anyone who would rush to her rescue if things went sideways and she found herself in a police cell. But it was a risk she'd decided she had to take. There was something going on between Lucius Gasana and Jean Kamanzi, and she wanted to be the one who worked out what it was.

She'd spent almost a week looking into both men, their rises to power and prominence, and any suggestion of skeletons hiding in closets that might be whispered about on Twitter by anonymous, faceless accounts or by Rwandan journalists who had found themselves labelled unpatriotic after one too many critical pieces about the country's great and good and now broadcast their views on what was happening in their motherland from afar on YouTube.

Some of what she read and watched was too bizarre to believe. The men were part of a secret pan-African government that was pulling the levers of power across more than fifty nations. The Nyungwe tantalum story was cover for the removal of a vast hoard of diamonds and gold that had been hidden since colonial times. They'd found a subterranean obelisk in a huge cave surrounded by concentric rings of skeletons with elongated skulls, and the obelisk was talking.

However, amongst these ridiculous stories and theories were enough probable ones to make her think she was onto something. Hopefully something that several international news sites would be keen to run, and maybe even get into a bidding war over first publication rights.

So, she booked a return Kenya Airways flight to Kigali, found a cheap hotel in the Rwandan capital's diplomatic quarter, and rented a white, mid-range rental car with just enough dents and dings in its bodywork to make it anonymous. When the person on the counter asked if she needed a baby seat installed in the back, she said yes.

Then she started stalking Jean Kamanzi.

Late in her first afternoon back in Kigali, Forte drove to the Ministry of Finance and Economic Planning and parked over the road from its entrance, close to a corner that no one could box her into or stop her pulling away from quickly if she needed to. She cracked the driver's side window open an inch for a little ventilation, turned the engine off and settled down into her seat, pulling the brim of the cap she'd bought at a store near her hotel down over her face. She nestled her phone in her lap and kept its screen turned on, sporadically flipping between Instagram and WhatsApp so she'd look to any curious passers-by like a bored mother or nanny waiting to do a pick-up.

She was in luck – Kamanzi had gone to work today.

An hour and a half after she'd arrived, a black Audi S8 pulled up to the ministry's entrance a minute before Kamanzi emerged from it. When he did, he walked straight to one of the rear doors and climbed in. Forte knew that most Rwandan ministers only got a mid-range hire purchase car with their position, so either Kamanzi had managed to negotiate a very different deal for himself as the person who controlled the government's purse strings, or he had the money to pay for a much more expensive car, and a driver to go with it, himself.

Forte waited until the Audi was back on the road before she started her engine and pulled out into the traffic. She kept at least two cars between her and her target as it led her through the city. Then, as they left Kigali's inner core and the roads got quieter she fell back further, keeping the Audi just in view so that she'd spot any corners it took without giving herself away.

She'd never had any proper training on tailing a target – most of her hunting was normally done along paper trails – but she hoped that she was being discreet enough not to be noticed. And that the mansion the Audi took Kamanzi to in the city's outer Kibagabaga suburb was his and didn't belong to someone else that he was either in cahoots with or having an affair with.

Half an hour after she watched a middle-aged man who was not the finance minister walk down the wide driveway the Audi had crawled up, unbuttoning the collar of the dress shirt that was tucked into the pair of jeans he was wearing, she decided that the finance minister was indeed home and wouldn't be leaving again.

To be sure she'd guessed right, and to get a handle on Kamanzi's regular daily schedule, she returned to Kibagabaga early the next morning, and the one after that, parking in different spots each time as she checked when Kamanzi's driver arrived and when the Audi left.

On the third morning, she made her move to doorstep the Rwandan finance minister and try to get him to confirm that something untoward was going on. He wouldn't actually have to admit to anything, just react in a way that made her confident that she should keep digging.

She woke up even earlier than the previous two days, gave the same smart trousers and shirt she'd worn in Nyungwe one more press with her hotel room's iron, twisted her hair into a low, tight bun, and set off for Kibagabaga.

The gated communities that had spread across Nairobi hadn't made it to Kigali yet, which meant that Forte had been able to drive right up to Kamanzi's house repeatedly and, now, stroll up the driveway to his front door.

If she suddenly came up against armed guards she'd be in trouble, but Forte guessed the fear of what happened to government critics was enough to keep anyone who might want to give its ministers a piece of their mind in person at bay. The only other thing she had to worry about was if Kamanzi somehow recognised her. But, again, she was willing to gamble that he had no idea who she was, and that the element of surprise would work in her favour.

She'd worn trainers, just in case she found herself needing to sprint back down to the street, and kept one hand in a trouser pocket, clutching her car keys. Her other hand was holding her phone, on which she'd already activated the voice notes app.

It was twenty minutes since the driver had appeared, and the past two mornings the Audi had left exactly twenty-two minutes after his arrival.

Forte hoped that she'd got her timings right and wouldn't be left standing on the edge of the driveway that led up to the mansion which, getting her first proper look at it, she saw was wrapped in verandas on its ground and first floors, as Kamanzi was sped away.

Again, she'd guessed correctly.

Kamanzi emerged from his front door just as she came alongside the Audi. He looked surprised, but not overly concerned, at the appearance of a well-dressed European woman outside his home.

*   *   *

Kamanzi was running out of patience. There was no reason to delay revealing the Nyungwe discoveries. It was a perfectly good news story for Gasana and Kamanzi. Especially Kamanzi. Whispers were starting to float around Kigali that the president was considering shaking up the cabinet again before the end of the year. And the sooner the story got out, the more likely it was that Kamanzi would become the first and only choice to take over as the next prime minister.

The only problematic detail – that Shaft B extended beneath the protected land of the national park – could be easily fudged until people were supportive enough that they'd forgive it, or simply not mentioned at all. In fact, Kamanzi had drafted several versions of the official government confirmation that would accompany Gasana's announcement that admitted they'd dug under the park but that its surface remained untouched, went into vague details about adjusting its borders at some unspecified point in the future, or just didn't reference it.

The press releases were ready to go, and had been for several days. But Gasana had dropped off the radar. He wasn't in Kigali and hadn't responded to any of the messages Kamanzi had sent him in between his endless meetings about subjects far more boring than the one he wanted to talk about – the one that would help seal Kamanzi's eventual rise to the office of the prime minister at the next election.

At least this morning he wouldn't have to go to the ministry straight away. After a breakfast eaten alone, because his wife had already disappeared off into one of the many rooms in the enormous home they didn't need but which she was constantly renovating, he had a cabinet meeting to attend.

The Rwandan cabinet was made up of almost thirty ministers, which meant it functioned like a mini parliament, complete with factions and agendas, and was populated by people who seemed focused as much on stabbing each other in the back as actually governing the country.

Kamanzi was already one of the cabinet's most senior and powerful members. But that just meant he knew he was the target of several other ministers' ambitions. He was likewise aware of at least three of his colleagues who also fancied themselves as the next prime minister. So, Kamanzi needed to make sure that no one had the chance of stopping everything he'd spent a long political career working towards from coming to fruition. He needed to go public with Nyungwe.

The news would be guaranteed to ruffle his opponents' feathers and knock them off balance. It might also put the president's nose out of joint a little, given it would be as much a surprise to him as everyone else. But, even if it made him begin to consider Kamanzi a direct threat, he'd still have to reward him as the world's largest conglomerates came begging at Rwanda's door. He could possibly even anoint him as his pick for prime minister straight away if public support for the discovery of the nation's new riches swelled enough.

At eight a.m. on the dot, he adjusted his suit jacket in the mirror next to his front door as he heard the engine of the Audi beyond it turn over. Then he opened the door, stepped outside, and found a woman standing between his house and his car.

He was not expecting a visitor, and people tended not to turn up at government officials' houses unannounced for fear of what might happen to them if the person they were intruding on didn't want to be disturbed. But Kamanzi kept his reaction to curious surprise.

He glanced at Lionel, his driver, silently telling him to stay where he was and keep the engine running, and turned back to the woman.

'Can I help you?' he asked her.

'I'd like to ask you about your relationship with Lucius Gasana,' she replied, her accent sounding like it belonged to somewhere Mediterranean.

Kamanzi should have said nothing. Brushed her off with a line about not commenting on private citizens or telling her to get in touch with his secretary with a request for an interview that would go unanswered. But the mention of Gasana's name from someone else caught him off guard and instead he said, 'Oh you would, would you?'

'Why are you protecting him?' she asked.

Kamanzi affected a smile despite the alarm bells suddenly ringing in his head and kept the tone of his response light.

'Protecting him from what?'

'From people knowing what's really going on in Nyungwe.'

Now Kamanzi had to fight to keep his smile in place. Did she know about Shaft B or something else Gasana had been getting up to? No, he thought, if word had got out about what was happening in Nyungwe this wouldn't be how he found out.

He looked her up and down, noticing the phone she was holding slightly in front of her, which he guessed was recording everything. He didn't want to say anything that had even the slightest potential to come back and bite him. The best thing to do was turn her accusation back on her – force her to reveal what she knew, or that she knew nothing.

'And what's really going on in Nyungwe?' he said, parroting her righteously indignant tone.

'Something that will bring you both down when it's exposed.'

It was a smart, evasive response. However, Kamanzi suspected that she'd used it because she didn't have a more precise answer. He decided she didn't know anything, though of course that didn't make her any less potentially dangerous. History was full of great leaders brought low by people who didn't know what they were doing.

Throughout the entire exchange he'd been trying to work out who this woman was, and where she'd come from. And then a name came to him. A name Gasana had given him.

'Are you Beatrice Forte?' he asked.

The question seemed to stop the woman in her tracks, knock the wind out of her sails and kick her legs out from under her all at once. Without another word, she shoved the hand holding her phone into her pocket, turned round and marched away down the driveway.

Kamanzi took her abrupt departure as confirmation that he was right about her identity. He watched her go, giving her enough time to disappear before he climbed into the back of the car.

Then, as Lionel drove him into the city he mulled over his partnership with Gasana and the increasing number of issues the other man was causing him.

Kamanzi had put up with Gasana and cowed to the man's expansive ego because he'd been the one to confirm the presence of tantalum under Nyungwe in the first place and offer to extract it for a fair enough share of the projected profits. He'd also, of course, found the deposits of iridium, rhodium, and palladium that had the potential to elevate Rwanda to the upper echelons of global mineral exporters and make the country a true industrial powerhouse.

But that had all been done now. Which meant Kamanzi no longer needed Gasana as much as he once had.

Their partnership had been forged on the basis of mutual benefit. But if Gasana was going to become a problem that could threaten Kamanzi's political ascent rather than help assure it, then he needed to put measures in place to quickly distance himself from the other man if necessary.

Kamanzi decided it would be prudent to draft another extra version of the Nyungwe press release – one that wouldn't need Gasana's approval before it was sent out.

CHAPTER 37

It was good to be home, Gasana thought, as he watched the sunrise from his bed.

He wasn't in Kigali. He'd travelled straight back to Nyungwe, the private jet dropping him off at Cyangugu late the previous evening before continuing on to wherever its next charter would take it. A four-by-four had been waiting for him at the airport, alerted to his impending return, and the extraction facility's senior scientists and the man Dusabe had left in charge of security were lined up outside the conference room next to his office when he arrived, ready to report just how well the place had been run in his absence.

Production and refinement was continuing apace, both in the main tantalum shafts and Shaft B. The sole chief engineer and senior mineralogist who knew the true extent of what had been discovered in Shaft B confirmed that the amount of precious minerals coming out of it was only increasing. Once they'd been dismissed the temporary head of security reported that worker morale was high and there'd been no more attempted thefts or any sudden disappearances of anyone who might relay anything not entirely complimentary about life and work inside Nyungwe.

After the last couple of days, Gasana appreciated being somewhere where people were eager to prove how highly they valued the trust they'd earned, and how committed they were to helping him achieve his goals even if they weren't privy to the full extent of his ambitions. They knew he had the power to make their lives good, and the faith that if they worked hard for him then he would.

He slept the contented sleep of a benevolent king in a happy kingdom, and indulged in a rare lie-in to watch the sun tumble its way over the national park, the source of the wealth he was going to use to transform Rwanda's place in the world, from his bed.

Once everything as far as the eye could see was blanketed in light, Gasana got up and dressed, lingering in the shower under the torrent of fresh water that felt so much better against his skin than the overly treated and chemically-ridden stuff he'd had to put up with in Europe.

Then he went down to his office and surveyed the other half of his realm.

The geodesic domes and polytunnels were all still where they were supposed to be, pulsing ever so slightly in a slow, undulating rhythm as air, bodies and extracted minerals circulated through them.

Gasana smiled to himself, then he reached into the pocket of his trousers, felt the angled edges of the fourth smart tag he'd taken from Pike in Marrakech, and reminded himself that while the possibility of reward was an excellent motivator, so was fear.

The Brit had brought it upon himself. Gasana had put his faith in him and he'd come up short.

Of course, fear rarely bred fealty, but Gasana didn't require that from Pike, he just needed him to get the private key. As soon as he had he'd be of no further use. Well, there would be one final job for him to undertake. It wasn't one that required his unique skills or that Gasana imagined he'd enjoy, but that didn't matter – he'd just need to do it, and Dusabe would make sure that happened.

Plus, the frustrated determination that had underscored Pike's outburst when he'd been confronted about the smart tags in the medina reassured Gasana that he wanted to get the task he knew was in hand done. Pike might not care about ingratiating himself to Gasana, but he did want to prove himself. And that was a quality of the man's personality that Gasana was more than happy to take advantage of.

His thoughts moved to the other two members of the trio he'd dispatched to Dubai.

After almost a quarter of a century standing by Gasana's side Dusabe's loyalty wasn't in question.

Ever since they'd first met, when one of Gasana's early prospecting trips had taken him to Dusabe's village in the north of the country, his *umuntu*'s wagon had been hitched to Gasana's star.

Gasana had read about a mythical source of gold near the village in the memoirs of an old German coloniser and had gone looking for it. The elders, Tutsis, who had learned to be extremely wary of outsiders, had refused to even meet with him. Dusabe, however, desperate for a more exciting life that better matched the scale of his already overdeveloped body, had seen an opportunity for escape in Gasana, and guided him the fifty winding kilometres across scrub and through forest to the deep ravine where the old mine was located.

The betrayal cost Dusabe his home, but opened up his world. And the sixty-five tonnes Gasana was able to mine by extending the single, small shaft that hadn't been worked for almost a century funded the creation of GME.

Since then, there had been no idea of Gasana's that Dusabe hadn't supported, no vision he hadn't shared, no problem he hadn't solved without hesitation or question. They were true brothers in arms.

Jones, on the other hand, was fully on board with to the plan to collapse the cryptocurrency market, but Gasana had never been completely sure of her commitment to him.

Jones had actually been there when he'd first decided he had to do something about the rise of crypto and the threat it posed to countries who were still struggling to harness the potential of their real, physical resources.

It had happened in Davos two years ago, at the World Economic Forum. Gasana had joined the Rwandan delegation – for the government it was a chance to show off their poster-boy of sustainable, responsible industry, for him it was an opportunity to scope out the competition.

Nestor Barrera, Elena Rivas's predecessor, had been invited to give a speech about his great crypto gamble in one of those evening slots where most of the delegates in the audience had already consumed a considerable amount of champagne and caviar and were in the market for a show to follow their dinner.

The chuckles and whispers that reverberated around the room every time the Salvadoran president took a breath between paragraphs of his speech only seemed to buoy the man behind the lectern and convince him that he was being underestimated by the very people who represented the 'unfairly rigged global financial system' that he wanted to upend.

They also solidified the fear that had long been swirling inside Gasana about the possibility of the world taking a giant leap forward before Africa had the chance to even catch up with where it already was.

He knew the people laughing now would stop as soon as they saw the opportunity in what the Salvadoran president was saying – they'd watch his experiment and then take whatever he proved, claim it as their own, and make themselves even more rich and powerful. Over the course of Barrera's speech it became clear to the Rwandan that cryptocurrency was the biggest danger that he, his country and his continent faced. It had to be stopped.

The only other person who left the auditorium with a dour expression on their face was a tall woman who, like Gasana, had attended the talk alone. She introduced herself at the post-talk drinks, where more joviality echoed around them as they shared their surprisingly similar worries about what they'd just heard.

They'd spent the next two years scheming to make sure the Salvadoran gamble didn't pay off. And then the Barrera government fell and was replaced by something worse: Elena Rivas.

Rivas was far more dangerous than her predecessor. She flaunted the hollow wealth she'd magicked out of nothing and done nothing to earn, and encouraged others to do the same with charming lies and charismatic promises. She was a symbol of everything that was wrong with the world and Gasana knew she had to be ruined, brought down in a way that would ensure the entire planet turned away from the evil of cryptocurrency for good.

Jones hadn't flinched when he'd told her what he was sure they had to do. In fact, she'd volunteered to insinuate herself into Rivas's close circle and spend months ingratiating herself with the woman, all the while plotting her destruction.

No, Gasana thought, Jones's belief in their mission also wasn't in doubt. And the question of her commitment to him could be answered once they'd accomplished it.

There was a fourth person Gasana had to consider as well. The man who had spent the last two days filling his secure inbox with increasingly over-the-top messages of concern and despair. The man whose resolve might need a little shoring up: Jean Kamanzi.

Gasana kept turning the smart tag around in his hand as he crossed over to his desk, and opened his laptop to check if he'd received a morning missive from the finance minister. He had. Two minutes ago, in fact. A single line, a little too close to an order, telling Gasana to call him.

So he did. He clicked on the video chat link the other man had added below his message twice – either by accident or out of emphasis – and a few moments later Kamanzi's face appeared on the screen.

'Where the hell have you been?' Kamanzi said before Gasana had the chance to sarcastically wish him a good morning.

'Greece,' he replied, after a brief, silent moment.

'Your plan was to go on holiday?'

'I wasn't sunbathing.'

'Then what were you doing?'

Gasana wasn't used to such direct questioning from Kamanzi, or the accusatory tone it was being delivered in. He'd always been the more cautious, nervous member of their partnership, but this was something else. Gasana decided that placating him a little might be a more effective response than leaping to put him in his place straight away.

'I was ensuring the future we've worked so hard for will last,' he said.

Kamanzi didn't need to know what that had entailed exactly, or that total success was still a little less than completely assured. He also didn't seem to want to.

'Well, we need to get on with it.'

Gasana was about to remind Kamanzi once more that the timetable for announcing the Nyungwe discoveries was entirely up to him, but the other man continued talking before he could.

'That journalist you insisted on inviting down there door-stepped me yesterday, asking me about my relationship with you.'

This made Gasana straighten a little in his chair. He'd suspected there was something more to Beatrice Forte than just being a puff piece writer when she'd come to Nyungwe, but had also assumed that the quiet words Ingabire Muhire had had with her Dutch counterpart had been enough to scare her off. Perhaps he'd been mistaken.

'Why?' he asked.

'I'm the finance minister; you were given exclusive rights to extract one of the largest recent discoveries of tantalum on government-owned land. It's not hard to put two and two together.'

As irritating as it was to admit, Kamanzi was right. However, the relationship between GME and the government was, at least on paper, entirely above board. As long as everyone kept to that line there'd be no salacious exposé that could cause any damage to either of them.

'She's just fishing,' he said. 'Upset that her precious little story was edited. It'll blow over.'

Kamanzi didn't seem satisfied with that answer. 'What if it doesn't?'

Gasana sighed loud enough for his laptop microphone to pick it up and relay it all the way to Kigali. 'If you want to be prime minister you'll have to deal with much bigger problems than some disgruntled foreign journalist. Are you sure you're still up to it?'

'I'm not the one that's delaying things,' Kamanzi replied, throwing the accusation straight back at Gasana. 'I should be asking what's wrong with you.'

And with that, Kamanzi crossed the line. Gasana leaned forward over the glass-topped baobab wood of his desk, his face twisting into a mask of anger and condescension.

'There's nothing wrong with me,' he spat at the screen. 'You need to find wherever your backbone has gone, and be ready for when I tell you we're going to go public.'

Then he slammed the laptop lid shut, threw himself back into his chair, and decided that the finance minister had just moved several steps closer to becoming disposable.

CHAPTER 38

TWENTY-FIVE YEARS AGO

Suddenly, after five years of near silence, the flat was full of noise.

The theft of the *Armstrong Hunter* made the local news, which was when Nathan discovered just how rare it was.

Delaney had been right – it was one of a kind. A twelve-thousand-year-old Stone Age sculpture that, according to the presenters on *Look North*, was 'the only example of semi-abstract human representation from the Magdalenian period of the Upper Palaeolithic that had been held in the collection of a British institution, and one of only four known to exist on the whole planet'.

From the moment the first story ran, Nathan's dad was either glued to the lunchtime and evening broadcasts with the TV volume turned high or stomping round the flat wishing violence on the criminals who had dared desecrate the Harbrook and muttering prayers for the security guard who had been rushed to the RVI and put in an induced coma.

'Those oiks will get what's coming to them, mark my words,' he said, over and over between glugs of Netto whisky, whether Nathan was in the room with him to hear or not.

Ken was now averaging a bottle a day, which was not good for him but at least meant he had to get out of the house a little more regularly.

When they were together, watching the news with their dinners on trays in their laps, Nathan kept his responses to his dad's comments to a minimum for fear of accidentally slipping up and mentioning something he shouldn't know or letting his mouth run and confessing the whole thing.

And when he was alone, Nathan kept going back over those last few minutes in the Harbrook, trying to work out if there was something else he could have done, and realising both self-ishly and shamefully that however he replayed it he'd always end up leaving the guard and saving himself.

He'd gone to the lock-up the night after the robbery, just like Delaney had told him to if things went sideways, but he wasn't there. Or at least he didn't respond to Nathan banging on the shutter doors for twenty minutes before giving up and slinking back home.

Nathan had expected his dad to be happy about the break-in, but he was furious. Nathan didn't understand how he could still be so loyal to something that had kicked him so hard when he'd been at his lowest.

But maybe, actually, he could.

Delaney had tricked and betrayed him, used him just like he said he would and then left him behind. But he'd also opened his eyes and given him a glimpse of the world that existed under the one everyone else saw. Yes, he'd been burned by his first visit to it but, like moths and flames, he could feel himself already being drawn back.

Perhaps he wasn't Oliver Twist, after all. What if he was actually the Artful Dodger? Had his brief time with Delaney set him on his own journey to becoming a hardened career criminal? He didn't remember the Artful Dodger feeling as bad as he did about his victims.

Over the course of the week after the break-in, the subject of the reports on *Look North* shifted away from the police investigation – it had apparently found nothing, and Nathan hadn't felt compelled to try to claim the modest reward that the Harbrook had offered for any information that might lead to the recovery of the statue – to updates on the condition of the security guard.

With each new bulletin and speculation about the long-term conditions the guard might suffer from if he ever regained consciousness, Nathan's anger at what Delaney had done to him transformed into guilt about what he'd let happen to the guard.

And the well wishes Ken had started offering up in his more lucid moments turned into slurred threats.

'If I ever get my hands on the gits that did that to him they'll wish they'd never been born,' he'd say, words running together, over beans on toast or Heinz ravioli, unaware that one of those gits was sitting on the sofa across from him.

Every mention of the guard by newsreaders or his dad made the knot that had started to twist up inside Nathan's stomach grow bigger, and he got to the point where he was one more report away from breaking down, bawling his eyes out and telling his dad everything.

But then it turned out he didn't have to. Miraculously, the guard woke up and all the vague scaremongering from the news about loss of memory or life-altering speech difficulties evaporated. It also quickly emerged he couldn't give the police any leads apart from confirming that they should be looking for two people, probably men, who owned balaclavas.

When the *Look North* presenter reached the end of the final piece on the drawn-out story of the *Armstrong Hunter* one evening, Nathan paused over his last bit of tomato sauce-sodden bread and finally asked another question that had been quietly burning away inside him.

'If it was so special, why was it so easy for someone to nick it?' he said.

As soon as the words left his mouth he realised there'd never been any mention in the endless reports on the theft about where the statue had been kept in the museum, or how securely.

But his dad didn't realise that his son had just admitted to knowing more about the Harbrook and what had happened to the *Armstrong Hunter* than he possibly could unless he'd been in the museum's basement at some point himself, which up until less than a month ago he hadn't.

Ken just sneered at the question as Nathan held his breath, turned down the TV volume and muttered, 'As if that's the bloody point.'

The news moved on.

The flat fell quiet again, and Ken withdrew from the world and his son once more.

For all the new eggshells he'd had to walk around the place on, Nathan missed the louder, angrier version of his dad – though not enough to bring up the Harbrook or the break-in ever again.

Nathan never received any more mysterious messages from ~~N£8F~~. He sent a lot of his own, asking where Delaney was and threatening to tell the police about what had happened if he didn't reply. But all his questions and hollow demands went unanswered and eventually he gave up. He couldn't bring himself to delete the conversation or the contact though, just in case Delaney ever decided that he wanted to get in touch and make things up to Nathan.

He tried to go back to his old life, poking around the internet and chatting with other people who at least claimed to also be bored teenagers. But it all seemed dull now. Safe.

Nathan tried to ignore the itch inside him, but he knew that eventually he'd have to scratch it again. And that, thanks to Delaney, the odd chocolate bar or comic from Woolworths wouldn't be enough to satisfy him.

Summer ended and he didn't enrol himself in a college. Instead, he started spending his days in the Newcastle Central Library, scouring the local and national newspaper archives for robbery reports that might give him some clue about where Delaney had disappeared to or at least some tips he could learn from.

Ken didn't notice his son's independent studies. Or his occasional overnight vanishings with the rucksack that was kept stuffed deep under his bed. Or the periodic upgrades Nathan made to his computer set-up. He mostly stayed in his chair, only leaving it to collect his dole money, buy his whisky, use the bathroom and go to bed.

The two of them lived like this for another year. Not really father and son at all any more. More like phantoms crossing each other's wakes.

Then, on a wet Tuesday in September, Ken Pike's years of drinking and bad diet finally caught up with his heart and his liver. And, a few weeks before his sixteenth birthday, Nathan Pike found himself an orphan.

CHAPTER 39

NOW

Pike had become a chameleon. He'd been a prisoner, a tomb raider, a punch bag, gone from the deep jungle to the heights of moneyed society, and hopped around four continents. Now, he found himself in another part-real, part-pretend situation: a work dinner with colleagues he didn't particularly like at a rooftop restaurant in Dubai.

He, Jones and Dusabe had landed in the city a few hours ago and had taken a taxi to a hotel that was both distinctly average and overpriced. They'd also flown via regular passenger jet, first back to Athens and then on to Dubai, which fitted their cover – again, part-true, part-not – that they'd been sent by Gasana to inspect the office space he'd rented at Malak Ali.

The restaurant they were at now was perched atop a much more expensive hotel, and offered a panoramic view of the Dubai skyline – that oversized, jagged metal and glass scalpel which sliced a narrow line between sea and desert.

The city was taller, shinier than the last time Pike had transited through it. But that wasn't unusual. The whole place was a monument to unrestrained ego and rapacious capitalism built on an endless supply of cheap, foreign labour. New buildings seemed to rise up from foundations built on shifting sands on a daily basis. And lording over all of them was the city's tallest, sharpest spire – the eight-hundred-and-thirty-metre-high Burj Khalifa, which was in the middle of its third dazzling light show of the evening.

They'd all dressed for dinner care of the fresh clothes they'd each found in the wardrobes of their three adjoining rooms. Jones was in one of her usual loosely draped suits, but with a subtle silver thread woven through its fabric. Dusabe had changed into a pressed polo shirt, and Pike was wearing light knitted Henley.

Dinner was a sombre affair. Conversation didn't flow over the platters of sushi that had been delivered to their table along with extended explanations of how it had been prepared and where exactly the fish and seafood that had been wrapped in or placed on top of perfectly plump rice had come from.

But, at last, after almost an hour of silent chewing and taking in the view, something exciting happened. Dusabe almost threw up.

Something in the feast of flesh, tentacles and roe disagreed with him, and Pike and Jones watched as, in very quick order, he began to sweat profusely, his face turned a deep shade of green, and he excused himself from the table and retreated to the nearest restroom.

Pike followed the giant man's frantic path across the restaurant – the first movements he'd seen him make that weren't intimidatingly measured – then turned back to the table, picked up a salmon-topped *nigiri* with his chopsticks and put it in his mouth whole.

'Don't worry,' he said to Jones once he'd swallowed it. 'I know better than to try to make a run for it.'

Jones picked up her next bite-sized morsel, an almost luminescent chunk of tuna sashimi. Then, once she was done chewing it, she asked, 'Why?'

'Sorry?' Pike replied.

'Why aren't you running? Why are you still here?'

Pike gave her a look of bemused surprise. 'Because Gasana said he'd kill me if I did.'

'His resources don't stretch as far as he thinks they do,' Jones replied, cleansing her palate with a sliver of ginger.

Pike wondered if she was testing him, or if Dusabe's departure was an opportunity for her to drop her guard a little too – a chance for the sarcastic Jones he'd met in Sihanoukville to make a brief reappearance.

'What does that mean?' he asked.

'It means I think that if you really wanted to disappear you'd be able to do it so well that he'd never had any idea where you went or if you were even still alive.'

'You found me easily enough,' he replied, letting her flattery bounce off him.

'You weren't hiding.'

Pike smiled. That was true.

He reached out for his own piece of ginger, and his chopsticks came back to him with a sizeable chunk of it – he was not as adept with them as Jones.

'I can make a pretty good guess at Dusabe's deal. Gasana rescued him from some bare-knuckle fight-to-the-death betting ring, or they've known each other since they were kids but have never been able to admit their feelings run deeper than simple friendship. But what about you? Why are you here? I'm not exactly feeling devoted acolyte or rose-tinted lover vibes.'

The right-hand corner of Jones's mouth curled a few millimetres. 'We share the same ambition.'

'You really don't like crypto. I get that much.'

'It's a mutually beneficial relationship,' she said, rebuffing Pike's next question about whether her personal motives for what they were doing aligned with Gasana's, or if they were something else altogether, before he had the chance to ask it.

Pike clocked the pre-emptive move, but before he could press her on it she turned the conversation back onto him.

'Are you going to betray us?' she asked.

'I've been shot at, had the crap beaten out of me, and threatened with being literally pulled apart, and I'm still here.'

'That doesn't answer my question.'

Pike picked up another piece of sushi before he responded again.

'Curiosity,' he replied eventually, drawing a raised eyebrow from his dining companion. 'Like you said when we first met. I want to get inside Malak Ali and see how it works. And I'm unlikely to get another opportunity.'

Pike couldn't tell from her expression if that answer satisfied Jones, but it seemed to at least be enough to get the conversation moving again.

'Well, you'll get your first look in the morning,' she said. 'After we check the office we'll be getting a tour of the storage facilities. They want to show them off.'

Pike nodded, though he wasn't sure if he should be more impressed by Jones's speed at arranging access to the most secure part of the free zone or by Malak Ali's determination to try to part Gasana from more of his money so quickly.

'What part will I be playing?' he asked.

'Assuming Dusabe's done emptying out his guts by eight a.m. he'll be reprising his role as the brawn. That leaves us to fight over beauty and brains.'

'I don't think I'm here for my looks,' Pike replied.

'In that case, I guess I'll keep our guide charmed and distracted while you get ready to rob the world's biggest safe.'

Jones looked like she was about to say something else, but before she could Pike saw her eyes shift focus beyond him and towards the rear of the deep balcony the restaurant occupied where the kitchen, restroom and elevators were.

Pike twisted in his seat and followed her gaze to where Dusabe was standing, bolt upright but ever so slightly swaying, his own gaze fixed on the solid lines of the skyscrapers that rose up past the restaurant like a delirious seasick sailor willing his boat towards the cliffs.

Jones raised her thick linen napkin from her lap and dropped it next to her chopsticks.

'Come on,' she said as she got up from the table, 'let's get our bodyguard back on solid ground.'

CHAPTER 40

'Two gigabyte download speed over WiFi, and each office unit has a dedicated server individually firewalled for security and privacy,' the young man said in his Arabic-inflected English, continuing the seemingly endless list of features that supposedly made office space in Malak Ali impossible to resist.

The man was wearing a three-piece black suit. The fabric had a slight sheen to it that was matched by his slicked-back black hair. He looked like a junior estate agent, which he essentially was.

He'd been talking almost non-stop for the whole half-hour since Pike, Jones and Dusabe had arrived at the first of the two staggered office blocks that flanked the entrance to the free zone on the western side of the E311 highway.

To the free zone's immediate right was the old Expo 2020 exhibition ground and Al Maktoum airport. To its left was the Persian Gulf, the free zone's docks, and the bigger of the two enormous land reclamation projects that had projected palm-tree shaped peninsulas out into the sea from the emirate's coast.

The free zone was both part of Dubai and also separate. Anyone could set up within its limits and take advantage of its low taxes and a time zone that neatly spanned the gap between Europe and Asia. But if you wanted to do business within Dubai itself you'd have to jump through several additional expensive and laborious legal hoops.

The office blocks were the first part of the economic microstate you saw when you arrived. They were also among its least remarkable features to look at, at least from the outside. They could easily have belonged on the downtown outskirts of a third-tier American city or to an out of town science park in the English home counties.

The man, who was still monologuing about the integrated climate control system that could be set to preferred temperatures, respond intuitively to the number of people in any room at any time, or even mimic the heat and humidity levels of wherever someone called home, had met them from their cab at the main entrance and immediately began his sales pitch, as if they weren't already tenants.

No attempted interruptions had derailed him from his script, so Pike and Jones had settled for just nodding as he ran through his spiel. Dusabe also kept his mouth shut, but from the looks of him this was the result of a return to his usual intimidating stoicism rather than a fear that he might throw up at any second.

The space was well-appointed. An open-plan area with sixteen designer desks and ergonomic chairs ready to be filled, a glass-fronted meeting room and single private office. There was art on the walls and plants carefully scattered around the place, both of which could be adjusted to taste at very short notice. Rental also came with unrestricted access to a high-end spa and gym and two dining levels, one more formal for entertaining visiting executives and clients, one decked out like a Disney-fied street food market, which both served cuisine from all around the world. However, none of these features were what drew people to set up an office in Malak Ali. They might help tempt employees to relocate here for a few years – along with the lack of local tax on their income – but it was the privacy and promise of absolute discretion about any business dealings that might take place within the free zone's limits that attracted CEOs and the super wealthy.

When the man finally paused to take a breath and it became clear that he was done espousing all the benefits of the office at last, Jones responded with a single word: 'Impressive.' The man missed the sarcasm. Then she went over to one of the desks, retrieved a gleaming Apple MacBook from her pristine Mulberry leather bag, both of which had been acquired the previous evening before dinner, opened its lid and waited for the prompt to connect it to the WiFi.

Pike, suddenly feeling compelled to fill the quiet that followed Jones's declaration, asked the man to explain the finer details of the office's entry system – something Dusabe probably should have done if Gasana had any intention of ever actually using the space he'd rented.

'Access to any office is limited to the people who are supposed to be there, and Malak Ali staff, of course,' the man said, suddenly reaching into his suit pocket and retrieving three keycards which he studied briefly and then quickly handed out in turn to Pike, Jones and Dusabe.

Staff, Pike guessed, included both the front-of-house team like him and the army of mute custodians they'd passed a couple of members of on their way to the office, dressed in spotless dark teal boiler suits, latex gloves, and rubber-soled boots with their eyes seemingly permanently fixed on the floor in front of them.

'These passes are temporary,' the man continued, 'but they will let you in here as well as into any of the facilities you might want to use.'

Pike made a show of looking at his keycard sceptically, and throwing the man an inquisitive look. A keycard was hardly the height of security. They could be lost, borrowed, stolen too easily – Malak Ali had to use something more sophisticated to stop people wandering where they shouldn't.

The man intuited Pike's thoughts. 'They're linked to bio-metric scanners that cover the entire free zone. Each card is matched to the record the scanners made of you when you arrived, encrypted of course. They work together through prox-imity, and the system tracks both of you in tandem so if you try to dash off to lunch and leave your keycard on your desk the door won't open for you. Or if you borrow someone else's.'

Pike had to stop himself from repeating Jones, but the sys-tem was impressive. It was also, thankfully, exactly the kind of set-up he'd thought it was going to be.

Another silence settled over the room and Pike looked at the others to see if they had any interest in filling it. They didn't. However, before he could come up with another ques-tion or observation the door to the office opened, revealing a woman in a cerulean blue suit who offered Pike, Jones and Dusabe a bright scarlet-edged smile and completely ignored the other man.

Their second guide of the morning had arrived.

* * *

The entrance foyer to the Archive, the name the woman used to distinguish the free zone's exclusive storage complex from its other warehouses, was considerably more elegant and refined than the bland corporate reception area of the office block.

Semi-circles of tan leather Barcelona chairs were set far apart from each other on huge, thick geometric rugs. On one wall was an enormous gilt-framed painting of a horse rearing up on its hind legs, on another a large video screen displayed a glitching visage of a man who alternated between laughing, crying and screaming with every pixel refresh. The ceiling was made up of overlapping sheets of impossibly thin alabaster stone cut into intricate fretwork patterns. A waterfall cascaded into a wide pool recessed in the floor in the very centre of the space, but it made no sound.

It felt like a cross between the world's most refined gallery and its most expensive members' club, which, Pike reflected as they were guided between two triple-height abstract sculptures that framed the route deeper into the building, was entirely apt.

Jones took the lead on this tour, playing the part of the deputy who had been tasked with relaying her boss's curiosity and questions about the facilities.

Meanwhile, Pike did his best to look impressed by everything they were being shown while paying extremely close attention to the details of the building. He cast casual glances at the occasional desk they passed which was staffed by another cerulean suit, clocked the doors at the ends of corridors that looked slightly more well-used than others and probably led to maintenance areas, surreptitiously counted up the number of levels in the twelve-storey building that were given over to client storage facilities as they took a lift up to the seventh floor.

For a moment he found himself fantasising about the collected value of the place and its contents and he very quickly reached a figure that was so stratospherically high it gave him vertigo.

'Each suite is entirely customisable,' the woman told Jones, bringing Pike's attention back inside the lift. 'And almost completely self-contained. Air supply is regulated centrally, but some clients prefer hermetic seals or even vacuums. It depends on what they're storing, personal heirlooms, important documents, priceless art.'

'Is there anything you won't store?' Jones asked, as they stepped out into a wide corridor that was painted and carpeted in a recessive grey and dotted with vivid pink and white orchids on clear plinths at regular intervals.

The edges of the woman's smile, which had been frozen on her face for the whole journey across the free zone from the office block in one of its autonomous, air-conditioned electric vehicles, dropped fractionally.

'We will, of course, refuse to accept anything that has been alerted to us as being illegal or dangerous, as it could pose a threat to our other clients' holdings,' she said.

They reached a doorway with a palm-sized digital panel on the wall next to it at chest height and no handle on its slightly darker grey door.

'We also don't accept anything if we know it's alive, in case you were considering moving in,' she added, her smile back at full beam.

It sounded like a well-rehearsed joke to Pike, but also a very carefully worded one, just like her comment about less-than-legal things. There was a clear message beneath what the woman was saying: don't tell us what you're keeping in your suite, and we won't ask.

Pike wondered what might be behind the other doors they'd passed beyond the kind of things they'd seen in the Acropolis Museum and the woman had described. Weapons caches? Nazi gold? Dead bodies? Nearly dead bodies?

The woman pressed her palm against the panel on the wall. There was the slightest click of a large lock disengaging, and the door swung slowly away from the corridor to reveal an entirely blank and featureless five-by-ten-metre box.

The woman beckoned the group inside the suite she'd just unlocked.

As he passed through the arch of the doorframe, Pike glanced at the unusual depth of it and the five deadbolt grooves that ran up its height. Then, just as the door was closing behind him his attention was drawn back out into the corridor. A small autonomous vehicle that looked like a cross between an oversized suitcase and a miniature futuristic fork-lift truck was slowly trundling past the door, a single crate balanced on the twin flat prongs that stuck out of its chassis, with another bowed-over figure in a boiler suit walking silently behind it.

Once the woman was done explaining to Jones the basic features of the vacant standard suite they were all now locked inside until she released them and how easy it would be to incorporate any particular individual enhancements, Pike asked her about the contraption he'd seen.

'Are those things how the lots from the Athens auction will be taken to their new owners?'

'Some of them,' the woman replied. 'Our worker bots are controlled by a mesh network that covers every square centimetre of the public and service areas of the complex, which tells them where to go and alerts them to obstacles.'

'Like those car computers that can tell if there's an accident round a corner from you, or shops that just know what you've bought and charge you when you leave without having to go through a checkout,' Pike said.

'Not quite,' the woman replied just about managing to cover her disdain at Pike's intentionally lowbrow comparisons. 'The Archive's systems are a little more advanced than those. Of course, some items are too heavy or delicate to be transported by them, and the insides of the suites are not covered by the mesh so everything always ends up being hand delivered by our extremely discreet team.'

'It's pretty quiet around here.'

'Our clients rarely visit in person.'

'Does anyone ever move their own stuff?'

'Only if they're removing an item. Clients aren't allowed in each other's suites without permission, and only when they're both physically present. Even if you were able to do everything required to vouch for your identity remotely, supply the correct personal security codes, and pass voice and facial recognition to prove you aren't a deep fake, the system still wouldn't let me give someone else access to your property.'

'The same as the offices?' Pike said, phrasing the statement as a question to make it sound like he was doing his best to keep up with all the technical wizardry the guide was describing.

This time she was clearly less offended by what he'd suggested, and gave him the kind of nod a school teacher might offer to one of their dimmer but nicer students when they finally grasped a basic concept.

'Exactly,' she said. 'Privacy and, if requested, anonymity are of paramount importance at Malak Ali.'

CHAPTER 41

They left the Archive after a few more questions from Jones about things like pricing and contract length. None of it was important – they had no intention of actually renting a suite, and Pike had already found out everything he needed to know about the numbers and kind of people who they might typically find strolling through its corridors at any time of day.

Another autonomous vehicle that looked like a golf cart with seamless perspex sides was lingering outside to take them back to the office block, but no one was waiting for them when they arrived.

Perhaps the man who had first shown them round thought his duties had been discharged and any responsibility he'd had had been handed over to the woman from the Archive. Or, now that the morning was in full swing, maybe he'd simply forgotten about them. Either way, Pike was happy to note that even in an environment as carefully monitored and controlled as Malak Ali human error could still creep in.

They passed other tenants on their way up to their office, who were either emerging from theirs for a mid-morning coffee or arriving to make a belated start to the day. They were the standard mix of ages, demographics, and professional and casual dress that inhabited rented office space all over the globe.

Once they were back inside theirs, Pike opened up his PADD and signalled at Jones and Dusabe to both keep their mouths closed.

After a few seconds studying the screen he said, 'Just checking in case there were any listening devices hiding anywhere.'

'That thing can detect bugs?' Dusabe asked.

'It can track live data networks. If it had found one it couldn't explain I might have suspected someone was engaging in a little live surveillance. But it looks like they meant what they said about privacy.'

'Good,' Jones said. 'So now what?'

'Now, I need the zero-day,' Pike replied.

She didn't look like she was prepared to hand it over just because Pike said he wanted it. Neither did Dusabe, who was still physically in possession of the USB stick that contained the code that would exploit the vulnerability that supposedly existed in Malak Ali's defences.

'Shouldn't we wait until it's a little quieter?'

Pike shook his head. 'We need to know it works because it's just the thing that'll open the door into Malak Ali's systems. I'll still need most of the day to do what I need to once we're in. And if it isn't going to work or set alarms blazing, better it happens now so we can fade into a confused crowd.'

'You said there were no live data networks, and our server's self-contained. How are you going to deploy it?'

'I said there were no networks I couldn't explain,' Pike replied. 'But there was one they were eager to show off to us.'

Then he pointed up at the air-conditioning unit.

'Centrally controlled,' he said. 'That's our way in.'

They all gazed up at the white, slightly concave disc that was elegantly embedded in the ceiling in the centre of the room for a few seconds before Jones nodded at Dusabe and he handed the stick over to Pike.

He slotted the stick's micro connector stub into a port on the bottom edge of his PADD and transferred over the code.

Then he held his breath and waited the couple of seconds the PADD needed to make friends with the air conditioner's little digital brain and upload the zero-day into it.

For several silent, pensive moments nothing happened. Pike felt his shoulders start to creep up slightly, and sensed his companions stiffening as well – getting ready to either make a break for the door or make good on Gasana's threats about what would happen to Pike if his plan failed again.

But then the screen in Pike's hands filled with multiple windows of data and he exhaled a deep sigh.

'We're in,' he said, inhaling fresh oxygen into his lungs.

Pike sat down at the desk opposite Jones's closed laptop and let himself become consumed by the access he had now to the inner workings of Malak Ali and setting the PADD to work gathering up all the information he needed about its security fail safes, staff rotas and client data.

After a couple of minutes he realised that Jones and Dusabe were still standing in the middle of the room, beneath the air-conditioning unit, watching him.

'This really is going to take a while,' he said.

'The private key?' Jones replied, apparently feeling the need to remind Pike of why they were in Dubai in the first place.

Pike navigated to the database that contained details of the people and organisations who used the Archive and a catalogue of all arrivals, removals and transfers of property. While the PADD copied the whole thing into its own memory for Pike's future reference, he scrolled through both lists, confirming the location of Liu's triple-sized suite and that it had received several deliveries from other units over the last forty-eight hours, including a single item from one that was currently being rented by the Government of El Salvador.

Pike smiled. 'Exactly where it should be.'

Seemingly satisfied, Jones sat down across from him and opened up the laptop as Dusabe took up position like a statue next to the door.

After two hours, during which time Dusabe barely moved a millimetre, Pike prodded and probed ever-deeper into Malak Ali's systems, and Jones occupied herself with whatever she was doing on her MacBook, she announced that she was hungry.

'Both of you go grab something,' Pike said. 'I'll need to work through.'

'No,' Dusabe said.

Pike smirked, pulled his keycard from his pocket and slid it across the desk to Jones. 'I'm really not planning on going anywhere.'

'I'll bring you something back,' she said, pushing the card over to him again.

Half an hour later, she did – a lunch that consisted of a bland cheese sandwich, a small bag of overly salted crisps, and an equally diminutive bottle of very sweet lemonade, which made Pike feel even more like a naughty schoolboy being kept in detention.

Once he was finished crunching the crisps, which he did more loudly and for longer than he really needed to, the room fell into another couple of hours of still silence. This one was ended by Dusabe, who had skipped lunch, saying that he needed to stretch his legs.

However, when he went to the door it refused to open for him. He took a step back and tried again, then fished his keycard from his pocket and waved it in the air in front of him, which also achieved nothing.

'Did you do this?' he asked Pike, turning to face him.

'No,' Pike replied, getting up and crossing the distance to the door.

He reached for the handle and it refused to move for him as well. Jones tried too with the same result.

'The temporary cards must time-out after a set period,' Pike posited.

'So we're trapped in here?' Jones said.

'Not necessarily,' Pike replied. Then he looked at Dusabe and said, 'I need the smart tags.'

He expected the other man – or Jones – to demand another explanation, but he handed them straight over.

Pike balanced the three hexagonal disks on one half of the PADD's opened out screen and tapped the command buttons that appeared in sequence on the other one. Then he handed one back to Dusabe and the other to Jones.

'Try the door now,' he said to Dusabe.

He did, and this time it opened.

'How?' Dusabe asked once he'd shut it again.

'I've coded the tags to give us full staff access,' Pike replied. 'But that's only half of it. I've also introduced an algorithm that automatically removes any record of wherever these go and whatever doors they might happen to open. More effort upfront, but much easier than trying to come up with a reason for every lock, scanner and security camera to go offline at the same time that doesn't make it look completely obvious that the free zone is under attack.'

'But the cameras will still see us as soon as we step out into the corridor,' Jones said.

Pike shook his head. 'I added a spatial element to the algorithm. It doesn't just delete the smart tags but everything within a two-metre, three-dimensional radius of them. Our biometrics are completely dampened and we'll be scrubbed from video footage before it's even been processed. As long as we're wearing the tags, we're ghosts.'

Jones looked impressed. Dusabe, however, was inscrutable as usual.

'Then we can get on with this,' he said, reaching his hand out to the door handle again.

'Not quite yet,' Pike replied, holding up the PADD that now displayed a heat map showing how many bodies were in each part of the free zone in real time alongside a colour-coded bar chart of staff and tenant numbers divided by sector. 'We need to wait for the place to thin out a bit.'

'What are we supposed to do until then?' the other man said, irritation finally filling his voice.

Pike crossed over to his desk, sat back down in his chair, turned the one next to it to face him, put his feet up on its seat and said, 'I'm going to have a nap.'

CHAPTER 42

Pike was nudged awake. He cracked one eye, then the other, slowly letting both focus on Jones standing over him.

He stretched his arms into the air as he twisted his feet off the chair they'd been propped up on and sat up straight.

'What time is it?' he asked the room, before he checked his own watch and confirmed it was almost six o'clock in the evening. 'Huh, I guess I needed to catch up on a couple of hours.'

Pike looked past Jones at Dusabe, who was still standing by the door, his face set in a deep frown that made his frustration at the lack of action over the last couple of hours extremely clear.

Pike hadn't actually been asleep all that time. For the first half-hour he'd been tilted back in his chair with his eyes closed, he'd been running through all the possible scenarios for what might happen when they did finally leave the office and go back to the Archive. Then he'd handed the most likely ones over to his subconscious for forty-five minutes to poke holes in, which he'd then spent the last twenty minutes calmly refilling, his eyes closed and breathing even.

No plan was ever perfect, even ones as thought-out as Pike's tended to be. There were always unexpected events, uncontrollable variables, blindsiding surprises that can't be fully predicted or managed and could threaten to derail things. The biggest issue they might face in the Archive would be discovering the private key was no longer in the false base of the headdress's container. But, this far into the operation, with so much at stake, and with no obvious evidence pointing to the private key having been discovered, it was better to imagine that simply wasn't a possibility. And Pike was confident he'd put enough contingencies in place to manage whatever else might happen next.

He stood up, stretched out his back and opened up his PADD. The same windows that had been on its dual screens appeared once more, this time showing a much cooler heat map and bar charts that were all steadily shrinking, pixel by pixel.

'Time to go,' he said, pocketing the PADD and starting for the door. 'And check that the smart tags are still working.'

'Wait a second,' Jones said, drawing a surprised look from Pike and a deepening of the groove across Dusabe's forehead. 'Explain the plan.'

'This is the easy bit,' Pike said. 'We head back to the Archive, go into Liu's suite, find the headdress, remove the private key, and then disappear into the night.'

They left the office one at a time, Dusabe first, then Pike, then Jones. Dusabe started marching towards the bank of lifts and Pike let him almost reach them before he said in a stage whisper that that wasn't the way they were heading and pointed to the door that led to the emergency exit stairs at the opposite end of the corridor.

The taller man stalked past Pike and Jones, through the door and down the stairs, only slowing his strides to glance behind him on each landing to confirm if he should keep going.

They reached the ground floor and didn't stop. The staircase continued to descend for at least four more storeys, but Pike signalled that they'd be exiting it on the second basement level.

They hadn't encountered anyone else so far, but Jones still only mouthed, 'Why?' at Pike, prompting him to retrieve his PADD and show her a keyline blueprint-style map of Malak Ali, centred over the office block.

He spread his fingers across the screen, zooming in on the image as the map moved through the building's floors until it reached its subterranean storeys and Pike revealed that the second one reached out beyond the limits of the office block's above-ground walls. It was a mirror of the roads and paths that spread throughout the whole free zone – an underground network of service and maintenance tunnels where all the messy and dirty work of keeping the place running was hidden away.

They stepped into the first section of painted concrete corridor which, through a sequence of turns, junctions and connections, would take them to the Archive. And once again Pike pointed them towards the less obvious of the two directions they could choose from.

'First stop,' he said, a little volume in his voice.

This time he'd gestured at a door which led to a large custodial closet that included several rows of shelves of toilet roll and cleaning products, and a stack of immaculately folded boiler suits and box of latex gloves above a row of boots.

'I can fool the digital systems but not people's eyes,' he said, as he started to root through the clothes and check them for size. 'So we need to keep a low profile and blend in.'

Five minutes later Pike and Jones were back in the corridor after finding a boiler suit and pair of boots that fitted them close enough. Dusabe, however, had refused to even look for one until they were done and he could be alone. Pike guessed his insistence on privacy wasn't a result of modesty or a fragile ego, yet he still felt compelled to stifle the laugh that welled up inside him when the other man eventually emerged in a suit that looked like it had been painted directly onto his muscles and might tear every single one of its seams with the slightest exertion.

Pike had memorised the path they needed to take to reach the Archive, along with two less direct routes in case they found themselves needing to make a detour for some reason.

He checked the PADD one last time before slipping it into one of the deep pockets of his boiler suit and pulling on his pair of latex gloves: the bar charts had dropped even further, and the heat map showed less intense blooms that were mostly confined to the buildings above ground, though not entirely.

He led them along the corridor, back past the door to the emergency stairs, and fifty metres further on to where it forked left and right. He turned left. Dusabe and Jones followed.

The corridor became wider, and seemed to stretch off to oblivion, or at least all the way to the docks on the far side of the free zone. Pike wondered how much of the contents of the Archive had been shipped into Malak Ali, tucked away at the bottom of the manifests of the container ships that used the free zone's port to exchange cargo and refuel.

They walked on for almost a kilometre, keeping a loose two-one formation, Dusabe and Jones taking turns being closer to Pike, to make it look like three people who just happened to be heading in the same direction instead of a trio on the same mission. Though they probably needn't have bothered with that particular precaution as they only encountered a handful of people, all heading in the opposite direction to them, before they reached the next branch tunnel they needed to turn down, and none of them took any interest in a few boiler suits strolling by the other way.

Pike had been keeping count of the tunnels that branched off the one that had taken them most of the way to the Archive, so when they reached their next turn he could take it with the confidence of someone who knew exactly where he was going.

Jones and Dusabe mimicked him, which unfortunately meant they were all already in the narrower corridor when Pike realised that there was someone else in it, ten metres away, walking rapidly towards them – the man who had shown them round the office block.

The branch tunnel was smaller and dimmer than the one they'd left, but there was no mistaking the man and even hugging the walls there'd be less than a metre gap between him and Pike, Jones and Dusabe once they reached each other, if they got that far.

There was no way Pike could warn the others or abruptly stop and turn one hundred and eighty degrees without drawing the other man's attention. All he could do was cast his gaze down at the floor, pray Jones and Dusabe did the same, and hope that while the other man wasn't at the top of the free zone staff's pecking order he considered himself far enough up it to ignore anyone dressed in dark teal.

Step by step Pike got closer to him, waiting for the man to recognise him, call out or break into a run back the way he'd come to raise the alarm.

But none of those things happened. The other man's shoes maintained their rhythmic pace on the concrete floor – a louder, strident counterpoint to the muffled, background shuffling of three pairs of rubber-soled boots.

Pike dared to glance up at him just as they crossed each other and saw that he was completely lost in whatever thoughts were occupying his mind, and which, from the tired grimace Pike could now see on his face, were not pleasant.

In an instant, Pike stopped thinking of the man as a threat. He was just someone finally finishing a long, thankless shift at a job he didn't really care about. Someone who had spent their day fending off complaints and condescending looks and wondering if it was all worth it. Someone who simply wanted to get away from Malak Ali as quickly as he could and back to the small, featureless box of an apartment he called home for a few hours of peace during which no one would make any demands of him.

The man passed Pike without breaking his stride, and he updated his prayer to the god he didn't believe in, asking him to guide Dusabe away from deciding to take the initiative and doing something that would cause more problems, like knocking the man out or worse. Stashing a body somewhere was one of the variables Pike had considered but definitely didn't want to have to actually deal with.

Thankfully, Dusabe resisted any temptation he might have been feeling to lash out and they all managed to survive the surprise encounter unscathed.

Pike, Jones and Dusabe rounded the next corner they needed to take twenty metres further down the tunnel, silently pausing for a second to acknowledge what had just happened and double-check they were in the clear.

Then, after three more turns, they reached another larger tunnel which had a loading bay cut into its side, the rear wall of which was filled by two double-width lift doors.

They'd arrived at the service entrance to the Archive.

CHAPTER 43

Jones stepped forward to the first lift. The wide doors refused to open in response to her proximity.

She looked up, searching for the blinking light of a sensor that should have registered her presence and summoned a lift before she was wiped from the system care of the smart tag that was now discreetly clipped to the inside of the buttoned-down flap of her boiler suit's left-hand chest pocket. There wasn't one. She glanced towards the doors' edges for a call button but couldn't see one on either side.

Pike and Dusabe cast their eyes around too, but couldn't see any means of commanding either of the sets of large slabs of brushed metal in front of them to part.

'I guess it makes sense that you can't just walk in there,' Pike said.

'You guess?' Jones replied. 'How big a problem is this?'

Pike retrieved his PADD from his leg pocket. 'Don't worry, I thought this would be the fastest way in, but there's a stairwell on the other side of the building we can use.'

'Is that another guess?' This time the question came from Dusabe.

'No,' Pike replied, checking the route and distance to the Archive's other entry point. 'All the emergency staircases in the whole complex work the same way. I suppose they just don't want people using the service lifts without one of those worker bots.'

Jones backed away from the lift doors and leaned her head round the corner to check the corridor was still clear. 'How far are the stairs?'

'About another six hundred metres,' Pike replied. Then he navigated up through the plans of each level of the Archive. 'Then Liu's suite is on the twelfth floor. It looks like they get bigger the higher up you go.'

Jones was halfway through asking which direction they should get moving in when a loud beep behind her made her spin round in shock and Dusabe almost burst out of his boiler suit as he readied himself to defend against a surprise attack.

It was a worker bot that had emerged silently from a doorway opposite the loading bay that none of them had noticed.

The bot moved a few centimetres forward, stopping before it hit Jones. It beeped again, slightly louder this time. Jones, composure returned, took it as a cue and stepped out of its way as Pike peered through the open door at a whole row of the mini forklifts that looked like they were powered down, waiting to be called into action.

The active bot moved again, coming to a gentle halt in front of the doors Jones had been trying to open, and they all heard lift motors beyond it start to whirr.

Jones and Dusabe looked relieved. Pike didn't.

'In there,' he said, pointing at the room full of bots.

Jones and Dusabe both shot him questioning glances. They'd just stumbled on a way into the Archive, so why wouldn't they take it?

'Someone could be coming to collect it,' Pike said, interpreting their expressions. 'Or be waiting for it on whichever floor they've called it from.'

'And we could just as easily be seen by someone down here,' Jones replied. 'That gets us inside.'

'But we can't guarantee it'll take us where we want to go,' Pike countered. 'Give me a minute and I can programme one of its friends to take us up to the twelfth floor without worrying about any unexpected encounters or tagalongs. It'll be quicker than walking.'

The hum of the motor in the shaft behind the doors in front of them started to quiet, signalling the imminent arrival of a lift. They only had a few more seconds to decide what to do, and Jones took most of them before she finally said, 'Fine,' gestured across the corridor, and they all piled in with the dormant bots.

The door shut behind them as the lift opened, which meant they didn't see if anyone had been sent to fetch the departing worker bot or if it would be making its journey up into the Archive by itself.

Pike's concerns about someone coming to fetch the bot, or waiting for it above them, had been entirely reasonable. However, he also wasn't going to pass up the chance to take a closer look at the inner workings of the worker bots given the opportunity – which he had just been given.

Thankfully, the room they rushed into didn't plunge into darkness once the door closed. It was large enough to accommodate all of three of them and, from a quick count, fifteen worker bots nestled in open-fronted alcoves with waist-height sides, and an empty station halfway along the row that belonged to the bot that had just left. The room was long and thin, the alcoves a single line down one wall. There was no repair area, no shelves of tools or pneumatic workbench. Apparently the bots didn't break down – or if they did, they were fixed somewhere else where they wouldn't get in the way.

Pike went to the vacant alcove first, checking the physical ports and pads that were used to transfer power to the bots, and hunting for any hard connections to the mesh network that was used to guide and instruct them. Then he turned his attention to the bot in the next nook. On closer inspection, it wasn't a completely blank white box with prongs. There was a touchscreen on the top of it which was faded to near invisibility but glowed to life as Pike hovered his hand above it, revealing its power level, identification code, and list of scheduled activity.

This bot was designated A-3, was currently at ninety per cent battery, and had no appointments until nine a.m. the next morning.

Pike pulled up the worker bot directory on his PADD and scrolled down to the Archive's section, impressed that the single building actually had forty-eight bots assigned to it, and they were currently in one of three charging and storage areas.

350

The directory confirmed the information displayed on the bot's screen, and it was just a simple matter of accessing the bot management program and issuing a command for A-3 to take a trip up in the lift to the twelfth floor – which could either be erased from the bot's and programme's records, ignored as an automated test, or left as a tantalising mystery no one would probably ever stumble over.

Pike inputted the order and a few moments later A-3 rose up slightly and trundled forward. Even though he'd now seen how the bots worked, Pike still half-expected it to keep getting higher in the air and hover its way out of the alcove.

'Good boy,' Pike said, as the bot turned towards the door.

The bot replied by beeping at Dusabe, who was standing in its way.

He moved to the side, the expression on his face suggesting that he equal parts wanted to knock the bot over and push it to go faster.

The door opened as A-3 approached it and, a second after it passed through, Pike leaned his head back out into the corridor, ensuring it was still deserted before they followed the bot over to the service lift. Then, as soon as the bot got within a metre of the left-hand lift, motors began turning again and, ten seconds later, that set of doors opened too.

Pike, Jones and Dusabe waited for A-3 to roll into the lift and turn itself round, then shuffled in around its sides, taking position behind it. They rode the lift up in silence, bowing their heads as they neared their destination level just in case one of A-3's siblings happened to be trundling past with its own subservient assistants when the lift doors opened again.

When the bot moved forward out onto plush carpet, the mesh network telling it there was nothing it needed to avoid or navigate round, the trio fell into step behind it as it began its pointless lap of the twelfth floor.

Liu's suite was on the other side of the Archive to the service lift, so they still had to walk about five hundred metres, but with each tentative turn they made and every stretch of corridor they entered that was empty of anything but more regularly spaced out orchids – deep purple to stand out against this level's putty-hued tones – Pike became more confident that they were past the point of being discovered or stopped before they reached it.

And then they did.

CHAPTER 44

There was no reason why the door to Liu's suite would look any different to all the others they'd passed, yet some part of Pike felt like it should. Given how much he'd gone through to reach it, and the astronomical value of what must be held behind it, Pike imagined it would be so much grander or more imposing than just another dark grey door with a palm scanner panel next to it.

A-3 kept on rolling straight past it, as if it meant absolutely nothing to the little automaton – which it didn't – reached the end of the corridor a further twenty metres away, completed a one-hundred-and-eighty-degree turn in front of the door to the emergency stairwell they hadn't had to climb up and began making its way back to the lift.

'Shouldn't we keep it here so we can take the lift back down?' Jones asked, her voice low.

Pike shook his head.

'Something else for someone to notice,' he replied, his tone equally hushed. 'A quick, random trip can be chalked up to command timing error or a diagnostic test, but keeping A-3 out of its dock too long might put a flag on a system

I haven't accounted for. We'll have to take the stairs on the way out.'

'Dealing with the computer systems is the only reason you're still here,' Dusabe said.

'I thought we were past the death threat stage,' Pike replied. 'No plan or code is ever completely perfect.' Then he put his hand up to the panel, let it scan his palm, and added, 'But the ones I come up with get pretty damn close.'

They watched the door open and reveal their first glimpse of what was inside. And it looked like chaos.

They stepped forward, mesmerised by what had been revealed and bumping into each other as they all crammed through the doorway at the same time.

The triple-sized suite was huge, but it couldn't be described as cavernous as it was almost completely filled with mountains of boxes, crates and objects haphazardly piled high on top of each other.

It took Pike a long moment to take even the tiniest fraction of it in.

He could see three enormous chests, each big enough to fit a person inside, that must have dated back hundreds of years covered in ornate fretwork and perfectly preserved lacquered illustrations, nestled up against boxes that looked like they came from a third-rate haulage company.

Gilt-edged frames were stacked up against each other ten deep against a wall, only the thinnest layer of foam draped over their tops to protect whatever priceless paintings they contained. Busts that had been sculpted from marble at the turn of the last millennium jostled for space on high shelves with more recently created ones made from pressed polystyrene that were being used as stands for an array of kabuki masks, crowns and tiaras. A display cabinet dwarfed by taller stacks that surrounded it looked like it was full of pristine examples of *saif* and *nimcha* swords. There was even a Roman amphora filled to the brim with gold coins.

Pike couldn't even begin to fathom the total worth of what he could see, let alone the entire contents of the suite, or the kind of reaction a museum curator or historian might have to being presented with it. There was no consideration here, no thought to display or even much of one to preservation. This wasn't a carefully grown and maintained collection of passion or interest. It was a grotesque, lumpen heap of wealth.

'Jesus,' Pike said, half to himself. 'The man's not a magpie. He's a hoarder.'

'Where is the headdress?' Dusabe asked.

The absurdity of the question made Pike laugh, which made Dusabe clench both his fists.

'How the hell should I know,' Pike replied. 'It could be anywhere in this mess.'

'Not anywhere,' Jones interjected, drawing Dusabe's attention before he was tempted to hit the other man. 'It's unlikely they rearranged the whole place just for that.'

'Good point,' Pike said. 'It'll probably be somewhere close to the door, or plugging an easy-to-reach gap.'

Dusabe unballed one of his fists, reached up to Pike's chest pocket and removed his smart tag. 'Then we should start looking.'

Pike pantomimed a bow at the order and started picking his way through the nearest gulley to him, between the lacquered chests and several upright dark brown leather trunks that were covered in a repeating pattern of the Louis Vuitton logo and Liu's initials. After a few seconds watching him, Jones and Dusabe chose their own paths and started working their way through the suite.

In theory, they could have spent all night searching for the headdress, and helped themselves to anything else that might catch their eyes, but even though no one was scheduled to deliver or remove anything from Liu's suite, that didn't completely remove the chance of someone turning up out of the blue – *they* had, after all. And, removing anything that might be on some inventory, however much it might feel like anything taken from the suite wouldn't be missed, might prompt a closer look at the Archive's security records and draw suspicion towards anyone who might recently have had a problem with Liu. Of course, that was more of a concern for Jones and Dusabe than Pike.

The three of them searched with quiet, thorough determination for the next half-hour, occasionally asking for a second or third opinion on a crate they'd spotted. At one point, Pike struck a vein of items he recognised from the Acropolis auction, but the headdress wasn't among them. He also never spotted the giant, cartoonish curves of the neon pink sculpture Liu had seemed so obsessed with, which got him curious about whether the Archive had an annexe somewhere for the pieces that wouldn't fit in its suites. Things like enormous balloon animals, ancient temple doors or complete dinosaur skeletons.

After another fifteen minutes of almost and not-quite finds, Pike could sense Dusabe losing what little patience he had left, and Jones getting closer to demanding he retrace every step of the journey the private key had been on since it left Perquin and work out any point where he might have missed it being diverted from its intended destination.

But an hour in, as he eased himself round a terracotta statue of a Qin Dynasty warrior stood to attention and clambered down onto his knees, he struck petrified gold.

'I think I've got it,' he called out, then started to slide the crate he'd found tucked in a gap between two more monogrammed trunks.

Out of the shadows, he recognised it as the one he'd last seen in a basement in an old rebel stronghold in the middle of the Salvadoran jungle, and it still looked more or less in the same condition – just a few light bumps and scrapes from its trip halfway round the world.

He gently slid it along the floor, past the terracotta warrior and the chests to the relatively open area in front of the door. Jones and Dusabe met him there, and at the sight of the crate the other man walked over to the display cabinet to retrieve one of the swords.

'Not necessary,' Pike said. 'It looks like they haven't bothered replacing the nails in the top after they scanned it for the hologram.'

He tested the edge of the lid and was proved right – it came up easily in his hands.

He put the crate lid on the floor and peered inside, at the top of the headdress's hermetic container.

'Is it there?' Jones asked.

'Give me a second,' Pike replied, reaching inside to unfasten the second lid.

He removed it, revealing an instantly recognisable alabaster curve. Now he reached both hands in, lifting up the headdress and handing it briefly to Jones as he retrieved the display stand and perched it back on it on the floor.

Pike gripped the edges of the hermetic container, pulled it up out of the crate and turned it over. Ever so slowly, the false bottom began to succumb to gravity and centimetre-by-centimetre started to half-slide and half-fall out of the container. He fought to keep his patience under control and the box completely level as any sudden jerks or changes of angle could wedge the metal panel against the glass.

Eventually, it reached the open end of the box and dropped into the dark shadow of the crate. Then, fully doubling over, Pike reached for the slit cut in the very centre of the foam that covered the back of the plate, found it, and felt the matte plastic of a USB stick.

Pike stood up, holding the private key almost aloft in victory. He looked at the other two and realised that neither of them was smiling, and that Dusabe was pointing a pistol at him.

It was the carbon fibre one that had been dug into this side during their brief trip to Morocco. Pike had wondered what had happened to it, and guessed it might have been the reason Dusabe had insisted on changing into his boiler suit alone. He couldn't imagine where the other man had stashed it, considering how tight his outfit had been, but then it occurred to him that Dusabe hadn't turned his back on Pike since they'd left the office block.

Jones held out her palm for Pike to give her the private key.

'I suppose there's no point in saying you don't have to do this, is there?' he said.

'No,' she replied. 'Are you really that surprised?'

He handed over the private key with a sigh. 'I guess not, but there really is no need.'

'You said yourself, no plan can be completely perfect. We might need a fall guy.'

'You're just making sure I'll tell whoever finds me what happened and who's behind it.'

'And you think they'll believe you, with no proof we were ever here? That's cute.'

Jones looked towards Dusabe, as if she was about to give him an order. Pike needed to say something before she did. This time he tried a different approach. An appeal to humanity. It was a long shot.

'Do you know what they'll do to me if they find me here?'

'It won't be pleasant,' Dusabe replied.

That was an understatement. Liu hadn't struck Pike as the forgiving type. And foreign nationals – especially foreign nationals who couldn't prove their identity and were found in places they definitely shouldn't be – tended not to fare well in the Dubai judicial system.

The handgun still trained on him, Jones reached into Pike's trouser pocket and removed the PADD.

'I meant what I told you about that,' Pike said. 'It'll blow up in your face if you try to do anything with it.'

'I don't need to do anything with it,' Jones replied, opening it up and tossing it onto the floor in front of Dusabe. 'I just need to make sure you can't use it to revoke our all-access passes and stop us from leaving.'

On cue, Dusabe stamped on the PADD, fracturing its screen into a spider's web of cracks and even sending a few chunks of it scattering between boxes. Then he pulled Pike's smart tag out of his own pocket, dropped it next to the broken PADD and obliterated that as well.

Jones and Dusabe backed towards the door, and Pike followed them until the angle of the pistol was raised to aim at his face instead of his chest and he stopped two metres from his only way out.

'You don't know where you're going,' he said.

'You're not the only one who can count turns,' Dusabe replied.

Then he took one more step backwards, prompting the door to open behind him, and he and Jones both stepped out into the corridor.

'See you around,' Jones said to Pike, throwing him one last sarcastic smile as the door shut again.

Pike didn't lurch to try and grab it, or bang on it to be let out, shouting that they'd made a mistake or vowing revenge.

He just silently counted the few seconds he thought it would take Jones and Dusabe to reach and go through the entrance to the emergency stairwell, leaned down to scoop up the broken PADD and smart tag, packed up the headdress again, and then made his way towards the deepest recesses of the suite to find something else he'd been looking for, for a long time.

It took him another two hours of scrabbling around and shifting priceless artefacts that Liu had once thought shiny enough to want but had since clearly forgotten he owned to locate the real reason he'd gone to so much effort to orchestrate getting inside Malak Ali: a velvet-lined box about the size of an old VHS tape that looked like it hadn't been opened in over twenty years and was wedged on a low shelf behind a crate marked with a ten-year-old American import stamp.

He held his breath as he opened the box.

Inside was a small figurine of a hunter, one arm held aloft, no bigger than the length of Pike's outstretched index finger and carved from the ivory of a mammoth tusk. It looked exactly the same as the last time he'd seen it, when it was being removed from a very different type of archive twenty-five years ago.

He delicately picked up the miniature statue, ran his fingers over the almost tessellating pattern that covered its middle section a few times, and slipped it inside his chest pocket.

And then, because he'd lied about the smart tags which actually did absolutely nothing, and it was only his individual biometrics that had given them access to every part of the free zone except the Archive's service lift and the emergency exit and would be wiped from its security records, he strolled out of Liu's suite.

CHAPTER 45

Gasana welcomed Jones and Dusabe to Nyungwe like con-
quering heroes.

Ever since he'd received the message from Dubai that
they had the private key, he'd been itching to hold it in
his hands. He'd been tempted to drive to Cyangugu and
meet them off their transit from Bujumbura Airport over
the border in Burundi, but after all the effort, planning and
working to acquire it he found he preferred the idea of the
key finally coming to him. So, he settled for lingering near
the floor-to-ceiling window at the far end of the conference
room next to his office through which the tops of the high,
main security gates of the complex were just visible.

Gasana was expecting two arrivals at Nyungwe this morning, but Jones and Dusabe's flight was scheduled an hour
before his second guest was due in from Kigali. They'd landed
on time, so when the gates parted he knew it was them.

He'd been in near-constant encrypted contact with Jones
and Dusabe since the second they'd left Malak Ali and confirmed that they had secured the private key. Yet, when they
both walked through the doors to the conference room, neither

of them looking like they'd spent all night travelling, he still breathlessly asked, 'Do you have it?'

Jones nodded as Dusabe raised up his hand, opened his palm and revealed the five-centimetre-long USB stick nestled within it.

Gasana carefully picked up the private key, holding it as if it was as fragile as a Fabergé egg. Then he placed it onto the conference table next to his laptop and the ice bucket that contained a bottle of 1996 Dom Perignon and four glasses at its head.

He resisted the urge to ball his hand into a fist and hammer down on the stick until it was broken beyond repair and the string of numbers it kept in its little memory core was obliterated.

Even if the billion dollars had come from bad means he could give it good ends. It could be used to fund GME's next wave of innovation and expansion, or drip-fed into the enhanced income the treasury would soon be getting from Nyungwe and invested in the kind of infrastructure that would help transform Rwanda into a truly modern nation.

Gasana also had to stop himself from slipping the end of the stick into the port on his laptop, uploading the key and kicking out the knees of the Salvadoran economy straight away.

He was going to do that second thing, but not quite yet. Not until the morning's second arrival.

So, the key stayed on the table, testing Gasana's patience as he poured out three glasses of champagne.

'To the future,' he announced, once he'd handed Jones and Dusabe their flutes.

They all took a celebratory sip, then Gasana asked, 'You didn't encounter any problems?'

'No,' Jones replied.

That wasn't strictly true. They had come up against a small issue once they'd left the Archive down the emergency stairs and were back in the tunnels beneath it: no more locked doors opened at their command. However, once they'd noticed this when they tried to change back into their own clothes in the supply closet, they simply followed a couple of other boiler-suited workers out of the staff exit and hitched a ride on the shuttle bus that took them to one of the city's nearby lower-level worker housing estates, from where they disappeared into the night. Jones didn't mention this to Gasana, and Dusabe didn't correct her omission.

'And the key was where it was supposed to be?'

'Exactly.'

Gasana asked more questions, back to their separation in Marrakech and going stage by stage to the present moment. He wasn't probing the details of the first-hand account of what happened in Malak Ali that Jones mostly told, trying to find any contradictions or fudges. He was vicariously reliving it, picturing it in his head as if he was there so that when it came to recalling it in the future his memories would tell him that he was.

Jones obliged, describing in precise detail their arrival in Dubai (she skirted Dusabe's allergic reaction at the rooftop dinner), the tour of the Malak Ali office block and the Archive, and then the late night visit to Liu's suite and the wonders it had contained.

Finally, Gasana asked about the character from Jones's story that his mind would eventually erase and replace with himself.

'Did Pike suspect you were going to leave him there?'

'Possibly,' Jones replied. 'But that didn't stop it from happening.'

Gasana's cheeks and eyes creased as he smiled, imagining Pike being trapped in the place he'd worked so hard to break into, surrounded by things of incalculable value that would be of no use to him – like a castaway floating in the middle of an ocean they dare not drink from.

'It's almost a shame. But he did know too much for us to just part ways amicably. I wonder if he'll end up in a prison camp in the middle of the desert, or thrown over the side of a cargo ship in the Arabian Sea.'

Gasana woke up the idling laptop in front of him, checked the time, and strolled over to the tall window. Right on schedule, he saw the tips of the complex gates pulling apart again.

He topped up the three champagne glasses – a lot for him, some for Jones, and barely anything for Dusabe – and filled the fourth flute. Five minutes later the door to the conference room opened, and Jean Kamanzi stepped inside.

The finance minister looked furious at having been summoned to Nyungwe on the first flight of the day out of Kigali. But his barely contained rage turned to incomprehension as

Gasana thrust a glass of champagne into his hand before anyone said anything.

Jones and Dusabe took Kamanzi's arrival as a signal to withdraw, and Jones was already almost out the door when Gasana told them to stay where they were.

'Our victory belongs to all of us,' he said.

'What victory?' Kamanzi replied, suspiciously inspecting the crystal flute he was now holding. 'Can I finally send out the press release I've had sitting on my desk for the last week?'

Gasana didn't answer him, but he did go back over to the laptop and pick up the USB stick.

'How much do you think this is worth?' he said, waving it in the air in front of Kamanzi.

The other man half-stifled a sigh and looked like he was about to either turn round and march straight to the land cruiser that had brought him from the airport and tell its driver to take him back there, or dump his champagne flute on the table and then storm out. He definitely did not look like he was about to indulge Gasana in a guessing game.

'A billion dollars,' Gasana said, the slightest pout creeping into his childish glee.

'Good for you,' Kamanzi replied.

Gasana affected a frown. 'Not for me. For us. For Rwanda.'

Kamanzi finally moved over to the conference table and put his still-full glass down. 'What are you talking about?'

Gasana took a long swig of champagne, then set his flute down next to Kamanzi's.

'It's not enough for us to just succeed. We must protect our success from people who could harm us or try to take our wealth from us.'

Kamanzi's eyes narrowed.

'Where did you get that?' he said, gesturing at the USB stick still in Gasana's hand with his chin.

'This,' Gasana replied, tightening his grip on the private key, 'is a quarter of El Salvador's cryptocurrency reserves.'

CHAPTER 46

Kamanzi's eyes widened in utter, total confusion. He shot looks at Gasana, Jones and Dusabe that implored them all to explain what he'd just heard, and his mouth tried and failed to form words for almost ten seconds before he at last managed to stutter, 'What?'

'Of all people, surely you understand the threat crypto-currencies pose to legitimate economies. Inventing wealth instead of earning it or building it. Using other people's hard work without—'

'I know what cryptocurrencies are and how they work,' Kamanzi said, interrupting Gasana before he reached full flow. 'This is too dangerous. I don't know how you've managed this but if what you've done was ever traced back to Rwanda it would do irrecoverable damage.'

Gasana wasn't angry that Kamanzi had talked over him, but he was disappointed by the man's myopic view.

'It won't,' he replied, dismissing the other man's petty concerns with a wave of his empty hand. 'Don't worry, you'll still get to be prime minister. Maybe even president.'

'Of a pariah state.'

'Not with what's under our very feet,' Gasana said. 'Once the truth about what we've found in Nyungwe is announced the whole world will be clamouring for our minerals. Any moral qualms will evaporate. They'll need us.'

'How did you get a billion dollars of another nation's reserve currency?'

'I liberated it from them,' Gasana replied. 'Actually, they did that for us. We just collected it.'

Kamanzi's head began to shake from side to side. 'You didn't have to do this. I want no part in it.'

'It's too late for that,' Gasana replied.

He gave the quickest glance and slightest nod to Dusabe. His *umuntu* understood the silent communication perfectly and moved closer to Kamanzi. Jones stayed by the door.

'We're all in this together,' Gasana continued. 'Nyungwe's minerals will make Rwanda rich, but destroying crypto is what will make sure our future remains in our hands. And the rest of the planet's too.'

At last, Gasana decided the moment had come. It was time to complete the final stage of a theft that had been in process for months.

He leaned over his laptop, unlocked the screen, and plugged the USB stick into one of the ports running up the right-hand side of the keyboard. The computer was hooked up to a larger screen at the far end of the room that hung suspended from the ceiling slightly in front of the wall, and as soon as it registered the presence of the mini portable hard drive in its side, a corresponding folder appeared on the laptop's screen and the larger mirrored one.

Gasana pressed a few keys and the glass of the conference room's windows immediately switched to a milky opaque frosting, then he opened the programme he would use to upload the private key onto the blockchain and transfer the billion dollars' worth of crypto into the anonymous wallet he'd set up.

The Salvadorans would know their reserves had been depleted as soon as it happened, but they'd have no idea who had done it or where the money had gone. Neither would anyone else, and that, as much as the actual theft itself, would be what would paralyse confidence in cryptocurrency.

Suddenly, Kamanzi lunged forward and grabbed at the wrist of Gasana's left arm. His movement was so swift and unexpected it took even Dusabe by surprise.

'This is insanity,' Kamanzi said.

His grip wasn't that tight, but the mere sensation of a hand on his skin sent a violent shock through Gasana's whole nervous system. He snapped his arm away from Kamanzi, then snatched at the other man's own wrist, pressing his fingers into it with enough force to leave a bruise.

'Do not do that,' he said, his eyes unblinking and his voice filled with so much cold fury that he sounded, for a split second at least, as if he might well be insane.

Then he threw the other man's arm back at him and glared at Dusabe, who clamped two large palms on the finance minister's shoulders.

'If you do this . . .' Kamanzi said, before his voice trailed off.

'There's no *if*,' Gasana said, composure returning to his voice. 'This is happening. We're making history.'

Then, his fingers moving rapidly across the keyboard as if he'd spent months practising for this exact moment, which he had, Gasana uploaded the private key. He generated a fresh public one and a wallet from it, then told the programme to direct its entire contents over to his anonymous one.

The whole process took barely five seconds, and when it was done the number one appeared as the sole dollar-equivalent entry on the anonymous wallet's transaction record. However, it wasn't followed by nine zeroes. It was just a single one, all by itself.

Everyone in the room was completely silent until Gasana said, 'What is . . .', his words now not managing to complete a sentence.

'That's not one billion dollars,' Kamanzi said, answering the unfinished question. 'That's one dollar.'

Gasana kept staring at the screen for another ten seconds, his mind still refusing to believe what he was seeing. His eyes went in and out of focus, the number appearing on the screen in horrific, sharp-edged clarity, then fading into murky, meaningless oblivion and back again. He stopped breathing, and it felt like his heart had stopped beating too, but then it started to hammer in his chest and he had to reach out both hands onto the desk to steady himself from the shock as he sucked in two deep lungfuls of air.

He'd failed. But worse than that, he'd been betrayed.

Someone had to be blamed. Had to be guilty of the worst kind of treachery.

His head spun round, his wide eyes searching for Jones. But she wasn't there. She'd vanished while everyone else's attention had been on the screen at the other end of the table.

'Find her,' Gasana spat at Dusabe, and sent him out of the room with a vicious point at the door.

Dusabe released Kamanzi's shoulders and sprinted away as Gasana turned back to the large screen and tried to calm the melee of thoughts and questions that suddenly filled his head and the rage that thumped through his body.

Had Jones never been loyal to him or the cause? Had she schemed with Pike to steal the real private key for themselves? Or had she always been working alone and, just as he'd wanted to see the look on Kamanzi's face when he revealed the true extent of his plans, she'd wanted to be there to watch them come crashing down after spending so long encouraging him to build them?

He'd lost months of work and millions of dollars. For nothing.

Gasana tried to calm himself, stop the despair and anger inside him from spilling out, breathe evenly. It was a blow, he told himself, but not a crippling one. There was still Nyungwe, and only a few people had any idea what had just happened, including Kamanzi who was now as complicit as him and would be tied to him forever, still a useful political puppet to control.

He rushed to reassure himself further, to shore up his ego. He could recover. It was a setback but he could overcome it like he had so many times before, and become even stronger and more resilient because of it. He'd flown too close to the sun, but next time he'd use wings that wouldn't melt.

However, while he'd been staring at the single one that refused to transform into one billion in front of him, he didn't notice Kamanzi removing his phone from his suit trouser pocket and sending a single, short email.

'This is over,' the finance minister said, re-pocketing his phone.

'No it isn't,' Gasana replied, his voice getting firmer with every word.

'Check your messages,' Kamanzi replied as he turned towards the door.

Gasana stared at the other man for a long moment, then spun back to the laptop. He opened his GME email account and saw a flood of new emails landing in his inbox, the unread count jumping up in tens and twenties every few seconds. His eyes shifted in and out of focus again, but he could make out several phrases repeating in the subject lines and preview texts of the torrent of new messages: *Is this true?* . . . *What's happening?* . . . *Congratulations!* . . . *Just saw the news* . . .

Gasana opened his web browser and loaded up the website of *The New Times*, Rwanda's biggest newspaper. The usual photo-led main story had been replaced with a 'breaking news' banner and a three-word headline in bold, double-height capitals: *NYUNGWE MINE NATIONALISED.*

Gasana staggered back from the laptop, only to look up and see the headline displayed even bigger on the suspended screen.

He desperately wanted his mind to refuse to believe what he was seeing. His eyes had to be playing tricks on him, or there was a glitch in his laptop. He refreshed the page, but it didn't change. He switched to his inbox – more messages all saying the same thing.

This wasn't what was supposed to happen. At this very moment he was meant to be a billion dollars richer and about to be announced as the man who had discovered the key to securing Rwanda's economic future.

Nyungwe was his. He'd convinced the government to let him have exclusive access to it, he'd built the extraction facility, he'd found the tantalum, and all the other minerals. And he was the one who had spent so much on stealing the private key.

'You can't do this,' he stammered to Kamanzi, who was already halfway out of the door.

'I'm the finance minister,' he replied, pausing. 'So, yes, I can.'

'I'll tell everyone about Shaft B,' Gasana said, desperation swamping his voice.

Kamanzi stopped, turned and took three steps back towards Gasana, squaring up to the man who was bigger than him but now seemed considerably diminished.

'No you won't,' Kamanzi said. 'Because if you even try to talk to anyone about that, you'll be stripped of all your other assets and either extradited to El Salvador or dumped over the border to find work in a Congolese coltan mine.'

Then the finance minister spun back round and marched out of the room.

Gasana slumped against the edge of the conference table, his eyes fixed on the doorway Kamanzi had left open, waiting for him to return, to apologise, to realise he was the one who had made a mistake and that Gasana was right.

But he didn't.

CHAPTER 47

TWO WEEKS LATER

Emma Bamford needed a splash. Her first four months as the new head of the Harbrook Museum had not been exactly edifying. Turning round the fortunes of a venerable but almost forgotten regional museum was always going to be a challenge – every single member of the several interview boards she'd sat through to get the job had seemed to be at pains to point this fact out, as had several of her friends and quite a few of her now-ex colleagues in the marketing department at the National Children's Science Discovery Centre in Manchester – but it had turned out to be even more of a slog than she'd prepared herself for.

It was halfway through the summer holidays and the tidal wave of tired parents looking for some way to stimulate their bored children or even just somewhere to take them where they wouldn't have to keep a constant eye on them was yet to blast the museum's doors open in a torrent of hopeful desperation.

Not that the Harbrook could handle it if it did – the traditional temporary summer staff of students from the city's two universities also hadn't materialised. Either they'd decided to spend their long breaks in nicer climes, were chained to laptops racing to deliver late essays and dissertations, or had found a better paid offer somewhere else.

The museum had a permanent staff, of course, but it wasn't large and they were a fatalistic bunch, all apparently content to occupy themselves with their individual curatorial or research-based peccadilloes as they ran down the time to either retirement or the museum shutting, whichever came first.

Bamford was determined to do more than simply manage the Harbrook's decline. There was an opportunity here. A chance to engage people by giving them a break from their TV, computer and phone screens and letting them get up close and personal with real, physical history. It was a big step up for her, taking charge of a whole institution instead of just a department. She was happy to lead from the front, but she would have appreciated at least an iota of back-up from the people whose livelihoods she was trying to protect.

She'd made it clear in the first couple of days of her tenure that she was open to any and every idea anyone might have about improving visitor numbers over the school break. When none had been forthcoming after a fortnight she organised a politely mandatory blue-sky breakout session to encourage some out-of-the-box thinking.

Someone suggested opening the ground floor for weddings, which wasn't entirely ridiculous but also wasn't the kind of cheap, quick fix Bamford was looking for. Someone else posited the possibility of late night opening, 'like down in London', then retracted the idea when it became clear that it would involve them giving up their evenings to work. A third voice tried to reassure her, saying they just needed a few days of bad weather before people got cabin fever at home and started looking for days out under cover.

'It's not our fault if kids want to waste their time TikTok-ing at each other instead of learning stuff,' Nigel, the Har-brook's seventy-something-year-old senior cataloguer, said when Bamford had asked him if there was anything buried in the museum's stores with an interesting story they might be able to build a mini exhibition around.

She resisted the urge to tell him that, actually, it was their fault. Everyone who worked at the Harbrook was a scientist of some kind and communicating their knowledge was as much a part of their job as collecting and protecting it.

She also stopped herself from asking him why he didn't have a list of several possible items he could cite off the top of his head given that he'd been at the Harbrook for fifteen years and, according to his yearly reviews, had catalogued and re-catalogued the entire museum's collection at least five times. Instead, she just asked him to let her know if anything occurred to him.

Then she'd looked through the long list of items that belonged to the Harbrook herself and had come to the reluc-tant conclusion that there wasn't any hidden gem buried deep in it, and that, in truth, the museum had only ever had one near-remarkable thing in its possession. The *Armstrong Hunter*.

And that was long gone, along with any possible mileage the museum could get from telling the story of its disappearance.

As Bamford checked her shirt and hair in the mirror of her en-suite, trying to work out if the slight creases and kinks in both made her look more relaxed and approachable than messy, she thought about how she could also use a little more emotional support from her husband, Steve.

He was still living in Manchester with their ten-year-old whirlwind daughter Maisie. They'd made that decision together and it had been a sensible one – there was no point uprooting the whole family if it turned out the job wasn't a goer, and Manchester was close enough that they could alternate weekends in the north-west and north-east. However, it also meant that it was up to her to make the Harbrook work, and find somewhere for them to move to if it did, while she spent almost every evening in her one-bedroom flat above a perennially busy Tesco Express in the Jesmond area of the city doing her best not to feel too lonely or whinge too much over FaceTime.

She decided that with a few well-placed yanks she could get away without having to iron her shirt, grabbed her bag and headed to work, treating herself to a *pain au raisin* from the Tesco on the way.

Jesmond was one of Newcastle's fancier inner suburbs. Its grand Victorian villas were homes to the families of doctors and lawyers, or divided up and occupied by the kind of rich students who didn't need summer jobs. It was also a ten-minute walk from the Harbrook, which gave Bamford time to enjoy her pastry, reply to last night's text message from an estate agent telling her that she'd lost out on the three-bedroom terrace she'd seen and loved two days ago that had been up for rent in Tynemouth, the upmarket town on the coast eight miles east of the city known as Jesmond-on-Sea, and prepare her psyche for another day spent convincing herself that she hadn't made a huge mistake.

She got to the Harbrook early. It didn't open to the public until ten a.m., but most of the staff kept regular office hours, and she liked to be in her office before everyone else, by quarter to nine at the latest.

Today, someone had beaten her to their desk. When she reached the staff entrance at eight forty-five the building's alarm system had already been deactivated. And as she walked along the corridor of half-glass doors that led to her own she saw who had turned it off.

Nigel was already sitting on a stool hunched over a rock on the examination bench in his office. Perhaps he'd finally taken Bamford's suggestion to heart and was trying to do something like decide for the sixth time if a groove in it was man-made and might prompt a complete rethink of how, when and where early humans started using sophisticated tools, or if it was simply a quirk of erosion. Unfortunately, Bamford thought it was more likely that he'd just woken up early and hadn't had anything else to do.

She let him be, passed his door without knocking on it and giving him a forced, cheery wave through the glass, and unlocked her own office as she ran through the mental to-do list she'd drawn up before she'd gone to sleep last night: check how much the local newspaper, *The Chronicle*, was charging for adverts and if the museum's charitable status would get them a discount rate for any spare space it had, send an email to one of the members of the board who happened to be a lawyer about the various licences that might be required for hosting large-scale events like weddings and corporate parties, and register with another couple of estate agents.

It wasn't until she sat down at her desk and reached her right hand out to open up her laptop that she realised something was perched on top of it that hadn't been there when she'd shut it down last night.

It took her a moment to realise what the object that looked like a small figure wearing a geometric-patterned tunic with a raised arm was. And then another to start shouting out Nigel's name.

CHAPTER 48

It was a warm afternoon. Warm for the north-east coast of England at least. And hot enough to send dribbles of soft-serve and raspberry sauce trickling over Pike's hand before he'd even reached the beach.

'Monkey's blood,' the man in the ice cream van had said as he'd held a pinkish squeezy tube over Pike's cone, more a piece of information than a question.

The man's Geordie accent was so broad and deep it made Pike smile and reminded him of his own which he'd erased long ago, a piece of old data written over to obscure it.

He licked the sweet, fake flavours off his fingers, and started descending the steep bank covered in long, brittle spikes of grass that gradually gave way to sand.

He followed a worn path that began along the side of a squat row of stone buildings that looked like they'd once belonged to something bigger. Stretching back into the deeper recesses of his childhood memories he recalled that they had – a Victorian pleasure plaza that had dominated the shoreline.

He could vaguely remember a grand ballroom that had become a roller-skating rink, and a fire that had gutted and collapsed the place.

Pike settled into a spot of soft, dry sand just above where the bank shallowed out and became beach proper, and looked out to the sea. There was a cluster of neoprene-clad children getting a surfing lesson almost directly in front of him. He couldn't recall anyone ever daring to dip more than their feet in the North Sea when he was a kid, even on the hottest day of the year. Maybe they were made of tougher stuff nowadays, or maybe wetsuits were just cheaper.

There were a couple of other notable differences to the view: the bustling cafe tucked against the headland to Pike's right, and the thin spires of a small offshore wind farm to his left. But for the most part, not much had changed.

It was the same with the Harbrook. Pike hadn't been sure he'd even be able to step inside the museum, or recognise what he found within it and remember his way around. But he'd managed to do all three, and finally go some way to putting right an old mistake.

Getting into the museum had been as easy as the last time he'd broken into it. Even without his PADD, which was still awaiting a replacement screen that would require somewhere a little more specialist than the usual shopping mall phone repair kiosk to install it, the Harbrook's security systems had been simple to hack and take offline for a half-hour window last night without setting off any back-up alarms.

Navigating with just the torch of his temporary burner phone, Pike could tell that most of the exhibits were still where they'd been twenty years ago, and for the ten before that.

He passed the scaled-down model of the solar system, which had a small plaque at its very end admitting that some astronomers no longer considered Pluto a planet because of its diminutive size but no recognition of the several larger celestial bodies that had been found orbiting the sun over the last fifty years. At least the Earth was spinning the right way now.

Then there was the galleried room of taxidermied animals – land and sea creatures still on the ground floor, airborne ones up on the balcony – that were now more dust and thread than feather and pelt. After that, the corridor lined with drawers stuffed full of unremarkable geological samples which led to the set of rooms dedicated to the north-east's coal mining history. And then, past the life-sized mannequins of a soot-covered coal miner and his crochet-shawled housewife, the museum's backstage area.

This too was almost exactly as Pike remembered it: a line of pokey offices carved out of a once much larger space, with partition walls cutting high window frames in half, cornicing and faded wallpaper not joining up, off-centred strip lighting, and tables, chairs and other assorted pieces of furniture so worn it looked like the rooms had been built around them.

The museum head's office – now labelled as belonging to its Chief Executive – was still at the end of the row, where it always had been.

The door to it was locked. It wasn't hard to pick.

Inside, the only thing that suggested time had moved on at all was the absence of the large off-white box of a computer monitor that had dominated the leather-topped desk, upgraded at some point to a closed laptop, upon which he delicately balanced the ivory statuette of the hunter.

He looked out towards the blurred line of the horizon where the sea mingled with the sky, and let himself feel good. It had been a long time coming, but he'd managed to put right something he'd once helped make wrong, and without causing too many problems for other people who didn't deserve it along the way. Exhilaration, relief and pride swirled within him, seasoned with just a little sprinkling of tempered guilt.

Pike had known that the *Armstrong Hunter* had been part of Liu Qiang's private collection of historical artefacts for over a decade, thanks to an old digital manifest he'd found in the days before the world's rich and corrupt fully understood the need to encrypt their incriminating data.

Delaney, however, he'd never found any trace of. Not a single whisper or shadow of the man in a quarter of a century – and he'd expended a lot of time and energy looking.

He was also fairly sure the Chinese magnate had been Delaney's original customer. Of course, he couldn't be completely certain that Liu was storing the statue in Malak Ali, but he'd spent long enough running the possibilities to make the gamble of breaking into the free zone worth it.

Would Liu notice it was missing, even if the Harbrook got a few news inches out of its mysterious reappearance? Maybe.

Would he be able to do anything about it if he did without incriminating himself in some way as the owner of stolen goods? Probably not. Would Pike enjoy thinking about the other man's impotent frustration at being beaten by someone he didn't even know he was up against? Definitely.

Pike had wondered what his dad might have thought about his recent achievements. So, after a long morning spent switching benches along the Newcastle quayside counting bridges, checking the local news sites and social media feeds, and testing the espresso of several coffee shops, he'd strolled up to a Metro station and headed east.

His first stop at the coast was the ornamental oval of water where his dad was spending eternity – the boating and bird pond where he'd told Pike his mum had died – the one sentimental location on the whole planet that the two men had shared.

Of course, Ken Pike wasn't going to be able to actually tell his son how he felt, and chances were that after so many years there were only a few specks of his ashes still mixed in with the sediment of dirt, stray sand blown up from the beach, sweet wrappers and bird excrement. Still, though, as Pike lingered at the edge of the pond, the water didn't recede from him, waves didn't suddenly rise up to drown him, lightning didn't strike him from above, and none of the swans attacked him. He decided to interpret all of that as a sign of forgiveness.

Pike enjoyed the mostly positive sensation he was experiencing for another five minutes, watching the waves roll in and licking at his ice cream until he heard the low, soft, elongated sound of feet descending behind him.

They were too close to be someone simply making their way to the beach, and after a few more steps that sent a stream of sand past him half a metre to his right, the person responsible for them reached his side and sat down.

CHAPTER 49

It was Jones.

She was holding her own cone of soft-serve topped with a generous splurge of monkey's blood. However, unlike Pike's, hers was still exactly where the man in the ice cream van had squeezed it.

Pike didn't turn to acknowledge her arrival, but from the side of his eye he watched as she leaned forward and took a single lick of her ice cream before wedging the cone in the sand next to her, apparently already done with it.

She didn't look at Pike either. But, once she was finished neatly discarding her soft-serve, she did speak.

'The private key never left Perquin, did it?' she said.

Pike let a smile spread across his face as he took his first bite of the edge of his cone and shook his head.

'I knew Rivas let us go a little too easily. How long did she know what we were up to?'

'Only at the end,' Pike said, between more crunching bites.

'The stick they found in the rucksack?'

'The decoy you brought me.'

'Why?'

Pike knew her question wasn't just about the dummy private key he'd pretended to steal. Or the motions he'd gone through to make it look like he'd stolen one of the real ones. Or the point about his analogue hacking skills he'd wanted to make to himself by cracking the safe that he hadn't technically needed to break into.

He could have told Jones that he'd thought Rivas had seemed like a decent person just trying to do the best for her country and he'd seen no reason to screw her or the people of El Salvador over.

But instead he said, 'I wanted to find out who was really after the billion dollars and why. Having Rivas play along was the best way to make sure we got out of El Salvador and I got to meet whoever you were working for. Although I don't think that was Gasana.'

'Nobody works for Gasana any more,' she said.

'I saw the story about Nyungwe. Such an altruistic gesture,' Pike replied, his voice full of sarcasm.

Pike had stayed in Dubai for two days after the Malak Ali heist, relaxing in one of the nicer apartments in the city owned by Alif while he waited for a clean passport that would be good enough to get him out of the emirate and through Heathrow's automatic scanners.

On the first day, he'd hooked up his PADD to one of the stack of clean laptops Alif kept in the apartment. The PADD's screen might have been shattered, but its inner components were still in pretty good working order, and the zero-day exploit still hadn't been caught by Malak Ali's diagnostics, which meant he was able to enjoy playing back the footage of two figures in boiler suits emerging from Liu's suite in the Archive and the subsequent flurry of encrypted messages between the free zone's security and staff chiefs trying to work out where the hell the undocumented workers had come from and if an investigation needed to be launched or the video file of them quietly erased. A hasty review of the Archive's records showed that everything Liu had registered with Malak Ali was still in his suite, and the free zone wasn't liable in case something undeclared had gone missing, so they opted for the latter.

On the second day Pike had seen an article at the bottom of the BBC News website's homepage about Lucius Gasana, the rising star of Africa's new industrial revolution handing over full ownership of the Nyungwe tantalum mine to the Rwandan government and announcing that he was going to dedicate himself to philanthropic work.

He skimmed the article, its references to the discovery of several other rare and extremely valuable minerals in the mine, and the comments by BBC political, economic and scientific correspondents about what the implications of this news might be for both the small African nation as well as global industry.

It was clear to Pike that someone in the upper echelons of Rwandan politics had got wind of what Gasana had been up to and had acted quickly to stop the man before he caused any more potential diplomatic incidents. Or perhaps whoever they were had been in cahoots with him, and this was their swift vengeance for the failure of his plan to collapse international trust in cryptocurrency.

The article's copious quotes from Jean Kamanzi, the country's finance minister, were a pretty strong clue about who Gasana's government accomplice might have been.

'I bet good old Dusabe is still by his side,' Pike added.

'I'd stay clear of him if I were you,' Jones said. 'He's still upset that you lied about the smart tags. And I'll be avoiding Dubai for a while.'

'No need to worry too much about that, they're not looking for you,' Pike said. Then he added, 'Or whoever they think you are,' reminding Jones that he still didn't buy the shell of an identity that she'd given him and, he guessed, most other people she encountered.

'Good to know,' she replied. 'How's the PADD?'

'It'll live. How long did it take you to realise about the tags?'

'The first door we tried to open after we left the emergency stairs.'

'Lucky I didn't bump into you on my way out then.'

'And how long did you spend looking round Liu's suite before you left?'

Pike took another few bites of his cone, removing the ring of wafer that still had some ice cream clinging to it. 'Just a couple of hours.'

'Why?' Jones asked.

'I'll answer that if you tell me something first,' Pike replied, pushing the dry leftover bit of his cone into the sand for some tiny creature to discover and feast on. 'Who do you really work for?'

Jones stretched out her legs, pressed her arms into the sand behind her and looked up at the cloudless sky. 'I'm guessing you're familiar with the concept of a DAO.'

'A decentralised autonomous organisation,' he replied. 'Basically the human version of crypto – groups of like-minded people who operate free of traditional governmental control or power hierarchies.'

'The tech crowd likes to think they invented the concept, but the principle has existed in the analogue world for centuries.'

'A kind of shadow state, secretly pulling the world's strings,' Pike said, finally glancing at the woman next to him. 'Are you about to tell me you work for the Freemasons?'

A smirk crept into the corner of Jones's mouth. 'No, but I do represent a very old DAO. One that's been helping shape how the world's progressed for a long time.'

'And Rivas is a threat to that?'

'Cryptocurrencies are, at least in their current form. We've put a lot of effort into stopping the entire global economy from collapsing recently and they're a destabilising force. We wanted to use Gasana to get rid of Rivas.'

'Sounds like using a snake to get rid of a spider. You're still left with a snake.'

'We'd have dealt with him too eventually.'

'Sorry I mucked things up for you. Are we enemies now?'

'Some of my associates wanted to make good on Gasana's threats about separating you from your limbs and throwing you in a river. I persuaded them that we can live with a fifty per cent success rate. When you're playing the long game it pays to be flexible. And if we can't bring down crypto then we'll find a way to make it work for us.'

'If you can't beat it, invest in it.'

'Something like that.'

'And I guess I owe you again now.'

'Yes, you do.'

'Any thoughts on how I can make us square?'

'I'll let you know. I'm impressed with you.'

'That sounds like interview feedback.'

'Maybe it is,' Jones said. 'Now your turn. Why did you really want to get into Malak Ali?'

'There was something in there that shouldn't have been. I wanted to return it to where it belonged.'

'See, it's when you say things like that that I start wondering how many steps ahead you might have been before I even showed up in Sihanoukville.'

'You flatter me,' Pike replied.

He didn't add that she was right to wonder, that maybe he'd got himself locked up in a Cambodian police cell precisely so she or someone like her could come and break him out of it. He was as impressed with her as she was with him. Probably even more. But he wasn't about to admit it.

'You know, you never told me how you learned to crack safes,' she said.

'Didn't I?' Pike replied, his question lightly dismissing hers.

Pike pushed himself up onto his feet, sending a mini avalanche of sand down towards the beach. Jones did the same, adding to the little landslide.

'One last thing,' she said. 'The zero-day. Were you the hacker the broker was middlemanning for?'

Pike thought about the six million dollars Gasana had handed over in Marrakech, which was now closer to five-point-eight after Alif and Elaid had taken their cuts, and that Pike had already spread across a variety of high-interest accounts, investment funds, and even some bitcoin.

He didn't feel guilty about taking it. After all, Gasana had paid a fair market rate for the zero-day, with just a little premium added on top for the repeated threats he'd made to kill Pike. But he also didn't want to give Jones the satisfaction of knowing that she'd guessed right again. So he just smiled, shrugged, turned away and started to walk down to the beach.

ABOUT THE AUTHOR

As a member of 22 SAS, Andy McNab was at the centre of covert operations for nine years, across five continents. Awarded both the Distinguished Conduct Medal (DCM) and Military Medal (MM) during his military career, he was the British Army's most highly decorated serving soldier when he finally left the SAS. Since then, Andy McNab has become one of the world's best-selling writers. As well as several non-fiction bestsellers including Bravo Two Zero, the biggest selling British work of military history, he is the author of numerous bestselling Nick Stone and Tom Buckingham thrillers, in addition to books for children. He continues to also be a spokesperson and fundraiser for both military and literacy charities, and in 2017 was appointed a CBE in the Queen's Birthday Honours List for services to literacy.